Jumper and the Apple Crate

By Kenn Amdahl

Jumper and the Apple Crate

Copyright 2017 By Kenn Amdahl

ISBN-10:

0-9627815-4-1

ISBN-13:

978-0-9627815-4-4

Clearwater Publishing

PO Box 1602

Eugene, Oregon 97440

Special thanks to Larry Jeannotte and his merry band of students in New York. In 2010 his class of fifth graders read *Jumper and the Bones,* then asked Mr. Jeannotte to arrange a video conference with Kenn Amdahl, the author. During that conference, they read their book reports into the camera and asked very interesting questions. Some of those are posted on the Facebook page for *Jumper and the Bones.* One student asked the author "Where did Jumper get his apple crate?" After thinking about it for a minute, the author hung his head in shame and confessed that he did not know. The question haunted him until he finally wrote this book to answer it.

Also thanks to several patient and kind early readers including people named Amdahl: Cheryl Amdahl, Paul Amdahl, Scott Amdahl, and Joey Amdahl as well as folks with alternate last names like Becca Owen, Liz Hill, and Lise Pyles. All their suggestions and cheerleading helped.

Finally, thanks to everyone who read *Jumper and the Bones* and encouraged Jumper to reappear in print. I hope the figments of your own imagination become the faithful sidekicks Jumper has been to me.

Contents

Chapter One
In which I remember an adventure with my Dad when I was a kid.

You're probably wondering where I got my apple crate, which I keep on my balcony. I sit on my crate to eat dinner if it's nice weather before I jump off a garage or tree. But if you ain't been to my apartment yet, you probably don't wonder about my apple crate all that much and everything I wrote so far, which you just read, is kind of a bonus.

Apple crates is wood boxes the apple farmer fills up and ships to grocery stores. You might guess I got mine at a farm or grocery store that was selling apples, but you'd be wrong. I got mine at a circus.

A lot of circus animals like apples. They also like carrots. Carrots and apples are like chocolate ice cream if you're a zebra or a elephant. Circuses buy so much apples and carrots they get lots of crates. Since circuses go from town to town, they always need boxes to pack stuff in and apple crates is perfect.

But you don't care about every single apple crate. You're just interested in mine.

When I was a kid, there was a circus that went from town to town. A few days before they got someplace they sent a guy ahead to put posters up on telephone poles with a picture of a tiger or whatever their circus had that was cool. When I seen a circus poster I got pretty excited like any kid would, but I didn't say nothing. My dad had already got sick by then and was always coughing a lot. He had to quit his job, plus there was doctor bills. Even being a little kid, I heard mom and dad talk about money and what they always said was they didn't have none.

A circus might be pretty fun, but it ain't as important as a doctor bill. Everybody likes a tiger, but cats that live in alleys is just like them, only they chase mice instead of deers. If you got stray cats, you can watch for free. Pretending you're in the wilds of Africa hunting tigers is a lot cheaper than going to the circus and about as fun. But everybody likes circuses, so a week before they was supposed to come, I asked Mom if I could go out the day after the circus left town and snag me one of them cool posters before somebody else got the idea and she didn't see no hidden flaws in that plan.

But that ain't what happened. Reading about my plan which I didn't do is another bonus for you.

A few days before the circus shows was going to start, my dad woke me up really early, while it was still dark. "Rise and shine, Jumper my man," he said. "We got some work to do."

"But it ain't even a school day," I said, which I knew even in my sleep because school had let out for the summer.

My dad laughed his deep laugh that sounded like a bear laughing. Then he coughed for a minute. When he stopped coughing he said, "This ain't school work. This is grown-up man work. Which, if you think about it right, is more fun than silly kid games. Get your jeans on. Your mom already made us sack lunches to take with. Eat some Cheerios and let's go. We don't want to be late."

"Where are we working?" I said, sitting up and rubbing my eyes.

"Jumper, it ain't much of an adventure if you know what happens before you even start."

I put on my clothes, went to the kitchen and ate my Cheerios. My mom was busy getting herself ready for work but she walked through the kitchen and give me a kiss on my forehead. The kitchen smelled like coffee.

"So Mom," I said, real casual. "What do you think about what me and Dad are doing today?"

She laughed a little and her eyes got sparkly.

"Mr. Jumper, I've always said you were a unique one. You're either going to be a detective or a lawyer when you grow up. I'm not falling for your tricks."

"Well, can you tell me if we're getting paid?" Lots of times things is more fun if you get paid.

"You know," she said. She tried to sound stern, but her eyes was twinkling. "For a kid who never said a word until he was four years old, you sure have a lot of questions now."

"I was mostly just listening. I listened pretty hard when you and Dad read me books."

"I think you listened hardest when your father read Huck Finn," she said.

"That's just the way: a person does a low-down thing, and then he don't want to take no consequences of it."

"Thank you very much, Mr. Twain," she said with a laugh. "I don't notice you quoting any of the books I read to you."

"Mr. Huckfinn sounded the loudest in my brain. Plus, Dad read it to me about eight times. He said it sounded the realest. But I think we was talking about getting paid. There ain't nothing wrong with getting paid, is there?" I asked.

"There isn't anything wrong would be the correct way to say that. Anyway, people get paid lots of ways, Jumper," she said. "Sometimes they get paid with money, sometimes with memories, and sometimes by learning something. If you try to learn something and always notice a good memory when it's happening, then you know you got paid. Money's a bonus."

She kissed me on the forehead again and messed up my hair a little. "I love your father," she said. "But he had a hard childhood and he's not the best grammar teacher." Since I wasn't trying to learn how to be someone's grandma I figured that didn't matter much. I just said Okay. She smiled and shook her head and then she went to finish getting ready for work.

Dad was already in the car. He looked pretty skinny but he never wanted to eat much. It was just part of the sickness he said, and there wasn't much anybody could do about it.

I tried to notice right away if there was any interesting memories happening around me, but I couldn't see none. The streets was dark as midnight even though it would get light soon. There wasn't many cars out yet, which made the empty roads look spooky, so that was kind of interesting. I didn't get to ride alone with my Dad in the dark too often so I watched him drive. The lights on the dashboard lit up his nose and forehead a little. He had a real careful look on his face. Sometimes I could tell he wanted to cough, but he kind of held it in and then his face looked like it hurt to do that.

"One thing I ought probably tell you," he said. "Them people we're going to work for today? Well, they don't officially know about it yet."

"Well, they'll probably be glad for some extra help then," I said.

Dad smiled. "Well, that's the plan. But if they ain't interested in our help, we can't hold it against them. They might have rules or something."

"Yeah," I said, feeling pretty grown up to be talking to my Dad like that. "Just about everybody's got rules."

I kept looking around for stuff that might be good memories, but I didn't see nothing. It was cool how the dash lights outlined Dad's face in white, like somebody drew him with chalk on a blackboard, but that probably happens to everybody. The car smelled like cigarette smoke, even if he didn't smoke that much any more except when Mom wasn't looking. The stoplights seemed extra bright. Maybe that's since there wasn't many cars driving around with their lights on. About the only light on the road was trucks. My Dad said they was delivery trucks taking stuff like donuts to stores so they'd have some when they opened. I never thought about how stuff gets to stores before that night. I decided to remember the night I learned about delivery trucks and if I didn't get no more pay for working that day I couldn't complain.

Dad pointed to the sky. "See? It's starting to get light already. Some people say it's always darkest before dawn, but I never got that. It just gets lighter and lighter and pretty soon the sun comes up."

"Why do they say it if it ain't true?"

He thought for a minute. "Bad stuff happens to everybody, Jumper. To me and also to you. No way around it. People say that thing about being darkest before dawn to remind you that no matter how bad you feel, you're going to feel better pretty soon. Even if it don't feel like it."

"Why don't they say it's always darkest before it starts getting lighter again?"

He laughed. "I like that better too," he said. "You should write them cards they sell for holidays."

Since we was having a grown-up kind of talk, I tried to think of something to say that Dad didn't already know.

"I found a quarter on the sidewalk," I said. I hadn't told anybody about that.

"That sounds pretty lucky," Dad said.

"It was like magic," I said. "I mean, I bet a hundred kids walk down that sidewalk and nobody seen it but me. It was like a magician made it appear just for me."

"Long odds," he said.

"Huh?"

"Before something happens, you think about how weird it would be if it happened. Like, out of the billions of people in the world, what's the odds your mom and I would meet? Pretty long odds. Billions to one. Or that you'd walk down one certain sidewalk on a Tuesday morning and find a quarter. Guys who write horoscopes or teach math at colleges would say the odds was so long it was basically impossible. Zero percent chance. But after something happens, they look back and say the odds was 100 percent it would happen, since it did. Just coincidence, no big deal."

"So me finding that quarter was long odds, not magic?"

"Pretty hard to tell the difference," he said. "A guy's life ain't nothing but long odds until stuff happens. When you tell about it later, like it was a story, people might say that ain't believable. The odds was too against it. Only it happened, so you gotta believe it. That quarter showing up on the sidewalk was long odds. Maybe you noticing it was the magic."

By now we was out past the main buildings of town, and even past the car stores. Now there was some fields that just had weeds on them and the road didn't have many stoplights. Dad started singing a song. It starts "Daisy, Daisy, give me your answer do." Well, that's a song we sung about a thousand times together, so I started singing right along. We both sang real loud, like it was a contest, only there wasn't no loser, and nobody was around to tell us to sing in our indoor voices. One time he started coughing so he had to stop singing for a minute, but I just sang even louder like I didn't notice he was coughing instead of singing and pretty soon he was singing again. We sung the whole song four times and after the last time we sung the words "bicycle built for two" I started laughing. It was pretty fun to sing like that. When you have a lot of fun, sometimes a laugh builds up inside you and you gotta let it out. He laughed a little too, and then we drove some more. It was still dark as a black cat, but it was starting to feel like morning anyway.

"Here's where we turn," Dad said, and his voice sounded a little tight, like maybe he was nervous. He leaned forward to see better. "There, I think that's it," he said. We turned into a really big parking lot that was empty except for some big trucks parked in one corner. We parked right next to them.

"Let's just leave our sack lunches in the car," he said. "We can always come back and get them."

"Yeah," I said. "It's pretty early for lunch."

He smiled and we got out. Even if it was the end of summer, the air was chilly and I shivered. Dad took hold of my hand and we walked past the trucks. I was getting too old to hold my Dad's hand. We both knew that. But in that dark parking lot, walking past those huge old trucks, it felt OK to me. Them trucks was about as big as dinosaurs. I know it was just a dumb kid thought, but I thought if one of them trucks came alive and started rolling toward me, it would be a lot faster for my Dad to pull me safe if he was already holding my hand. So it was kind of a safety issue.

Past the trucks was a big empty field with dirt and dead weeds. In one part of that there was some trailers and RVs and tents, like they was getting ready for the big picnics before Denver Bronco football games. I ain't never been to a Bronco game, but I seen them all on TV with my Dad. They always showed the big picnics people had in the parking lot and this looked pretty much like that.

"Are they getting ready for a football game?" I asked.

"Something like that," he said.

For a second I was surprised as heck and then I decided he was joking on me. There wasn't a football field around and nobody had pickup trucks with picnics on them. It would of been cool to go to one of them Denver Bronco picnics, but the tickets were expensive as heck so I put my foot down on even pretending that one. My dad was a pretty good joker, but I'm pretty good at figuring out clues. Sometimes it took me a while to figure out his jokes, but that was OK. Mom said it took her a while too. When you ain't sure, the best idea is not to say nothing, so that's what I said.

Some men was moving around doing stuff. A couple was pounding wood stakes into the ground and tying string with little plastic flags to each stake.

"They're laying out the ground," Dad said in a soft voice so nobody else would hear him. "If everybody knows where the paths are and the tents and booths, then nobody has to move things around later."

I figured that was more clues.

One guy was just standing drinking a cup of coffee. You could see steam coming off it. He didn't notice us but was yelling at two guys pounding stakes.

"No, no!" he shouted. "People walk down that path, what are they going to see? Think about it. Oh for crying in the night! Do I gotta do everything around here?" Then he walked away from us toward the guys who wasn't thinking good enough.

"Let's stay away from that one until he's had more coffee," Dad said.

I giggled and nodded.

One guy was pushing a wheelbarrow. Then he stopped, shoveled something into it, then pushed it a little bit farther and stopped again.

"How good are you at operating a shovel?" Dad asked me.

"It's one of my best things," I said. "Are we gonna ask him if he needs help?"

"No," said Dad. "People who really want to help somebody, they just help. People who ask if they can help just want credit for asking. Come on, before the boss comes back."

We walked toward the guy with the wheelbarrow. When we stepped on dead weeds they crunched like toast. You could smell that somebody was cooking bacon. Some extra shovels was leaning against a pickup truck.

"Here, this one looks like your size," Dad said, and he handed me one that was shorter than the one he picked up. As we got close, you could see the wheelbarrow guy was loading up little piles of mud from the dirt. When we got even closer you could tell from the smell that they wasn't mud.

"Pew!" I whispered. Dad just smiled and breathed in real deep, like he was smelling Thanksgiving dinner.

"Smells like an adventure to me," he said.

It was easy to see what to do. Before we even got to the guy there was a big pile of poo. Dad got most of it in his shovel; I got the rest in mine. We didn't say a word but just walked over to the wheelbarrow and dumped our shovels into it. The man looked surprised and started to say something, but Dad just smiled at him and nodded. The guy wasn't a full-grown man. He was just a teenager and really skinny but to a kid like me teenagers who was only five or six years older than me looked pretty scary, so I didn't say nothing. He looked at me, and then at my Dad, then closed his mouth and went back to work.

It was pretty fun. After a minute I didn't even smell the poo hardly at all. We'd clean up the piles in one spot, the guy would drive the wheelbarrow a little farther and then we'd load it some more. After it was full, he pushed it out past all the workers and dumped it in a big hole in the ground. We followed right behind him. When he turned to go back for more, my Dad said the first words any of us had said all morning.

"My son Jumper here has never gotten to push a wheelbarrow," he said.

The man looked at me and you could tell he didn't think that was the best idea anyone ever had.

"I'll help him, of course," Dad said.

The guy shrugged and pointed his finger at my face. "Don't you break my wheelbarrow," he said. His voice was deep and kind of rough sounding. It might of seemed mean except he was saying I could push his wheelbarrow, which sounded like about the most fun thing in the world.

I stood between the handles with one hand on each one and my Dad stood right behind me with his hands on the handles too.

"The trick is to keep moving forward," he said. "They're kind of hard to get started but once you get them moving, they want to keep moving. So, think ahead to where you're going. You want to have time to aim, and then just keep moving forward. Lots of things work like that."

At first he did most of the pushing, but once we got up to full speed he took his hands off. I couldn't keep it going in exactly a straight line since I could hardly see over the top of it, but nobody yelled at me or anything.

Dad laughed. "That's a pretty big grin you got on your face, Jumper," he said.

"It's just like driving a car," I told him. "Or maybe a spaceship."

The guy we was helping kind of coughed when I said that. For just a second I seen he was smiling, but then he wiped his face like he had soup on it and then his face was ordinary again.

"It's harder when it's full," Dad said. "You better let the grown-ups do that part."

"OK," I said and picked up my shovel. I was shoveling poo into the wheelbarrow when I come across a really big pile. "Wow," I said. "A dinosaur must of done that one."

"Not a dinosaur," Dad said. "An elephant."

"But where would an elephant …?" I stopped and Dad nodded.

"That's right," he said. "The circus."

I stared at Dad, then I stared at the big pile of elephant poo. Then I looked at the guy we was helping.

"So, you work for the circus?" I asked him.

"Guess so," he said.

"Wow!" I said. "Do you think it would be OK… I mean, I ain't a circus kid or anything. I ain't ever even been to a circus…" I looked back at the elephant poo. The man cleared his throat.

"I ain't got a lot of authority here," he said, which I didn't know what that was but I was pretty sure I didn't want any of his. So I decided to just ask him straight out.

"Do you think I could do that one all by myself?" I asked.

"The elephant sh…" the man stopped himself. "The elephant poo?"

"I'll do my best job," I said, "even if it takes me eight shovel fulls! I bet I'd be the only kid in my whole school who cleaned up an elephant poo all by himself."

The guy started to laugh.

My Dad didn't laugh. He was pretty serious when he said, "Jumper always does his best job. He'll do as good as any circus man, I guarantee you."

The guy stopped laughing. His face got serious and he rubbed his chin like he was making a hard choice.

"I never once in my life let a town kid clean up after an elephant," he said. "That's the truth. But maybe just this once."

"Thank you, sir," I said and got to work. It was pretty heavy, and it smelled more like the inside of a barn than any barn I ever visited. It took me a bunch of shovels to get it all, but when I was done you could of sat down on that spot and ate your lunch.

While I was shoveling, Dad and him started talking, which they had not done much of so far. The wheelbarrow guy started first. He said, "Why?"

Dad didn't answer right away, which is usually the smart thing. He nodded and thought for a minute, which I would of done too, since I didn't understand what the guy was asking.

"Every father wants to give his kid something," Dad told him, and then he coughed. "Something that will last a long time. But some of us don't have much money." Then he coughed a whole bunch and turned his head so I couldn't see his face. When he could talk again, he talked pretty soft. "And some of us also don't have much time."

15

The man nodded, as if he understood. I still didn't even get the question. The man reached out to shake my Dad's hand. "I'm Gus," he said.

My Dad told him his name was John Cable Senior, but Gus laughed and told him that wasn't a good circus name. Then he turned to me. "Now Jumper," Gus said. "that's a circus name. You sure you ain't a spy from Ringling Brothers?"

"No, sir," I said. "I ain't a spy and I ain't got no brothers."

"Well, we gotta think of a circus name for your Dad too," Gus said.

While we was talking, I was memorizing that elephant poo just like Mom told me. It had its own smell, and had little bits of straw in it and other stuff you might not like to hear about. Some of it was green. If I was ever on trial and they was cross examining me about today, they wasn't going to trick me with some little thing about elephant poo as if I just made it up to sound cool. Dad always told me, don't make the mistake of memorizing every bad thing, like toothaches or nightmares instead of memorizing the cool stuff.

We kept shoveling for a while, only now Gus and me took the full loads to the dump spot while Dad stayed behind and waited for us to get back. Since he was sick, he got tired pretty easy, but he made a joke on it. "Somebody's gotta plot the strategy," Dad said

"Most important part of the job," Gus said, which made me like him. Other guys was putting up tents and signs and stringing lights onto poles. That empty field was starting to look like a real place, like a town or a funny kind of shopping center with little roads to walk on and shops in tents. That really big tent that was going up in the middle of everything told you that it wasn't a town it was a circus. The sun was up but it was still a little cold.

When Gus and I got back to Dad with the empty wheelbarrow, there was a kid standing next to him. It was a girl with long black hair so curled and confused maybe she didn't even own a comb. She was wearing jeans and faded red shirt with some paint stains on it. She moved from one foot to the other like she was getting ready for a race. Her head was tilted way back, like she was looking at the sky and she had a yardstick balanced on her nose, sticking straight up. I thought it would fall off in about one second, but even though she was moving around, it just kept sticking straight up.

Gus started talking kind of loud to her while I was still pushing the empty wheelbarrow.

"Thumbelina, this is Jumper. Jumper, that's Thumbelina. But everybody calls her Thumb." The girl tilted her head forward real quick, the yardstick flipped into the air and she caught it with one hand without even looking. She looked at me like she already didn't like me much.

"Jumper ain't a townie name," she said.

"Thanks," I said as I put down the wheelbarrow. "That's a cool trick with the yardstick."

"Every circus kid can do that," she said. "Or this." She held her hand flat, with all her fingers together and put the end of the yardstick in the middle of her palm. She moved her hand from side to side, but the yardstick kept pointing straight up."

"Here, you try," she said. I tried it on my hand but the stick fell over right away. I laughed pretty hard about being so bad at it, but she just made a face at me.

"Townie," she said, when she took it back from me. Her voice told me that circus people like other circus people better than they like people who live in towns. You can't hold that against them; everybody likes people like theirself. You just got to find out how someone else is like you and then you'll think they're OK too.

"It's like magic," I said. "You must of practiced a lot to be that good at it."

"It's easy," she said. "The top is going to keep falling over. Keep watching the top. When it starts to fall, you just move your hand so it's always under the top. Every circus kid knows that."

"What's up?" Gus asked her.

"Busted pipes," she said. "They musta froze when we went over the mountains."

"Those idiots!" Gus said. "I told them to drain everything before we left Nevada. The seasons are different at this altitude."

So Gus went walking pretty fast and we all followed him. We went to where they had a bunch of garden hoses and pipes and valves by one big truck which was the water truck.

"What a mess!" Gus said. The ground was muddy from all the water that leaked out. Some of the pipes had big rips in them. I would not of believed water freezing in them could do that. Dad said that when water freezes it gets bigger and will bust just about anything that tries to hold it in. I figured that was maybe what I was supposed to learn from today, so I memorized it extra hard.

"Do you have an extra torch?" my Dad said.

Gus looked at him funny.

"I done some plumbing in the Navy," my Dad said. "I'd like to show Jumper how to sweat solder. Plus, it will go faster with us helping you." When he said this, he said "sodder" which is how the word "solder" sounds when you say it. I only tell you that since it took me so long to look up how to spell it.

"Sure," Gus said. "I've got several. This isn't the first time they put clowns in charge of draining pipes."

I won't tell you all the boring parts, but I memorized how to solder. Soldering metal is dangerous which makes it even cooler than elephant poo. I bet Dad would of got in trouble with Mom for letting me do it, but it never come up in conversation, so we was off the hook. While Gus was getting stuff together, Dad picked up two little brown pipes, each one about as long as my thumb. "Let's practice on these scraps," he said. He used steel wool to clean the end of one copper pipe and then let me clean the other one. They got real shiny where you rubbed them, which was interesting. One was just a tiny bit smaller than the other. He helped me gunk up the shiny ends with sticky stuff called "flux" and then slid the little one inside the bigger one.

"This part's cool," he whispered, and it felt like we was magician inside an old pyramid and he was teaching me his best trick. "It's called a torch," he said. It was just a blue metal bottle with a little pipe coming out the top. He twisted a knob on the torch and it started to make a hissing sound. Then he held some wire thing in front of the tube part and squeezed it until it clicked. Right away, the hissing changed and now there was a blue fire coming out the end of the tube on the torch. The flame was about one inch long and looked like it was alive. No matter how he aimed the torch, that little blue flame come straight out of it.

"I get to use the torch, since I'm the grown-up," he said. "But if you're careful, you can hold the solder." He handed me a roll of wire made from soft silver-colored metal.

"Solder melts easy," he said. "And when it cools, it's as hard as metal. So you can use it to glue metal pipes together. But both pipes have to be very hot or else the solder won't stick." He held the torch so the blue flame was on both pipes where they was inside each other. The flux got hot and started to bubble like boiling water. After a while he decided it was hot enough and told me to touch the end of the solder wire on the spot the two pipes went together.

"But don't touch it with your hand. Plus, it can splatter and that hurts like heck, so use a long enough wire so you can stay back from it. And keep your face back too."

That sounded scary, so I was extra careful. When the end of the solder wire touched the hot pipe, the wire just melted. It looked like a drop of liquid silver for a second, the kind of magic thing you'd see in a movie. Then as quick as anything, it all ran between the pipes, like it got sucked in.

"A little more," Dad said. I touched the end of the solder wire to the pipe again and the same thing happened. The tip of the gray wire of solder turned into a shiny ball that jiggled and dripped and then got sucked between the pipes.

"That's how you do it," Dad said. "It's called sweat soldering. It takes a while to cool down, but once it does, those pipes are held together by metal." He looked at me and smiled. "And we done it together, Jumper, you and me. Pretty hard to separate things that are held together by metal."

It did take a long time to cool down, but when it did, he picked it up and gave it to me.

"You put this practice one in your pocket," he said. "If you ever forget how to sweat solder, it'll remind you."

But I was memorizing stuff about a hundred and ten percent. You don't see magic like that every day.

"I ain't ever forgetting how to do that," I said.

After that, Dad and Gus mostly did the soldering and I mostly handed them stuff, but sometimes I touched the solder to the pipe, and once when we had to start up a new torch, Gus let me use the starter thing. At the end, Dad let me hold the torch and aim it at a joint we was fixing. He said

I done a good job. By the time we fixed all the busted pipes, the sun was straight above us and it was time for lunch. Dad give me the keys to our car and I ran to get our sack lunches. Then Gus led us over to where the other guys was sitting around eating their lunches. Some was sitting on the dirt; some was sitting on wood boxes.

"You guys sit there, on those two apple crates," Gus said. Just then a loud voice yelled right behind us.

"Hey!" the man shouted. "No townies!"

We all turned around. It was the boss we seen when we first got there. He was mad when we first seen him, and he was still mad. Some guys ain't happy unless they're mad.

"They're with me," Gus said. He didn't seem scared of the boss at all.

"I don't care if they're with the President of the United States," the boss said. "No townies unless they pay admission."

We stood there next to Gus while the boss walked real fast right up to us. He was red in the face and waving his arms. But Gus didn't move, even if he was only a teenager. The boss was kind of fat and a lot older and wearing better clothes, but Gus was taller. I thought they was going to fight, but Gus just folded his arms across his chest.

"I don't care who your uncle is," Gus said. "I'm starting to lose patience with you. I said they're with me. They worked hard all morning for us, and now they're going to have lunch with us." His voice was real calm but he was about as firm as my second grade teacher when she was explaining how I should follow rules. They stared at each other for a minute, but you could see the boss wasn't moving Gus unless he got onto a bulldozer to do it.

Finally the boss turned to all the other men and yelled, "What are you looking at? Finish your lunch and get back to work!" Then he walked off real fast, like he just remembered a appointment.

We sat on the two boxes where Gus told us to sit and opened our sacks. We each had a peanut butter and grape jelly sandwich, plus an apple for dessert. The other men didn't say nothing, but they was kind of smiling. I think they all liked Gus a lot more than they liked the boss and thought it was funny that Gus wouldn't do what he said.

We was about half finished with our sandwich when that girl Thumbelina come walking over. She was dressed just the same and she still hadn't combed her hair. This time there was a lady with her. I figured it was her mom because their faces was sort of the same and they both had long black hair. Only the mom's hair was about as smooth as chocolate pudding. The mom was skinny and wore really tight jeans and a tight black shirt. Her belt had some little round metal things that sounded like bells when she walked. The men all watched her. It was like their eyes was puppets and she was pulling all their strings at once, only she didn't pay no attention to them at all. She had a kind of sleepy smile on her face.

"This is Jumper and his dad," Thumb said. The mom reached out her hand to shake mine.

"I'm Charm," she said. "Gus says you're the best workers on the whole crew."

"Thank you, Mrs. Charm," I said. She winked one eye and I couldn't look away from her face, just like all the men. Her eyes seemed extra wet. She made me feel like I probably just swiped a cookie I wasn't supposed to swipe and she knew I done it but didn't care and wasn't going to turn me in. I was kind of glad when she turned to shake Dad's hand.

"So, you're the mastermind behind the whole operation," she said while she smiled that same sleepy kind of smile at Dad.

"Pleased to meet you, Charm," he said. "You've got a sweet daughter there." You could tell Mrs. Charm liked that he said it.

"So, Thumb," Dad said to the little girl. "Who's your little assistant?"

I looked at the ground next to Thumb and about fell off my apple crate. She was holding a leash and on the end of the leash was a little bitty monkey. He was moving around, picking up stuff and putting it in his mouth, then grabbing at the little collar around his neck, then sniffing at Thumb's shoes.

"What's the monkey's name?" I asked. I ain't never seen a monkey that close up before.

"Not monkey," she said. "Chimp. He ain't a pet."

"Thumb's helping it get used to people," Mrs. Charm said. "Maybe when you're done with your lunch you can hold his leash and walk him around a little bit. Would you like that, Jumper?"

"I ain't never walked a monkey," I said. "Not even in a dream."

"Chimp," Thumb said.

I took a big bite out of my sandwich. Charm laughed. "Take your time," she said. "He's not going anywhere."

21

One of the men had already finished his lunch and he started tapping his fingers on the box he was sitting on. Another guy did too. Them boxes sounded just like drums. The first guy started singing a song about a drunken sailor. Everybody else knew the same song and they all sang along. More guys started tapping on their boxes. I didn't get the idea of the song, but some parts was funny because everybody laughed. Charm started kind of dancing in one place and the bells on her belt kept time with everything else. She was about as flexible as a snake, so I bet she done lots of stretching exercises like you see on TV. She had bracelets on both hands that also made clinking sounds in time to the singing.

I never seen people start singing and dancing and beating on boxes right in the middle of their peanut butter sandwiches, but everybody acted like it was as ordinary as watching TV.

Then Thumb jumped up and yelled, "Get back here!" which surprised everybody so the people near her stopped singing. The rest kept singing and didn't pay much attention, but I was right next to her so I heard her extra good. I turned to see what she was yelling at. She waved her hands over her head. One hand held the leash, but Chimp the monkey wasn't on the other end. I looked where she was looking and seen him standing next to a truck on the other side of everybody. He was looking back and jumping up and down. You could tell by his face he was laughing. Then he turned and run under the truck.

Thumb took off running after him. I had just started to bite into my apple, but I stopped with my teeth holding onto it. The grownups was all still singing about drunk sailors early in the morning, but when I seen that monkey start running, and then that girl start running, I didn't have much choices. With that apple still partway in my mouth I started running after them. Maybe Dad seen me and told me to stop, but I didn't hear him if he did. Just like you can't blame a cat who chases a mouse that starts running, you can't blame a kid goes chasing after a girl and a monkey even if he ain't got permission.

Chimp the monkey was fast. He got pretty far ahead, then stopped and turned around. He jumped up and down and laughed at us with his big white teeth and saying "Hee-hee-hee!" Then he run off again.

Thumb was a good runner and a few years older than me, but running is one of my best things so I caught up easy. Chimp run under one of them big moving trucks and scooted to the left. Thumb turned way left so she'd catch him when he come out. You didn't need to be smart as a circus clown to figure out what was going to happen. She was going to catch up with Chimp at the left end of the truck and he was going to stop and then go screaming right as fast as he could, back under that truck. If he come out running fast, he'd probably just keep running to the next hiding place, which was a blue and brown pickup truck a little ways away.

I run over to that pickup truck. It had a beat up camper top on it. It seemed like, if I was a monkey and people was chasing me, I'd want to climb up on top of it so that's what I done. I climbed up on the hood, reached up and pulled myself up on top of the camper top. If you don't know me you might think that was weird, so I'll tell you I been climbing stuff all my life. Once I was on top, I moved to the back so you couldn't see me as easy. That's when I remembered I still had a apple in my mouth and I got the rest of my idea.

I took out my red Swiss Army knife and cut of piece of apple. Then I leaned back like I was really comfortable and started to eat it. I don't know if monkeys is much like cats but I know this about cats: you can't catch one. They're faster than you, they climb stuff better, they crawl into hiding places better and they'll scratch you a lot harder than you want to scratch them back. Chasing a cat ain't ever your best plan. It probably wasn't your best plan with a monkey either. Your best plan is to outsmart him, but monkeys is pretty smart, so you also got to be cool as a watermelon.

I was just swallowing the piece of apple and cutting me a new piece when I heard a sound on the pickup and Chimp pulled himself onto that camper roof. That's when I learned that monkey faces look just like human faces when they get really surprised, except monkeys have big pink ears that stick out like clown ears and a pinkish tan face in the middle of black hair everywhere else. But the surprised part looks just like you or me look if we get surprised.

Chimp got over being surprised and went "Hee-hee-hee" at me and jumped up and down. Only I didn't even look at him. I just cut two more apple slices and put one in my mouth.

"Mm, " I said. "That's about the best apple I ever tasted." I smacked my lips together, which Mom says ain't polite but I figure monkeys got different rules about being polite, since they throw poo at each other. I kept making sounds like it tasted good, and even chewed with my mouth open. Chimp seemed pretty interested but I didn't pay no attention to him. I looked the opposite direction from him and flicked a little piece of apple toward him like it was an accident.

He tried to pretend he wasn't interested for a minute, but he didn't fool no one. In a minute he was eating that apple like it was his favorite thing.

I know what you're thinking. You're thinking I gave him some more apple pieces and then he come over and we became buddies and lived happily ever after. Which might have been a good plan and you can use it in your own book if you want. What I thought was that if I just kept feeding him, pretty soon he'd get full and then he'd run away again. So I put my Swiss Army knife back in my pocket, put the apple in my teeth and stood up real slow. Chimp got nervous and was chattering at me, but I kept looking away from him. I was standing right at the edge of the camper, looking down. I seen Thumb a little ways away with some of the grown ups, but nobody was coming toward us.

And then I jumped off the camper.

I probably should of told you that I like to jump off stuff, and that's been my sport since I was about old enough to walk, so if you're worrying that maybe I killed myself jumping off the camper, I didn't. I ain't saying it to brag. I'm just saying there's a reason everybody calls me Jumper.

The ground was soft and I landed good. I turned around and looked back up. Chimp had that really surprised look on his face again. I didn't really have a whole plan worked out, but that ain't stopped me before. I took the apple out of my mouth and started jumping up and down going "Hee-hee-hee" at Chimp. Then I started running around the truck about as fast as I could go. By the second time, Chimp climbed down from the camper and was running after me. Before he could catch me, I climbed back up on the truck hood and back on top of the camper. Chimp come around the corner of the truck and seen I wasn't there so he stopped. I went "Hee-hee-hee" at him and he come racing up. Only by the time he got there, I'd jumped off the other side and was on the ground. This time he didn't wait but started climbing down the side of the camper. Monkey's feet are about like hands, with fingers and everything so they can climb like the dickens. As soon as he started climbing down, I was already climbing up the other side.

It was pretty fun, and I maybe could of kept ahead of him for a little bit more, only I started laughing too hard. I just lay down on top of that camper and laughed my loudest and couldn't stop. Chimp stood on the other side of the camper roof going "Hee-hee-hee." Finally I sat up. "Hee-hee yourself," I said. I cut him a good slice of apple and held it out for him.

He pretended not to see. "Not this time, buddy," I said. "We gotta go back to work."

Finally he come over and took the apple from me. He stood right by me and ate it and I petted his back. While he was still eating, I picked him up and climbed down off the camper. While I was climbing down, Chimp was climbing up my arm so he could sit on my shoulders like we was playing piggyback. I kept my hand around one of his ankles though. Even if we ain't known each other very long I had my suspicions that he'd make another getaway if I didn't make good rules for him.

We walked over to Thumb and the grownups. Chimp kept messing with my hair, like maybe I had snacks hid in there.

"You're wasting your time, buddy," I told him. "If I had snacks I'd of ate them already."

Maybe you done lots of stuff that's as cool as walking around with a monkey on your shoulders, but it's one of the coolest things I ever done. One part of me said it would be more fun to just keep walking with Chimp. But the big opera star voice in my brain said we was just on our lunch break and there was probably still chores we needed to do. The smart plan was to memorize how cool it was right that second and then I could remember it a whole bunch of times.

When we got close to Thumb, everybody was staring at us. Dad was right behind Thumb and Mrs. Charm, her mom, was next to him. Gus was a little to one side and all the other guys who we was eating lunch with was behind him.

That's the first time I figured I was maybe about to get in trouble. They probably got as much monkey rules and circus rules as the government and chasing one around and feeding them human food and letting him ride on your shoulders probably breaks every rule in the book. Nobody was saying nothing, which ain't ever a good sign. I started to try to think up an excuse, only an excuse is extra hard to make up when you don't know what rule you broke.

Then my Dad clapped his hands one time, which he sometimes done to get my attention. He sure had my attention this time and I stopped walking. Then he clapped again, only this time Charm clapped one time too. Then my dad clapped again, and Gus clapped, and pretty soon everybody was looking right at me and clapping their hands like I just pulled a tiger out of a hat or something. I could feel my face get hot, so I looked down at my feet and walked toward them. When I got right up to them, Thumb put Chimp's collar back on him and took him off my shoulders.

Charm put her hand on my shoulder. "So, you're Jungle Boy, eh?" she said. "What does that make your Dad?"

"Jungle Boy's Dad was Tarzan," I said. "My mom read me that book three times."

Everybody laughed.

"Well, maybe Tarzan is a good circus name for your Dad then," Gus said.

"It fits him pretty good," I said. "Except for swinging through the trees."

"Tarzan it is then," Charm said.

I looked at Dad. He smiled a little but he didn't look so good. "Tarzan and Jumper," he said. "Sounds good to me." His skin looked white and he didn't seem real steady. Only he knew I was having fun so he didn't want to leave early, even if he should of been resting on the couch at home.

"Hey, Tarzan," I said. "I'm getting kind of tired. Maybe we should go home now and finish our circus chores a different time."

"There's still a lot of work to do," he said.

Gus stepped close to us.

"No more work. Not for you guys, not today. We got a union rule: anybody catches a wild monkey we gotta give 'em the rest of the day off. You don't want me to get in trouble with the union do you?"

The way he said it, God wouldn't want to be in trouble with the union. Dad nodded.

Gus turned to me and handed me a little envelope. It had three tickets to the circus inside.

"You get to bring your Mom and Dad to the circus for free," he said. "You earned it." He looked at Dad. "Both of you did. Tonight, tomorrow, next time we're in town — whenever. These tickets don't expire."

My eyes got wide. "Thank you, Mr. Gus," I said. "I ain't never been to the circus."

"Sure you have," Gus said. "I'll walk with you to your car, make sure no one hassles you."

We walked past all the apple crates where we ate lunch.

26

"I'll practice that box drumming thing too, " I told Gus.

"Will you now?" Gus said.

"Oh yeah, that was pretty cool."

"How you gonna practice if you don't have an apple crate?" he said. "You're just saying stuff, aren't you?"

"No sir, I never just say stuff. I'll get me a cardboard box and practice on that and then when I'm really good I'll get me an apple crate."

"Pish!" Gus said. "A cardboard box ain't even a musical instrument. You'll get bad habits. Wait here."

Dad and I stopped and Gus went over to the apple crates and picked up one. He held it up to his ear, tapped it a few times, then shook his head and put it down. He done the same thing to another one. This time he nodded his head, smiled, and brought it over to us.

"Now this one's a C sharp model," he said. "It's a good one for beginners. Only it don't play sad songs. How would that be?" He looked at my Dad.

"I don't want him to ever play sad songs," Dad said. "That one will be perfect."

Gus carried the apple crate over to our car and put it in the trunk. Then he shook our hands.

"It was a pleasure to meet you, Jumper," he said. "And it was an honor to meet you, Mr. Tarzan. You did a good job."

And then we drove away.

Chapter Two
In which a crime is committed and I put on my detective hat.

All that stuff at the circus happened a long time ago, when I was a kid. I just told you about it because I was thinking about it and we was talking about my apple crate, which now you know how I got it. I'm a grown up now and I live in my own apartment near Colfax Street in Denver. I ain't got a wife or any kids. I had a car once, but they ain't practical when they break, so now I walk or ride buses. I still like to jump off stuff, and I practice it all the time, which is why I don't get hurt the way most guys would. I mostly train at night since I figured out that people think you're weird if you do stuff they don't do. They ain't right about that, you and me both know that, but you don't need to make them feel bad about it. So everybody calls me Jumper but only a couple of my friends know why. Plus, I have a parakeet bird, which is a whole different story.

I was walking back home with a sack of groceries when I seen two police cars parked in front of my apartment building with their lights flashing. "Uh oh," I said and started walking faster. One car means they caught somebody in the act and they was probably speeding. One car plus an ambulance means somebody got sick, or maybe hurt in a fight. Two cars mean somebody done a crime. Four or five cars mean someone done a crime in a rich neighborhood. I ain't ever seen even three cars in my neighborhood.

A bunch of people was standing on the sidewalk in front of the building. Mostly they was other people who lived there like me, but some was people who just wondered what was going on. Before I even got up to them, my friend Holly, who was standing with everybody else, seen me and started running toward me.

"They won't let us in until they investigate," she said.

"OK," I said. Even if I got to know Holly pretty good when I was dealing with a crime done by a gang called The Bones, it still seemed like I had a lot fewer words in my brain when I was talking to her. Holly is a pretty nurse who lives in the apartment right below mine. I'm on the third floor, she's on the second floor. Holly has brown hair which she mostly wears in a ponytail. She was wearing blue jeans and a light blue work shirt like a man would wear, only it was ironed smooth. It wasn't tucked in.

I was going to ask her what was going on, but she answered before I could say anything.

"It was burglars," she said. "They broke into every apartment, I think. Even yours."

"Why would burglars want into my apartment?" I asked. The biggest thing I own is a couch I got off the sidewalk when somebody put a big "free" sign on it. I ain't got a lot of fancy stuff, like books or a computer.

"I don't know," Holly said. "They knocked on the doors and if anyone answered, they pushed their way in, tied them up and put tape over their mouths. Then they ransacked the apartment. They pulled out all the drawers, threw stuff on the floor and threw the valuables into a box. They broke the doors of people who weren't home and did the same thing. Only a few older people were home, most of us were at work. They cleaned out the whole building in two hours."

"Wow," I said. I was thinking about the cash I had hid in my freezer. You gotta figure that smart burglars probably found that pretty easy so I could kiss that goodbye. Next time I had some cash I'd use my whole brain to think of a better hiding spot.

On the good side, I'd already paid my rent, I had a whole sack of groceries in my hand and I probably still had sixty-two bucks in my shirt pocket as change from the grocery store. So I wasn't too worried.

We walked over to where the police was talking to people. One policeman had a notebook. He started talking to Holly in his most official voice.

"Name," he said. I knew right away he was making a mistake. He thought she'd think he was cool if he acted tough. You can't blame a guy for that, but it was dumb.

"Don't you people even talk to each other?" Holly said.

"Well, of course…" he said.

"If you can't keep track of who's been questioned and who hasn't then how do you know the burglars aren't right here, in this crowd?"

"So you're saying that an officer has already interviewed you?"

"It doesn't give a victim much confidence in our criminal justice system," she said and went on to say some more stuff, but you probably get the idea. The officer looked over to his buddy who was interviewing Mrs. Trumble from the first floor. That officer made a motion with his hand that said "It's OK" and pointed at himself and then pretended to be writing stuff down for about two seconds, then pointed at Holly. Which all meant, "Yeah, I already interviewed her." The whole time they was doing this sign language, Mrs. Trumble never stopped talking to that officer and Holly never stopped talking to this one. So if either one had good clues, the policemen missed them.

"I ain't been interviewed yet," I said.

"Thank you," the officer said. "And what's your name?"

"Jumper," I said.

He looked up at me like I was joking on him.

"Jumper? That's your name?"

"Well, my official name is John Cable which was also my father's name. Only he ain't alive anymore so it ain't that confusing. Everybody calls me Jumper."

"Why do they call you that?"

"Probably cause they heard someone else call me that. Or else I told them hi my name's Jumper." OK, so that was the truth but maybe not the whole truth and nothing but the truth. There wasn't much point in saying extra stuff for his brain to work on.

"Were you at home when the incident occurred?"

I looked down at the grocery bag I was holding and then back at him. He just stared at me, waiting for me to answer, while I just waited for him to figure out how dumb a question it was. But his brain wasn't even thinking about that.

"No," I said. "I was at the grocery store."

"Is anything missing from your apartment?" he asked, real serious.

"Well, air conditioning is missing. That would be a good feature."

"I mean did the burglars take anything?"

"Probably," I said. "Usually burglars take stuff. It's part of their job, so I bet they did. Unless they was really spies looking for government secrets. I could give you a better answer for your investigation after I go look at the apartment."

He looked up kind of sudden and stared at me like I just appeared out of a magic hat. Then he looked at my grocery sack.

"So, you were at the grocery store and haven't been inside your apartment since the incident?" He said it like it was a question, but also like he just figured out the mystery of where I been.

"Yeah," I said. "I probably should of been clearer about that."

Holly was getting red in the face listening. She tried to step between me and the officer but I moved my arm into her way so she couldn't. Maybe he wasn't as smart as a TV cop, but then he wasn't getting paid as much either. I figured he was doing his best job and you can't get mad at a guy when he's doing his best job.

"If you want to come up with me I could tell you what they swiped in about a minute."

"That's a good idea," he said. "It looks like the evidence team is finished. Ma'am, you can probably go to your apartment now too. I'm sure you'll want to straighten it out."

Holly looked like she was going to say some extra stuff to him, but then she just shook her head and walked in. Me and the officer followed her and walked up the three flights of steps to my floor and down the hall to my door. The door was open and the wood on the frame was busted. But the door wasn't busted at all, so it would be easy to fix.

Everything was a big mess. The couch cushions was on the floor, drawers was open and mostly dumped out. My apartment is all one room, with a couch where I sleep and a kitchen on one end, so it was easy to see it all without walking around much. The cigar box I kept my best stuff in was right on the floor. I don't let anybody even see my cigar box and now some burglars had thrown it on the floor like it was nothing. I felt like somebody kicked me in the stomach. It's a cool box all by itself, all brown and red and yellow that looks pretty fancy. It says "El Roi-Tan Mild Cigars" on the top with two gold colored unicorns. On the side, it says, "The cigar that breathes." I opened the lid, feeling nervous. Inside the lid it says "10 cent fresh panatelas."

Then I smiled. Inside was the two little pipes my Dad and I had sweat-soldered together at the circus, and the three circus tickets Gus gave me which I never got to use, and a lucky wood nickel I got from my uncle, and a bird skull I found, and some other cool stuff.

"I don't think they took nothing," I said. I relaxed a little and looked around again.

There is a black birdcage on a metal stand in the corner of my apartment. The birdcage has a green parakeet in it. "You was a witness, wasn't you, Mr. Silver," I told the bird. Sometimes I clean apartments for the building owner, and one time the old tenants had left their bird behind so I adopted him. I remembered a story about a pirate who had a parakeet on his shoulder all the time, and his name was Mr. Silver, so that's what I named my bird too. "You gonna use your right to remain silent again, ain't you?" I said. Some birds talk, but Mr. Silver never got the hang of it. But he was always chirping and flapping and kicking his birdseed around, so I liked having him as a roommate. He ain't much of a guard bird, but since he was still there, and so was my cigar box, I felt like them burglars missed all my best stuff.

"Don't you want to check your valuables?" the officer said. It took me a minute to figure out he meant dollar bills and jewelry and other stuff a burglar could sell.

"Right," I said. I closed the cigar box and put it back in the top drawer. "Looks like they didn't get my art collection."

You could tell he didn't know what I was talking about. I pointed to all the drawings I did on printer paper that was taped up all over the walls. They was mostly drawings I made with a pencil of interesting stuff, like a coffee can or a garbage sack or a dandelion flower. When I got some colored chalk as a present I started putting color on some of them too, but that's tricky. I mostly put one thing in color, like the yellow flower on a dandelion or the tie on the trash bag, and leave the rest just pencil with paper showing through. Using too much color seems kind of show offy. The officer looked at them and nodded.

"Well, it's hard to fence stolen art in this market," he said. So then I was glad I didn't joke on him before. We both knew my art wasn't in big demand, but he was nice to pretend maybe it was. Mr. Silver squawked, but you can't take his opinion all that serious since he's a bird.

In the kitchen, my refrigerator door was open and all the stuff I keep in there was on the floor. The ketchup bottle wasn't closed good enough and ketchup was leaking on the floor. I picked it up and tightened it. "That one's on me," I said. "Sometimes I forget to check the lid." The freezer part is on top and that door was open too. I already told you I seen that one coming. The whole freezer was empty except for the ice that grows on its sides. Some of the frozen stuff was on the floor, so I picked that up and put it back.

"You really like liver, don't you?" he said.

"Yeah. Plus it's pretty cheap. I hated it when I was a kid, but mom said I should be careful because 'hate' is kind of a permanent word. She didn't like liver when she was little but when she grew up she did. She said that might happen to me too. I never believed her but if you put enough ketchup on liver it's pretty good. It took me a long time to learn the lesson about using permanent words."

"You've got eight packages of liver," he said.

"Yeah," I said. "Them burglars didn't get none of them. I've always been pretty lucky."

"Is anything missing?" he asked. He looked around like maybe he'd guess where I kept my diamonds in case they was gone.

"I don't think so," I said. Then I seen that the sliding glass door to my balcony was open. It ain't a big balcony by rich people standards, about eight feet long and three feet wide, but I seen right away that something was missing out there. I stepped out onto as if maybe I was wrong, but there wasn't room to hide nothing.

"Oh, no," I said.

"Did they take something?" he asked.

I couldn't say nothing. I just pointed to the spot on the balcony where nothing was.

"What was it?" he asked.

"My apple crate," I said. My voice was pretty soft.

"What?"

"My apple crate," I said. You could tell he didn't get it. "You can play it like a drum, and you can sit on it." That blank space didn't look real to me. It was like looking down at my leg and seeing I didn't have a foot. I sat on that box to eat dinner almost every night, and sometimes I'd sit on it to drink a cup of coffee in the morning. I practiced tapping my fingers on it to songs in my brain, only real soft so I didn't bother the neighbors. Sometimes if I couldn't sleep, I'd sit on it and talk to the stars and moon and it felt like I was talking to someone who could hear me.

"Several residents said the burglars threw their valuables into a wooden box. Maybe they took your box to use for loot. It could be a clue."

I just kept staring at that empty space. My face got hot and my stomach hurt.

"It ain't a clue," I said. "It's a crime."

"If we catch them, maybe we'll recover it. But it's pretty long odds. I'll make a note so the detectives all know about it," he said.

I heard him and nodded my head, but when I talked I was talking more to myself than to him.

"It's only long odds til it happens," I said. "If you break the rules, you gotta take your consequences."

"What?" he said.

"Them burglars was wrong to go into apartments that wasn't theirs. And they was wrong to take stuff. If you break rules, you gotta take your consequence."

"Right. Well, thank you for your help. Maybe we'll get lucky and find them."

Mr. Silver chirped and kicked his birdseed around like he didn't believe the cop. I didn't either.

After the cop left, I didn't know what to do. The sun had went down and it was a nice evening. I opened a can of minestrone soup, which would have been good to eat sitting on my apple crate. Instead of feeling good about a can of soup and a nice night, I felt like I used the wrong word and somebody I didn't even know was making fun of me for it. I stood on my balcony holding the can in one hand and my spoon in the other and ate it anyways.

Well, you can't keep feeling bad about stuff you can't change. That's just dumb. So, even if it was hard, I didn't have much alternatives. I was going to have to find them burglars and get my apple crate back. I just needed a plan.

I probably should of gone down to the park and done some tree climbing that night. There ain't much better ways to come up with plans as climbing a tree at night when there ain't nobody else around and then jumping off a branch onto soft grass.

But I didn't. I just lay on my couch trying to go to sleep. I would of gone out onto the balcony, which is a good place to think, only there wasn't an apple crate out there to sit on. My Mom probably would of told me to just let it go: there's lots of boxes in the world and just because you like something don't mean it's worth a lot of money or time. One mistake people make is thinking every little thing is worth something. If you can't let go of any little thing then you won't notice when big stuff goes missing on you. She told me that lots of times when I was a kid.

So one voice in my brain was saying it was no big deal. Be smart, be a grown up, let it go.

But the big opera star voice in my brain was saying I don't care about being smart. I want my apple crate back.

Only I didn't know how to get it.

The apartment building creaked around me. Doors slammed down the hall. The walls of my apartment had soft shadows from the little bit of light that come in the window from the moon and cars. The shadows drifted around like an old black and white movie all out of focus, or maybe like ghosts. Finally it got all the way quiet, except for sounds from outside, like cars on Colfax Street a couple blocks away. After about three, when the bars was closed, even Colfax got pretty quiet. I tried to pretend I was a real good detective, like one of them guys who had TV shows. What would they do?

I decided the problem was I didn't have no good clues. The cops talked to everyone in the building but they didn't tell me nothing. I didn't know what the crooks looked like, or what kind of stuff they took from other people. The easiest way for me to find out would be to ask the other tenants. And since Holly was a tenant, and I knew her pretty good, I could start with her. People probably already told her stuff, plus I bet she had stuff swiped from her apartment too, so it wasn't just an excuse to talk to her. Plus, it would be good practice for me. That idea cheered me up pretty good. You always feel better when you got a plan. Right away, I started working on the details, which is where the Devil is. I decided I should take notes when I talked to the tenants. Then I thought it would sound better if I said "interview the victims" instead of "talk to the tenants." At first I thought maybe I'd take notes on three by five cards, which I had a bunch of. Then I decided it would seem more official if I used one of them legal yellow pads. Writing on a legal pad don't make you a lawyer, but it makes a guy feel like one.

I heard Holly come home in the apartment below me. She's a nurse and sometimes works the night shift. She'd eat something and watch some TV and then go to bed. She wouldn't get up until about noon.

That gave me plenty of time to go buy me a legal yellow tablet.

35

The next morning I walked over to the grocery store to buy one. Which they had, but they only came wrapped in bunches of five pads. I sure didn't need five pads. That would last me about two lifetimes, unless I decided to write another book, which don't seem that likely. But if one legal pad makes you feel like a lawyer, five might make you feel like a judge and I only needed to get up to feeling like a detective so I spent the money and bought the pads. I also bought two bunches of bananas and walked over to the thrift store where my friend Jim works.

"Hey, Jumper," he said when I walked in. He was sitting on a stool behind the counter by the cash register.

"Hey, Jim," I said back. "Did you hear about the excitement at my building?"

Jim nodded before he said anything. He ain't a guy who says stuff before he knows it's what he wants to say. "Yeah," he said. "Everybody's talking about it."

Jim is an interesting guy. He's only got one leg and he's really skinny. I know he don't make much money at the thrift store so he might be skinny from not buying enough groceries. But he's the nicest guy you ever met and he knows that thrift store like he was Noah and built it shelf by shelf to keep all his animals. Plus, he's the best driver I ever rode with if you can stand getting scared to death by how fast he goes. If we lived in a bigger town, he'd of been a taxi cab driver, but Denver don't have that many taxis. Once he gets talking, he talks as much as anybody. It just takes him a little bit to get warmed up to full speed. Jim sat there for a minute, nodding his head. He didn't say nothing but he looked like he might so I just waited. Pretty soon, you could see he decided what else he wanted to say.

"Did they get anything from your apartment?"

"Not too much," I said. "Mostly they just made a mess like they was looking for something I ain't got. Like my jewels and gold bars. But they did swipe my apple crate."

"The one on your balcony?"

"Yeah."

He looked down at the countertop for a minute.

"You owned that since you were a kid," he said.

"I know," I said back.

"Probably makes you sad. I'm sorry."

36

"At first it made me sad. Then it made me mad. But now I figure I'll find it and get it back."

He nodded for a minute. "Hmm," he said. "What's your plan?"

"Well, I got me some legal yellow pads."

Some guys would answer that one right away by joking on you or saying that was dumb, or asking how in the heck legal yellow pads would get your apple crate back. But Jim's smart. He just thought about it for a minute before he talked.

"You're gonna write down clues?"

"Yeah," I said. "I figure I'll interview the victims and take notes." I took off my backpack and got out the pack of pads.

"That's a lot of pads."

"Yeah, it's the only way they sell 'em."

"There were three of them."

"Nah, they come five to a pack."

"No, the thieves. I heard a couple of cops talking about it this morning outside the shop. They said there were three of them, young white guys in their twenties. They talked with an accent."

"Lots of cops have accents, like from New York."

"No, not the cops. The thieves had accents, but not the usual ones. Not Mexican or German, but from some foreign country. No one recognized it for sure."

"Hey, that could be a clue right there!" I said. I opened the pack of pads and took a pencil out of my pocket. "I better write that down before I forget it."

"Good idea."

"Yeah," I said. It made me feel good that he thought about what I said before he just started talking himself.

"Well," he said. "You're a pretty good detective. I bet you already got some ideas."

"You give me the best clue so far by saying there was three of 'em and they talked with accents. You already get some credit when we solve the case. I'll probably make you answer the questions at the news conference."

Jim smiled. "I'll keep a clean shirt handy."

37

"I was thinking about the burglars last night," I said. "And one thing don't make sense. It seems like they done a lot more work than you or I would of."

"Anybody would do more work than you and me," he said.

"Yeah, but criminals is lazy even compared to us. They always do the easy thing, which is what made them criminals in the first place. Only these guys didn't."

"They didn't?"

"Nah. Easier to break in when nobody's home, for one example. Maybe somebody's got a gun, or a cell phone to call the cops. These guys went into every apartment whether someone was there or not. That don't make sense."

"I see what you mean."

"Plus, my building ain't got very rich people living in it. If you wanted money and jewels, why wouldn't you pick a place where people had money and jewels? Instead of apple crates. So these guys picked a dumb place to rob and they let lots of witnesses see them. And they done it in the middle of the day. Either they're really dumb, which lots of criminals is, or else that stuff is all clues."

"You could be right. What's your next step?"

"I figure I'll interview all the victims. I might start with Holly, since I know her and all."

Jim smiled. "The Department ain't gonna pay you overtime to talk to pretty girls."

"That's OK. I won't even charge the Department nothing for this one." We was both joking. There wasn't a Department and nobody was going to pay me a dime for investigating. On the good side, nobody could be mad at me for not solving the case, which they would be if they paid me.

"Well, good luck," Jim said.

"Oh, wait, I almost forgot." I got one of the banana bunches out of my backpack. "The store was having one of them buy one get one free sales. I was gonna skip the free one cause it'll just go black on me before I can eat it and I'd have to throw it away. Then I thought, hey, maybe Jim'd like the free ones. So here you go."

"You don't have to buy me food," he said.

"Wasn't you listening? I didn't buy 'em. The store threw 'em in for free and I can't use them." I set a banana bunch on the counter and closed up my backpack. "If you want to let them go to waste and make some kid in China starve, that ain't my business. As long as you can sleep at night from starving some kid. See you later."

I walked back to my building and knocked on Holly's door. I noticed I was holding my breath, which I sometimes do when I'm nervous, so I let it all out just when she opened the door.

"Hi, Jumper," she said. "What's up?"

Well, I'd just let out all my air so I had to breathe in real quick to answer, which made me cough and then I couldn't say nothing for a second. I could feel my face getting hot.

I got to know Holly better when I was detecting on The Bones drug gang and they thought she was a person of interest to them, so you'd have to say we was friends. She's a little younger than me and real pretty, with brown eyes and a brown ponytail. I like her a lot, and we even kissed one time, but that was during a turtle release party, which ain't an ordinary time so the kiss maybe don't count. Anyway, you can like someone pretty much and even kiss them one time and it don't mean they're your girlfriend or something.

"Hi," I finally answered, even if she maybe forgot the question. "I was wondering if we could make an appointment so I could interview you about the incident." It sounds smarter if you call stuff an "incident."

"You mean the break in? Sure, I'm not busy now, come on in." She opened the door wider and smiled.

OK, so I wasn't really ready to interview anybody. I didn't make up my questions yet, for one thing. But I already noticed that pretty much whenever Holly smiled and told me to do something I didn't have much alternatives except to do it. I went into her apartment and sat down on her couch.

"You want a soda?" she asked.

"Well, thanks, but I'm sort of on duty…"

She give me a look that said, no, you ain't on duty and stop being a idiot. She pulled two cans out of her refrigerator.

"Here you go," she said. "Diet Dr. Pepper, right?"

"Yes, ma'am," I said.

"So I see you've got a legal pad and a sharp pencil. You probably want to ask me questions while you take notes, right?"

"Well, I ain't got all my best questions thought up yet," I said.

She smiled again. This would be a lot easier if she didn't keep smiling. It made it harder to think. But she didn't need no questions to tell what happened. She just started talking.

"They took some jewelry I got from my grandmother," she said without me even asking. "One was a pair of emerald earrings in the shape of a fish. I always loved them."

I wrote down "emerald fish earrings."

"I'll sure keep my eyes out for that," I said. "What color are they?"

She smiled again. "Green, like a piece of shiny green glass."

"That's a pretty good clue," I said. "I ain't ever seen a fish earring."

"I wasn't home when they broke in. The police said they used a crowbar to pop open the doors so it wasn't as loud."

"At least it don't look like they messed your place up too bad," I said.

"It was a total mess. I've been cleaning nonstop."

"Oh. Well, you done a good job. Was there anything unusual?"

"Unusual? Except for the fact that someone broke into my apartment, stole my grandmothers' jewelry and completely trashed the place?"

"Well, that stuff's all unusual compared to a day when nobody burgled your apartment. I get that. I'm just trying to notice if these particular burglars done something that other crooks might not of done. Like, they took all the liver out of my freezer and threw it on the floor. What kind of burglar messes with a guy's liver? Maybe that's a clue to their true identity."

"I see what you mean. No, I can't think of anything like that."

I stood up.

"OK, then. Thanks for the Dr. Pepper."

"Sure, Jumper. I'll let you know if I think of anything else."

"One more thing," I said. "Do you know what order they used?"

"What order?"

"Yeah. Like which apartment was first and which one was second."

"What does that matter?"

40

"I don't know. Maybe it don't. A guy can't just look for the clues he already knows what they mean. The best clues is the ones you don't know what they mean."

"Right. No, I don't know what order they used."

"OK. Well, thanks."

I decided that if I was burgling an apartment building with no elevator, I'd start on the top floor. That way I wouldn't have to carry the stuff I stole upstairs, just down. I went up to the third floor, which is where I live to the apartment on the end and knocked on the door.

"Hey, Mr. Stevens, it's me, Jumper from down the hall," I said when I knocked on the door. People was probably nervous about answering their door to strangers. Mr. Stevens opened the door a little bit and looked out. I seen he'd already got his chain fixed even if the first one didn't do him much good.

"What do you want?" He said. He was a skinny old guy with white hair. His hands shook all the time. He never smiled and didn't say hi to me in the hallway. He always figured somebody was about to do something bad to him. Now that somebody had, I would of thought he'd be in a pretty good mood from being right and all. Maybe it just hadn't sunk in all the way because he still seemed in a bad mood.

"I said what do you want!" he said again.

"I just wanted to ask you about the incident."

"You mean those hooligans? Police already asked all their questions."

"Yeah, I figured they did. But you know, cops is part of the government. I ain't sure I trust the government to solve any problems. How 'bout you?" Guys who think something bad is about to happen usually don't like the government, so I was just guessing he was one of them guys too.

"Bunch of lazy bureaucrats!" he said. "Not one of 'em worked a day in their life."

"Well, Officer Mike was pretty good, you gotta admit that. But he retired, so we're kinda on our own. But if you'd rather trust the government bureaucrats, that's up to you. Have a nice day." I turned and started to walk away when he opened his door.

"All right, but make it quick."

I went in and sat on his couch. His apartment was really neat and clean. He had heavy black curtains on the window so it was dark inside.

"What's your plan?" he asked.

"My plan is to figure out who those guys are, then find them and get back the stuff they stole. Then I'll turn 'em over to the cops."

He sat across from me on a big stuffed chair. His apartment was a lot bigger than mine. He nodded his head real fast. "Good plan," he said. "Excellent plan. How are you going to do it?"

"The hard part is figuring out who they is. The next hardest part is where they is. The first thing is just getting clues. I'm going to talk to everybody in the building and maybe somebody knows something that's a clue. So, what do you remember?"

"I was sitting right over there at the kitchen table, eating my oatmeal…"

"I ain't never liked oatmeal too much," I said

He looked at me like he was mad for a second and then I seen that I'd stopped him in the middle of his story. Nobody likes that.

"You gotta mix a lot of fruit in it," he said.

"I shouldn't of stopped you," I said. "Go on with your story."

"Right. I was sitting at the table when I heard a knock on the door. It was soft, so I thought it was maybe a Girl Scout or something. I went over and looked out the peephole, but I couldn't see anybody. So I yelled, "Go away! I don't want whatever you're selling." I turned to walk away and bam! They busted in the door. It hit me in the back and knocked me down. Before I could do anything, they were on top of me. They tied my hands together behind my back with plastic straps and covered my mouth with tape."

"What kind of tape? Did they use duck tape?"

"No, it was masking tape, like painters use."

"OK, see, that could be a clue right there. Then what happened?"

"They're just lucky they surprised me or I would have taken a couple of them out. I've been in a fight or two. Back in the war, me and my buddies…"

"Man, we ought to save that story for when I got a new legal yellow pad," I said. "I want to keep this one just for clues."

"Right. They taped me to the kitchen chair, right in front of my oatmeal. They taped each of my legs to a different chair leg and a few loops around my waist holding me to the chair back. You'd think you could break masking tape, but it's stronger than you think. They used a lot of it."

"What did they take?"

"First thing, they took all my pillowcases. They used them to carry out the rest of the stuff."

"They didn't have a box?"

"No, they took my pillowcases. Then they took my guns."

"You had a gun?"

"I had six guns. One revolver, two pistols, two rifles and a shotgun. They wrapped the long guns in a sheet and threw the rest in pillowcases. One guy carried those down to the getaway vehicle. Oh, and a dozen boxes of ammunition."

"Wow," I said.

"Yeah. They're just lucky I wasn't holding one when they broke down the door. Then they trashed the place. They found some silver dollars I'd been collecting. Here, I made a list for the cops and printed up a few copies."

"Thanks," I said, taking the paper from him. "Did they say anything?"

"Not to me. When they talked to each other, they used a language I didn't recognize. Maybe Russian. They had a kind of communist look to them. Or like terrorists. They're lucky I didn't get off a couple of shots."

"Interesting. There ain't that many communists in Denver, so that might be a good clue."

"There's more than you think."

I stood up to go.

"Thanks, Mr. Stevens. If you can think of anything else, I'll sure write it down in my pad." I walked to the door and opened it. He followed after me, but he kind of limped along since he was so old.

"After they tied me up," he said. "They turned on my stereo, just to mask any noise. They could have left it on the talk radio station I always listen to. But no, they switched it to some public radio station. I don't think they even liked it, they just knew it would irritate me. These guys are mean."

"Yeah, that sounds pretty mean." I stepped out the door. "OK, thanks a lot," I said.

"One more thing. It's probably nothing. They looked at all the photographs on my wall. Got their noses real close to every one. That's just being snoopy. I'm pretty sure they're communists."

"I wouldn't bet against it," I said. Once Mr. Stevens decided to talk to you, it was pretty hard to get him to stop. I was out the door when he reached out to shake my hand.

"Bless you, Jumper," he said and I thought he was going to cry. "Please get my guns back. I just don't feel safe without them."

"I'll try my hardest," I said and pulled the door closed behind me.

Next I talked to Jacob and Sophia who was a nice young married couple. They both was at their jobs when the burglary happened so they didn't see the perps. The word "perps" is what cops sometimes call "perpetrators" which means "the guys that done the crime." But I ain't giving a test, so you don't need to remember it. Jacob and Sophia was about as broke as me. The suspects tore up their apartment and threw stuff out of their freezer, but Jacob said he didn't think they swiped anything. Sophia thanked me for my detective work and said if they ever had a baby, they'd sure let me babysit it. That was a nice thing to say, cause people like their babies pretty much. I looked at my shoes.

"I could sure babysit him while you guys was around," I said.

They laughed and said that would be a good start.

I went from door to door interviewing victims. Not everybody was home, so I knew I'd have to just keep detecting every day until I talked to everybody. I figured the suspects did start on the top floor, just like I guessed. If somebody was home, they tied 'em up with masking tape and turned up their stereo. They took stuff out of people's freezers and threw it on the floor, they dumped out everybody's drawers and broke stuff they wouldn't of had to find valuables. Which makes you think they wasn't poor guys who needed money real bad but that they was mean just like Mr. Stevens thought. I didn't have enough clues yet to decide if they was communists.

By about 6:23 I felt like that was enough detecting for one day so I went to my apartment. Mr. Silver chirped and squawked until I give him some new seeds to eat. "If you wouldn't kick it out of the cage, it would last a lot longer," I told him. But you can't use logic on a bird, you just got to put up with them the way they are. They got their own ideas and you ain't gonna change their little bird brains. He just chirped at me and flapped his wings.

I decided I'd eat a can of Dinty Moore stew and wait for it to get dark. My mood was improving a lot, which happens after you decide to start doing stuff instead of just thinking about stuff. I knew the thing that would kick my mood up the next step or two. After it got dark, I was going to find something good to jump off of.

Chapter Three
Jumping off a church roof can get complicated.

If you're going to jump off a building at night, a church has got some natural advantages. Usually nobody lives in them, so you're not going to scare somebody or have them shoot you or call the cops for trespassing. Lots of them have some grass, which is a lot better to land on than a parking lot. And they usually have some lights in the yard so you can see where you're landing but not so many a neighbor might notice you. Plus, since God belongs to everybody, you gotta figure His house is partly everybody's too, so it ain't really trespassing, which He forgives you for doing anyway, as long as you forgive people who trespass on your stuff too.

I like this one church. It's got one really tall pointy roof plus a smaller flat roof part. It's got stained glass windows in the front and they leave enough lights on inside so they look pretty cool at night. I like the red glass and blue glass the best, but they're all fancy. One good feature of this church is a tree by the corner of the flat roof part, which is easy to climb. So I climbed up the tree and stepped onto the flat roof.

When I'm training at that church, I usually jump off the back of the short building part with the flat roof. There's a garden area which only has a few little bushes with a bunch of wood chips between them. Wood chips is about the easiest thing to land on for not hurting your ankles or knees. When I'm done, I can just smooth out the woodchips and not even Columbo could tell I'd been there. That was my plan for tonight. I figured I'd do maybe seven jumps, but first I like to just sit up there where nobody knows I am. I like to notice what the air smells like, and if bugs is singing to each other. Everything looks different from on top of a building, especially a church, and sometimes that makes you think of different stuff too.

Since I was working on a mystery, what I should have been thinking about was all my clues, but I gotta admit I was mostly just noticing stars and smells and bug sounds. Crickets chirping was the most popular sound that night, but there was some buzzing bugs too. The chirpers and the buzzers didn't pay attention to each other. They was like two guys who was each telling their own story at a party and it didn't matter what the other guy chirped, they was gonna just keep buzzing on.

I was doing some stretches before I jumped when I heard people talking. That wasn't very ordinary, so I stopped to listen. Two guys was coming across the parking lot and they was talking about vandalizing the church.

"Look," one said. "Let's just tag it from the outside. What if it's got an alarm?"

"I told you, I already checked. No alarm. I checked the whole place out last Sunday."

"You went to church? To a service?"

"Don't be an idiot. They open the doors an hour before the service and anybody can wander around. There's a meeting room back here. I unlocked the window. If nobody checked it, we don't even have to break the glass."

"You think this ladder will fit through that little window?"

They was getting closer to me by now and I could see they carried one of them fold-up aluminum ladders that lots of workers use.

"It doesn't have to," the other guy said. "I'll climb in the window then unlock the side door. We'll just carry the ladder through the door like we own the place. Then we can improve that stained glass with some spray paint."

"It's gonna be so cool!"

"Yeah, that priest is gonna be surprised!"

"It ain't a priest. It's a minister."

"Like I care what he calls himself. It'll take 'em weeks to clean the glass. And we can walk by every night and admire our art."

I gotta admit I had some conflicts, listening to that. First, I'm an artist myself so I don't like to be too judgy about another guy's idea of art. On the second hand, I seen a lot of graffiti guys do stuff that ought to be in a art museum instead of on the side of a train. Maybe these guys was like that. But on the third hand, messing up somebody else's stuff ain't right even if you call it art. Them perps who swiped my apple crate and Holly's ring and Mr. Stevens' guns could say they had a good excuse if burglary was their kind of art. But they'd just be making up stuff so they feel better about being crooks, which every crook wants to do. These graffiti guys was pretty young, so they probably didn't even know they was making it up.

I walked real quiet on the roof til I was right above where they was standing. There was a big patch of wood chips right below me. I stood right on the edge of the roof and watched them.

"Look, the window's still unlocked." He grunted and pushed it open. "There," he said.

"It's a pretty small window."

"No problem. I'll take off my backpack. But first let's make sure no one's around."

They took a couple steps away from the building. The one guy took off his backpack and handed it to the other guy. They looked every direction except behind them, toward the building. I aimed to land right between them and the building.

And then I jumped.

While I was falling off the church roof, I could hear the chirping and the buzzing bugs, and some cars a few streets away. It smelled like some neighbor dug up dirt in their garden. I seen that the moon made some shadows from the trees on the parking lot. I kept my arms straight out to each side like wings, to help with my balance. I hit the woodchips perfect. My knees was bent a little and I kept bending them more after I hit until I was crouching on the ground. It was an excellent landing and I give myself about an eight. I had to take off points for letting one hand hit the ground.

The graffiti guys heard the crunching sound of my feet hitting the wood chips. They turned around real quick. I was still crouched low when they turned, so when they turned they was looking above me at the window they just opened. So they wasn't looking in the right spot to see me. Plus, I was in the shadows next to the building, in the exact spot they was just standing two seconds before, so they figured nobody was there.

I stood up slow and their eyes got real big, like I just sprouted out of the ground. They took a step back.

"Who… who are you?" the taller guy said. He tried to sound all tough and scary but I wasn't buying it.

I smiled, but I was still too much in the shadows so they probably couldn't see it.

"Well, I ain't a priest," I said. "And I ain't a minister either. But I do kind of think of this as my own special place. So I don't like for people to mess it up."

Their eyes got even bigger and their mouths was open like fish mouths. They backed up another step. I took one step toward them and raised my arms to the sides, like I was about to jump again. I was going to tell them I wouldn't turn them in, only they shouldn't make up stuff to make them feel better if they knew they was breaking rules. But when I stepped forward, I come out of the shadows and the moon hit me kind of sudden. It startled them to see me get all light like that. I figured that out later. But what really startled them was that just when I raised my arms, the bells in the church started to ring. They ring every hour like a clock, only soft so it don't bother the neighbors. It wasn't any big deal but it might of seemed spooky to have a guy suddenly light up and have bells ring when he lifted his arms.

Them two graffiti guys yelled and turned around and started running away about as fast as they could. They didn't even remember to take their ladder.

So I picked it up. It said ABC Construction on the side. Maybe them guys bought it from ABC but maybe they swiped it. I carried it around to the side door, where the church guys would find it easy. The priest could call ABC easier than me, since I ain't got a phone. Plus, nobody'd think a priest swiped their ladder, but if I took it to them they'd probably call the cops on me.

I was in the middle of a case and I didn't need the distraction.

I jumped six more times and mostly got nines. You can't complain much about a night like that.

Chapter Four
In which I'm investigating pretty hard

I talked to most of the people in my building. It took longer than I thought because they was all interesting and I wound up asking them about stuff in their apartment or their dog pictures. Everybody will talk about their dog or whatever they think is cool, and pretty soon it sounds cool to you too. I always remember what my Mom said when I was little. She didn't talk about "God" but she talked about "the universe" and it sounded about the same to me. She told me that you should always notice cool stuff. If you do, then the universe will send you more cool stuff.

"Like a puppy?" I'd asked.

She laughed. "I don't think you're quite old enough for a puppy."

"I don't mean that," I said. "I mean is the universe like a big puppy? So if it does something funny you should give it a bite of your hot dog and then it will know to do something else funny."

She laughed again. "There's no puppy as funny as you," she said. "And if you want to share your hot dog, don't let him take a bite out of it. Cut off a little piece. Dogs can have germs."

I was pretty sad when my Mom died, especially since my Dad was already dead by then too. I should of gone to some foster home and stayed in middle school. It was kind of breaking the rules that I didn't. But there wasn't nobody to notice whether I was in one place or someplace else and nobody complaining about me. I'd already did some work cleaning apartments for this one old guy and he kept letting me do it and pretty soon I was living in one of his units. I always done my best job and I never stole or broke any of the important rules. Pretty soon I was a grown up man.

I ain't seen much bad consequences of staying out of school, so it worked out pretty good. I still clean apartments for the same guy when someone moves out. I also collect cans, which you can turn in for money. Sometimes I can make a whole bunch of money by being in a drug study. That's where they hire you to take medicines that ain't legal yet so they can test you for side effects. Some people are afraid to do a study since they think a new drug might make them crazy or stupid or something, but I never had a problem.

Mr. and Mrs. Simpson took all Saturday afternoon to interview. They was from Texas, which you could tell by the way they talk and the Dallas Cowboy poster on their wall. I'm pretty much a Denver Broncos fan but you can't hold it against someone if they like a different team, or even a different sport or a different God. I used to think you couldn't hold it against someone if they liked a different political guy, but these days I got my suspicions about that one.

Mr. and Mrs. Simpson decided to retire in Colorado since the summers ain't as hot, but they still sound like everything is better in Texas. Mr. Simpson don't get around too good after his hip surgery and they couldn't get their shower curtain up, so I helped them do that when I was supposed to be interviewing them. Then a burner on their stove wasn't working, but Mrs. Simpson couldn't see good enough to figure it out. The connection needed to be cleaned, so I done that. Then their window was stuck closed, which you could see because they painted it shut. That's pretty easy to fix and it didn't take much time.

The whole time I was fixing stuff for them I was casually asking questions about the burglary. They wasn't home at the time so they didn't know much. The burglars took two hundred bucks Mrs. Simpson kept under the flour can on her kitchen counter and some earrings and a necklace. They wasn't too worried since they had insurance, but they wasn't all that helpful to the investigation either.

Mrs. Comanici was maybe the most interesting. She's lived in the building for almost twenty years. Mrs. Comanici is my buddy. She's older than my Mom would have been but she ain't old enough to be my grandma. She's got long black hair, with lots of gray hairs, and really dark eyes. The middle part of her eyes is brown, just like most people's, but hers are extra dark brown. When she opens her eyes real wide, she looks kind of scary, like a witch. She opens them real wide like that pretty often, but she ain't a witch. She's about the nicest person I ever met. She likes to wear bright colored dresses and bright scarves and she laughs really loud, if you can say enough jokes til she thinks one is funny. Most of the time she's quiet. She retired from being a substitute teacher and I think she got used to being quiet on account of her job and now that she ain't working she maybe wears the stuff she wishes she wore her whole life and laughs loud to make up for not laughing so much before.

"Shar-sen, Mrs. Comanici," I said when she opened the door.

She smiled big and said, "I'm fine, Jumper. Shar-sen?"

"Well, I ain't as good as a full bag, but I'm a lot better than a empty one," I said.

Shar-sen means "how are you" in Moldova, which is where Mrs. Comanici's parents came from. Teachers don't ever stop teaching all the way, even when they retire. She was always teaching me new words and stuff and I done my best to remember them. She had a round globe of the world and she pointed to Moldova, but I don't think I could find it again. She smiled at my bag joke, but she didn't laugh out loud. It had to be a pretty good joke for that, like I said.

"Well, I just baked some chocolate chip cookies," she said. "Please come in and help me eat a few."

"Thanks," I said. I come in and sat on her couch. She put a plate full of chocolate chip cookies on the coffee table and brung me a big glass of milk. Even if I been a grown man for several years, she always treated me a little bit like I was her kid. You could tell it made her feel good to do that. And if I was telling the whole truth and nothing but the truth I'd have to say I didn't mind it either. Plus, it's just mean to stop someone doing something they like if it ain't hurting anybody.

"To what do I owe this honor?" she asked and sat on the chair. She'd used that line on me before so I knew it meant, "why did you knock on my door?"

"I'm investigating the incident. You know, the burglary."

"I see," she said, kind of frowning. "Don't you think that's a job for the police?"

"Yeah, they're working on it too. Theirs is mostly the official investigation and mine is sort of the extra one."

"Did they take something from you?"

"Yeah," I said. "Only it wasn't something that would be expensive to anybody but me. I think cops work harder to find stuff that's expensive to rich people."

"You're probably right."

"Anyway, I'm just interviewing all the victims in case the alleged suspects made some mistakes the cops missed. So, was you here when the incident happened?"

She looked away, like she was remembering. She was drinking a cup of tea, but she put it down on the coffee table real slow.

"Oh, yes," she said softly. "I was here. It was awful."

Right away I felt bad that I was making her remember something awful.

"I'm sorry, " said. "You know, I talked to most of the victims already and I probably got enough clues…" I started to get up but she stopped me.

"No, Jumper, that's all right. Everyone knows how you managed to catch that terrible drug gang. Sometimes it takes a person who looks at things a little differently. My mother called it 'glasso.' It means 'different kinds of melodies'. The world needs many glassos. I'll tell you about it. Just promise you'll be careful."

"Yes, ma'am," I said. "I'll use my best glassos. Even little stuff might be clues. "

She smiled and picked up her teacup again.

"It was about three in the afternoon," she said. "Someone knocked on my door. When I got up to answer it, I stumbled a little and spilled hot tea on my favorite blouse. I should not have lost my temper, but it was my favorite blouse. I said "ban khul" just as I opened the door, which is a very naughty phrase my father said when he hit his hand with a hammer." She smiled at me. "I know you don't like to curse," she said. "And I don't either. But it's an old habit. At least I stick to words no one understands."

"It probably ain't really cussing if nobody knows what you said," I told her.

"Anyway, I was a little distracted. When I opened the door these three ruffians were standing there. One had a crowbar. There was a wooden box beside them, full of jewelry and cash and envelopes."

"That's my apple crate!" I said.

"It had pictures of peaches on the side…"

"That's it! Peaches and a pretty girl with a red handkerchief around her head. I'd know my apple crate anywhere!"

She looked at me like she was going to say something then changed her mind and just nodded. I got a lot more interested in the interview now that she give me that clue. I felt like I was hot on the trail for sure.

"OK, then what happened?" I asked.

"Nothing happened for a few seconds. They looked at each other like they were surprised I answered the door. The tallest one put his fingers to his lips, telling the others to be quiet. Then they moved quickly, pushing open the door, pushing me back, and covering my mouth with their filthy hands. They tied me to a kitchen chair and started tearing the place apart."

"What did they take?"

"I had some cash in the refrigerator, pushed in a jar of feta cheese. I thought it was safe there, but they found it. A few earrings, a bottle of good poteen — that's whiskey from the old country — and some galbi. My laptop was in the shop for repairs, thank goodness, so they didn't get that. My backup thumb drive was in the case with it. From now on, I'm going to keep them in separate places. Pretty stupid to make it easy for someone to steal your computer and your backup at the same time."

"Galbi?" I asked. Mrs. Comanici spoke about perfect English since she was a substitute teacher and all. But when she got excited she used old words nobody knows.

"Sorry. Gold coins. They might be valuable by now. I kept them to remind me of home."

That was a clue right there.

"Home? You mean you ain't from America?"

"America is my home now. I was born in Moldova. That was a different life and a very long time ago."

"Cool," I said. "So then they just left?"

"Yes. And they left the door open and the place a mess. I couldn't get loose until the police came."

I got up to leave.

"Thanks for the cookies," I said. "If I find my apple crate, I'll look extra hard for your gold coins."

"I know you will, Jumper. You be careful."

"Yes, ma'am," I said. I went out into the hallway. There was only two apartments left before I got to the back door. I went up to the next door, but before I could knock on it, Mrs. Comanici opened her door again and stepped into the hall.

"I forgot one thing," she said. "They took my photo album, right off the coffee table."

"Your big book with pictures inside?"

"Yes. Pictures from my whole life. It doesn't matter; I've scanned them all into my computer so I can print up new copies. The point is an old woman's pictures aren't worth anything to anybody. They just took them to hurt me. They're just nasty men. They're kanniecho. You know, chicken thieves." You could tell she was working herself up to be mad all over again. "You be careful."

"Yes, ma'am," I said. "Plus I'm glad I ain't got chickens."

She didn't laugh but said some other foreign words without explaining them and went back inside her apartment.

The next apartment was Mr. Mitchell's. I knocked on his door. I only met him a few times in the hallway or outside on the sidewalk. We knew who each other was, but we wasn't buddies. There wasn't nothing wrong with him, we just ain't clicked as friends yet. He was really polite like you imagine a serial killer would be. He was maybe forty years old, real thin, and he dressed better than anybody else I knew. Holly told me she thought he got a divorce and was just living here til that was finished. But I don't know. Once I asked if he liked the Denver Broncos after they beat Oakland. He said he didn't know, he was more of a hockey guy. In Denver, lots of guys like the Avalanche hockey team but only if they got extra time left after liking the Broncos. So that was suspicious, but people is different.

He opened the door and you could tell it took him a second to think who I was. Then he did.

"Mr. Jumper, isn't it?" he said. "How may I help you?" He talked about as soft and smooth as a serial killer would, too, but that's just circumstances evidence.

"Hi, Mr. Mitchell. I'm trying to figure out the burglary incident, so I'm asking all the victims about it."

"Fascinating," he said. "And probably noble. But I'm afraid they didn't invade my space at all. I can't tell you anything about it."

Only instead of saying 'about' he said 'a boot.' That was the first time I noticed he said some words different than I did. Since the suspected perps had accents, I was paying extra close attention to that. You couldn't decide somebody was a suspected perp because he talked funny. But you gotta notice anything that might be a clue.

"They didn't come in at all?" I asked.

55

"No. I was home all afternoon, reading a book. No one even knocked. I consider myself lucky, eh?"

"Yeah. That's pretty lucky."

OK, that's what I said. But what I was thinking was, 'why was you reading a book? In the middle of the day? When it ain't some kind of homework punishment?' But I didn't say that. I also didn't say it was weird he didn't hear the perps messing up Mrs. Comanici's apartment right next door. Nobody gets so interested in a book they don't notice real stuff. But a good detective don't say everything he's thinking. Instead, he asks questions and sometimes people say extra stuff that turns out to be clues.

"So, what book was you reading?" I asked. "Maybe I read it too."

"Have you read much Margaret Atwood?"

"The name is kind of familiar. What state does she live in?"

"She's not an American."

"Oh yeah, I forgot."

"Good luck with your research, Mr. Jumper. I'm sorry I can't be more help."

Even though he said it as quiet and polite as a guy who works for a funeral parlor, by the time he was done talking, the door was closed and he was inside and I was out in the hall.

Before I even knocked on the last door, I sat down in the hallway and wrote my notes about Mr. Mitchell on my legal yellow pad. I even numbered my big points.

1. Funny accent, which I ain't heard before, which is how witnesses said the perps talked.

2. Everybody else got busted into except him.

3. Reads books by ladies who ain't American.

4. Talks like a serial killer.

That was a lot of clues against a guy but they was all circumstances. What was the most interesting is that he wore nice clothes and a nice watch. If I was gonna break into one apartment in my building, I'd pick his because he's probably got cool stuff to steal. That was a hard clue to explain.

I knocked on the last apartment door and Mrs. Trumble opened the door just a little bit. You could see the chain was keeping it from opening more.

"What do you want?" she said, like she was mad at me for knocking. Mrs. Trumble just likes to be mad, so you can't feel bad about it. Some people think she's crazy, but she seems OK to me. She just has a hobby of being mad, which is a cheap hobby and you can do it anywhere. If you practice it, pretty soon you can get mad at about anything. Maybe someday I'll try it as a hobby, but I ain't had time yet.

"Hi, Mrs. Trumble," I said. I could see a little bit of her face trying to look mean behind the door. "It's me, Jumper, from the third floor. I'm interviewing victims of the burglary incident."

"Can't help you," she said, and she made it sound like I done something bad, like maybe I killed her cat or ate her last piece of pie without asking.

"Anything you remember might help," I said.

"I said I can't help you! They didn't break into my place. At least not yet. But they will. They probably think I'm some helpless old lady. Well, they'll learn a thing or two. I'll be ready for them."

"Have you ever met Mr. Stevens from the third floor? I bet you guys'd like each other. They didn't break in at all?"

"Are you deaf? That's what I said, isn't it? Are you calling me a liar?"

"No, ma'am. I'm glad they didn't perpetrate on you. Well, you have a nice day."

"Fat chance of that," she said. Then she slammed the door the rest of the way shut.

OK, so her story was a clue that give Mr. Mitchell some bonus points. The perps didn't just skip him; they skipped the last two apartments. Maybe my apple crate got full, or maybe they heard a siren, or maybe they had a appointment so they had to stop burgling. Or maybe they just got bored and decided to knock off work early. Mr. Mitchell still talked like a serial killer but it might be a total accident they skipped him. You can't decide your facts before you get all your clues.

I went back to my apartment to think, which is the hardest part of detecting. Mr. Silver had kicked all his birdseed out of the cage and onto the floor, plus he'd splashed water onto the newspaper at the bottom of the cage and then pooped right in the middle of it. "If you can't be a little neater," I told him, "I'm gonna make you hire your own maid. I never signed up to be a bird maid." Mr. Silver just flapped his wings at me while I changed his newspaper and gave him clean water. Then I filled his jar lid with new birdseed and he made angry bird sounds. "You ain't got a right to be upset at me," I told him. "You're the one acting like a baby." But Mr. Silver didn't care. They say birds is just little dinosaurs with feathers, and that's about how he behaved. "If you ain't careful," I said, "I'm sending you off to Jurassic Park."

Mr. Silver just kicked some more birdseed and stuck his face up in the air like he wasn't scared of no dinosaurs.

"We'll see," I told him. "You don't settle down, we'll just see."

Chapter Five
I do some jumps and get the idea for a sidekick

I do my best thinking when I'm training and night is the best time to train because people don't see you and think you're weird.

I sat on the floor of my balcony and ate a can of minestrone soup. I could of got some other box to sit on or even got a cheap chair at the thrift store but I didn't want to. That would be like admitting I wasn't gonna get my real box back. You get good at what you picture and what you practice. Some of them new Bronco receivers must of pictured themself dropping the ball a lot of times because as soon as they catch it they fumble like it was a snake they caught by accident. They practiced dropping balls so good in their brains they could fumble in their sleep even if the ball had glue on it. I wasn't going to practice sitting on some new box.

So I sat on the floor of the balcony to eat my can of soup. My back touched the wall of the building and my feet touched the outside wall of the balcony, so it was pretty comfortable. It was starting to be summer so the sky stayed light a long time. It had been a few days since the Dumpster in the alley got emptied, so you could smell old food rotting in it, but just a little. I don't mind that smell if it ain't too close.

I had a good view. Mostly it was a view of sky, which changes all the time, but also I could see the trees and the alley and some tall Denver buildings. If I looked between two trees I could see a little bit of mountains. We get cool sunsets in Denver above the mountains and it's a different one every night. Down below, I could see the back yard of the apartment, which used to have grass but dogs and kids pretty much killed that so now it was dirt and weeds. Sometimes my boss had me mow the weeds as if it was grass, but mostly he didn't want to spend no money on lawnmower gas.

Right below my balcony is a garage that he rents to someone to store a car in. There's a mattress on the roof, so that's where I aim my regular jumps. A one-story jump onto a mattress ain't a big deal if you do it all the time, but even I have to be careful every single jump or I'd hurt myself. Especially at night.

I waited a while until the sunset changed from yellow and red to gray and you could see a few stars. Then I jumped up onto the railing and practiced balancing there for a while. I like to stand on one foot for about a minute, then on the other. It's a lot harder when you close your eyes, so you should practice that on a board on the ground first. One cricket was chirping, so I listened to him for a minute.

Then I jumped.

Sometimes, while I'm falling through the air I picture that I'm flying. Sometimes I'm a rocket ship going through space. Sometimes I'm diving in a submarine in the ocean. The one thing it ain't ever like is my ordinary life of picking up cans and cleaning apartments and doing drug studies.

If you ain't got a hobby like that, you should find one. Nobody should have to live just their one ordinary life.

I was maybe thinking too much and I lost my balance a little when I hit the mattress. I give myself about a seven which ain't that good. My excuse was I had lots of clues to think about, so I didn't get mad at myself. I thought about them while I climbed the downspout back up to my balcony.

The first clue was why the perps burgled our building in the first place. Maybe they was just driving around when the mood came on them to burgle and they said what the heck. But maybe there was some special reason, which if we knew what it was we could figure out who done it.

The second one was why they stopped burgling when there was still two apartments left. Maybe they was lazy, but maybe it was a clue.

The third clue was the stuff they swiped. Some of it made sense, like jewelry and cash. But swiping Mrs. Comanici's picture book was just taking something heavy to carry that wasn't worth a buck at a garage sale. That was a clue they was kind of dumb.

And the fourth clue is that sometimes perps will do stuff to give you extra clues that lead in the whole wrong direction. Good detectives have to figure out which ones is the extra clues. I ain't saying I'm the best detective in the world, like that guy in the Pink Panther movies. But I seen enough TV shows to know that you gotta notice clues, even the ones nobody else thinks is cool, and you also gotta figure out which ones is the extra clues they just threw in to make the show long enough.

By now I was back up on my balcony and I had to stop thinking. This next jump I wanted to get me a nine point five.

Sometimes I accidentally get free cable TV and get to watch lots of old shows which is good research for being a detective. One thing every TV detective has is a second person. Maybe they bring in some big shot from the FBI who never figures out the crime. But mostly detectives have side-kicks, which is a guy they can talk to about the clues, and who reminds the detective about the twin sister everybody else forgot about. Mr. Monk has Natalie, Sherlock Holmes has Watson, and Rockford had his dad Rocky. You might as well not even start detecting something if you don't have a sidekick. Step one was for me to get one.

I had lots of choices. Jim at the thrift store is pretty smart and he don't talk too much. I give art lessons to this kid Greg who is what they call 'troubled.' He's really smart too, but he's got issues that make him say stuff before they're ready to be said. Officer Mike is a cop, so he's got lots of bonuses to him, only he retired and he forgot to give me his address. So it would be extra detecting just to find him.

Then I had a better idea. Wouldn't it be good to have a sidekick who lived really close? That would cut down on commuting time. It would be a bonus if they had an extra reason to help. Like maybe something got stole from her apartment, for one example.

Mr. Silver chirped at me from inside and I smiled.

"No chance, buddy," I said. "I need someone with a brain bigger than a Cheerio."

I decided Holly would be about the perfect sidekick. But when I pretended asking her in my brain, it didn't go so good. You can't just go up to a girl and say, "hey, would you like to be my sidekick?" Even when I pictured James Bond doing it, he got a shook but not stirred drink thrown in his face and I ain't usually as cool as James Bond.

By the time I done three more jumps I had that part of my plan all worked out. I didn't see no hidden flaws in it.

Chapter Six
Plans ain't much like predictions but I get some clues

I practiced what I was going to say to Holly about nineteen times. I even practiced what she'd say back. So when I knocked on her door I felt like I was in a TV show playing a part I done every day.

"Hi, Jumper," Holly said when she opened the door. "Just the man I was looking for. Do you have time to do me a favor?"

"Well, I ain't got much appointments right now, but I was gonna ask you something…"

"Great. This will just take a minute. Come on in."

I went in and she closed the door behind me. This was even easier than I pictured, only none of the times I practiced started out like this, so I didn't feel as much like a guy playing his regular TV part. I was playing somebody else's part. I followed her in while she kept talking. I felt like Spock trying to pretend he was Captain Kirk. She walked over to her couch, which was blue. Her apartment smelled like vanilla.

"My couch wobbles," she said. She pushed down on the end of it and the whole thing moved. "It's the back leg. I think if I put a book under it that'll fix the problem. But I can't lift it and slide the book under at the same time."

"Sure," I said. "I could slide the book under for you easy."

She looked at me like I said the wrong thing, but she didn't say nothing. She just put her hands on her hips and kept looking at me like she asked me a question and I ain't answered yet. Then I had another thought.

"Or, I could lift up the couch and you could slide the book under."

"Let's do it that way," she said. "Ready?"

It wasn't any big deal to lift one end of the couch. When your sport is jumping off stuff you spend a lot of time climbing back up whatever you jumped off, which is good exercise. So I'm pretty strong. I could of used one hand but that seemed show offy. I held it up real still so she could get the book under.

"I'm not trying to slide a cow under it, Jumper," she said.

"Oh yeah," I said. I lowered it back down almost to the carpet.

"There, now let it down."

I did. It didn't wobble any more.

"Thanks," she said.

"That's a pretty good use for a book," I said. "I'll have to remember it."

"Great. Now, what did you want to ask?"

"What?"

"You knocked on my door, you said you wanted to ask something."

By now, most of the stuff I was going to start off with would sound dumb. Like, how are you and is this a good time to ask you something. Finally I just threw all my practice lines out the window.

"Do you ever watch TV?" I said, but it sounded dumb the minute I said it.

"Sure," she said. Lots of times people say a lot more when you ask them a question, which makes the next one easier. But she just waited. She was going to make me do all the work of this conversation.

"Do you ever notice something on detective shows?"

"Like what?"

"Well, the really good detectives always come in teams. It ain't like one guy is the boss detective, it's like they got different specialties. See what I mean? They're like thinking partners."

"I guess that's right."

"Well, I kinda run into a brick wall trying to figure out who busted into everyone's apartment. There ain't many clues and the ones I got ain't very good ones. I was wondering if I could just sort of talk to you about it."

"You want me to be your thinking partner?"

"We could call it whatever you want. Magnum PI had his team, and Andy Griffith had his buddies and Sherlock Holmes…"

"You're saying you want a team like Andy Griffith's team?'"

"Well, he solved a lot of crimes even if he didn't detect full time…"

"So you want me to be your Barney Fife? Is that what you're saying? You see me as a sort of Barney Fife character?"

I could feel this wasn't going perfect.

"Barney had some good ideas and he took his job extra serious, plus he was funny. But I can't see you as Barney Fife, that was just one example. I was thinking more you could be the Sherlock Holmes part and I'd be Dr. Watson. Or maybe you could choose either Rizzoli or Isles and I'd just be the other one. They was just for examples."

"I know. I was just teasing you. Sometimes people tease their friends. What are the clues?"

I had the clues mostly memorized even without my legal yellow pad, but what she said took over my brain for a minute and stopped me. She said friends tease each other, and she was just teasing me, which was like a long way of saying we was friends. Which is how I seen us too, but it was cool that she seen it that way.

"You said something about clues?" she said. She sat on one end of the couch and so I sat on the other end.

"The first clue is, how come they robbed our building instead of another one?

"That sounds more like a question than a clue.

"Yeah, clues and questions is a lot alike."

"Why does it matter? People get robbed every day."

"Maybe there was a reason. Like maybe they grew up in this building so they knew all about it. Or maybe they hated a tenant and wanted to rob him."

"I see what you mean. So they robbed everyone else to confuse the police."

"Yeah. So if that was it and we figure out who they really wanted to rob, we could track them down."

"That's a good idea. What are your other clues?"

"Did you ever notice Mr. Mitchell talks like a serial killer?"

Holly laughed. She had a loud laugh, but a cool one. Whenever she laughed I felt like somebody tickled me and I wanted to laugh too. But she seen I wasn't making a joke on her so she stopped laughing.

"I don't think he's a serial killer. He's just a little different."

"Well, he's got an accent and so did the perps."

"OK, so maybe that's a clue. But maybe not. What else?"

"They didn't rob Mrs. Trumble or Mr. Mitchell."

"So what?"

"I don't know. That's why I need a thinking partner. Maybe one of them was in on it. Maybe they both was."

"You don't really think that."

"Nah. I don't think nothing yet. I'm just collecting clues."

"All right. So why else would they skip two apartments?"

"The last two. They done em in a row and them was the last two."

"Maybe they got tired," she said. "Maybe they finally figured out no one had anything valuable."

"Yeah, that makes sense."

"What else could it be?"

"I don't know, I'm just trying to think of every answer. Maybe they had to catch a bus or get someplace by some time. So they ran out of time."

"That's pretty good, Jumper. If you can figure out exactly what time they left, maybe you can figure out what happens at that time."

"Thanks. But that's just one idea."

"OK, so why else would they skip the last two apartments?"

I thought for a minute, then I had an idea.

"Maybe they was looking for something. And when they found it…"

"When they found it they left," Holly finished my sentence for me. Her voice was soft and kind of surprised. She looked right at me. "That's pretty good, Barney Fife," she said.

"Thanks, Andy," I said back. I noticed that we was sort of teasing each other again and my face got hot.

"So, who was the last person they robbed?" she asked.

"That's easy. It was Mrs. Comanici. I talked to her already, but that was before I knew she was the last one."

Holly stood up.

"I get off at noon tomorrow," she said. "Shall we talk to Mrs. Comanici in the afternoon? Say, two o'clock?"

I stood up too. You could tell our meeting was over.

"I'll meet you in front of her door," I said. "I got a new legal yellow pad that needs some clues."

"Perfect," she said. "I'll see you then."

Chapter Seven
Holly and me get an interesting history lesson, not like the ones in school.

The next day I was in front of Mrs. Comanici's apartment at about six minutes before two. The hallway had short red carpet and smelled dusty, the way carpet always does right after you vacuum. For a while I thought maybe Holly forgot our appointment, but at about one minute before two she come walking down the hall. You can't really say somebody's late if they're a minute early, even if it feels like that.

"Hi, Jumper," she said with a cheerful voice. She was wearing a red shirt which I ain't seen before and blue jeans. They was both ironed so they didn't have wrinkles. When she got close, I could smell her shampoo plus a little bit of the vanilla smell from her apartment.

"Hi, Holly," I said. "Nice shirt."

"Thanks. I see you've got your note pad. Did you bring a pencil?"

"Yeah, I got two."

"Good," she said, and she knocked on the door. We both stood back a little bit so Mrs. Comanici could see us better. Everybody was careful about looking through their peepholes since the incident. In a minute, Mrs. C. opened the door.

"Well, hello Jumper," she said. "I see you've brought reinforcements. Does this mean I'm under arrest?" She was smiling when she said it so I knew she was joking on me.

"You're just a person of interest, which means we ain't got to follow the rules so close."

She laughed. "It's Holly, isn't it? From the second floor?"

"Yes, ma'am," Holly said and reached out to shake her hand.

"Holly and me are helping each other with the investigation," I said. "We was wondering if we could ask you some more questions?"

"Of course. Come on in."

Holly and me sat on the couch. Mrs. Comanici sat in the chair.

"You was the last person they robbed," I said.

"I was? That's interesting."

"Well, it might be," I said. "We was wondering why."

"I have no idea."

Holly seemed impatient. "Jumper had a thought," she said. "What if the robbers were looking for something specific?"

"Like what?"

"We don't know. But maybe it was something they took from you. Once they got it, they left without hitting the last two apartments."

"I see. Well, I told Jumper what they took. Some cash, a few earrings, a bottle of whiskey and a few gold coins. Maybe once they got the whiskey they decided it was time to drink some of it."

"Yeah, that could be it," I said. "Crooks like their poteen."

Mrs. Comanici smiled and turned to Holly. "Now he's showing off his vocabulary. In Moldova, they call whiskey poteen."

"Did they say the word 'about' like 'aboot'?" I asked.

"I don't think so. In fact, come to think of it, I don't think any of them said a word."

"How about the gold coins?" Holly asked. "Were they especially valuable?"

"Not really. They were never rare and they didn't have an ounce of gold between them. Not worth enough to risk all the burglaries. Would you two like some cookies?"

"I never said no to a cookie," I said.

"That would be lovely," Holly said.

Mrs. Comanici got up to get some cookies and I sat on the couch and looked around her living room. Sometimes you know something ain't right, only you can't say exactly what it is. There was a clue in Mrs. Comanici's apartment but I couldn't find it. Maybe it was something in the apartment, maybe it was something Mrs. Comanici said, or the way she looked. Or maybe some dog wasn't barking that should have been yapping like he seen a squirrel with a squeaky toy, which is how Sherlock Holmes solved one case. But I couldn't figure it out. I might of been distracted by Holly, since she always distracts me. Mrs. Comanici put a plate of cookies on the coffee table and sat back down. "So, you been in this building a long time, haven't you?" Holly asked her.

Mrs. Comanici laughed. "Far too long, I suppose," she said. "Twenty years." She looked out the window but her eyes was looking at stuff she remembered instead of what was outside.

"You must love it here."

"Not really. A person just gets settled." Mrs. Comanici sipped her tea.

"I bet there's an interesting story in there somewhere," Holly said.

"Interesting?" Mrs. Comanici said. "Not really. It's just silly."

"It was a man, wasn't it?" Holly said.

Mrs. Comanici looked out the window at her memory. After a minute she answered. Her voice was soft.

"Sort of," she said. "It was my son."

"I didn't even know you had a kid," I said. Holly looked at me as if I said something dumb, which means I probably did. So I got quiet.

"Eat a cookie, Jumper," Holly said. "I want to hear the whole story."

Obviously, I sat back down on the couch. Mrs. Comanici sighed.

"Well, it's a short story. I was a young and foolish girl, a country girl in a very old country. I fell in love with the sweetest boy in the world. He worked at his father's winery. He tended grapes, he supervised the workers, he took care of the horses. He even ran their little still, where they turned some of the wine into brandy. There was never a man who looked so dashing on a horse. I was too young, but we loved each other." She was looking far away again, and you could tell she felt like she was still that young girl and she was talking about stuff that happened last week.

"Beneath the winery buildings were ancient caverns, so old the Romans had quarried stone out of them. Now people used the tunnels for storing the wine and brandy. Dobre knew all the secret passageways where the oldest wine was stored. We spent many afternoons in the cool tunnels..." She was looking out the window again. Then she shook her head.

"Dobre, my boyfriend, ran the winery when his father grew old and forgetful. It should have been his when his father died. But my people have their own laws, laws that have never been written. Dobre's younger brother Vidal got the winery, even though he never worked there a day in his life. Vidal was a true gypsy, in the way outsiders use the word; he worked handyman jobs and traveled from town to town, always looking for a shortcut to money. The jobs were just his excuse to be in a place. He would paint your house, then return that night to steal your jewels, and your bread as well. His little boys were worse than him, stealing anything that wasn't nailed to the floor, then lying in your face about it. They went with their father from town to town, splashing their own paint on walls and floors, just as often painting their employer's cat."

"I thought you said gypsy was a bad word to call someone," I said.

"Yes, Jumper, I did and it is. But in this case, it fits. Vidal was charming, I have to give him that, and their father loved his rascal grandsons. He probably thought the responsibility of the winery would settle Vidal down, maybe give the grandsons a head start on a straight life. But once a gypsy, always a gypsy. The winery business did not interest Vidal. He had neither head nor heart for it, like my Dobre. But he knew how to sell the casks of brandy that were aging in the tunnels. Quick cash is what a gypsy knows best.

"Vidal was cunning. He moved his family of thieves into the main house and banished Dobre. Instead of settling into a life of hard work but financial comfort, Dobre had nothing.

"We didn't care. Dobre had saved a little money; we eloped to Chisinau. I'd never been in such a big city. For a month we just honeymooned. He took me to restaurants for breakfast— I'd never heard of such a thing. We went on boat rides, we visited the Chisinau Circus. It was still a new building back then. Elephants and clowns and tightrope walkers and trapeze artists. It was magical."

"I went to the circus once," I said. "I met a monkey there."

"Well, then you understand," Mrs. Comanici said. "Dobre loved it too; he could handle a horse like any circus performer. He said it was in his blood. His grandfather trained horses. Some gifts arrive the day you're born."

Holly looked at me pretty stern so I didn't say nothing else. Even if there wasn't going to be no clues about the burglary from Mrs. Comanici's honeymoon, it was her turn to talk. Sometimes people would rather talk about themselves than listen to me, believe it or not. It's about the easiest favor you can do somebody to listen to them, even if it's kind of boring and they use words you don't know. I liked Mrs. Comanici so I listened to her story, even if part of my brain was still looking around her apartment for clues.

"But you can't honeymoon forever," she said. "The country was in turmoil— it's always in turmoil — there wasn't much left for us there. Dobre thought he could make his fortune in America. Wine was still a new industry in California and Dobre knew everything about wine. We flew to New York and took a train west.

"Immediately, I got sick. I threw up across a dozen states. The train broke down in Denver, we had to stay in a motel for several days, and I seemed to feel better. We decided maybe the train ride had made us sick. Money was running low. Dobre saw an ad for a job at a coal company and they hired him on the spot. We thought we'd stay a few months, let me get my strength back, save a little money and then continue to California."

She stopped. "Of course, I wasn't really sick."

"You were pregnant, weren't you?" Holly said.

"Of course."

"People throw up when they're pregnant?" I asked. They both smiled.

"Sometimes they do, especially at first. It's called morning sickness. Sometimes eating dry crackers helps."

"Man, they should warn people about that," I said.

"They usually warn the girls," Mrs. Comanici said. "Boys do better if you don't tell them too much." After a minute she started talking again.

"Dobre's job was in the coal company's office, keeping their books. He shouldn't have been in the mine at all the day it collapsed. He didn't belong in the mines," she said "It was cold and dark and the bosses worked the men like mules. But workers got sick, they were on a deadline, he had to go. We thought it would only be for a few days. "

"The other men tried to bully him. They called him names, made fun of his accent. Twice he came home bruised and bloody. He said it was an accident with equipment but I knew better. The others had fought him. They would not have had an easy time of it. He was strong as a bull and stubborn as the Devil, but he was alone. They hated him because he seemed different, but they also wanted his grandfather's ring. It was made of gold, with a green emerald. Miners don't wear nice rings. It wasn't worth much, but it reminded Dobre of his old home. It was always passed down from the head of the Comanici family to his oldest grandson and Dobre never took it off his hand.

71

"The second time he came home bloody I told him he should not wear the ring to work. He agreed with me and said he'd find a safe place to keep it. Soon, he said. The third time he came home bloody, he wasn't wearing the ring.

"He said nothing about it and I didn't either. There was nothing to do and talking would only make him feel worse. Words can't call the water back upstream."

"Well," I said. "If I'd been there, I would of helped him fight them other guys."

Mrs. Comanici smiled.

"If you had been there, no one would have even tried to fight the two of you." She looked off into the distance. "Then there was the accident. No survivors." She stopped talking for a minute and Holly and I didn't say nothing.

"Suddenly I was alone in a strange country with no money, no job. I barely spoke the language. And I was pregnant." She stopped and you could see she was deciding how much she should tell us. Finally she shrugged.

"I made mistakes. I admit that. But I did what I could. When little August was five, the police decided I needed to spend some time in jail. So they moved me out of this building and into a government facility. They sent my boy to live with strangers. In jail I studied English and all the other subjects. I was going to be the best mother in the world. I was gone for three long years. By the time I got out, the couple who took my boy had moved to Texas or Oklahoma and changed their names. They just vanished. I tried everything to find little August but I couldn't. So I moved back into this building. If I couldn't find him, maybe someday he could find me. My old apartment had been rented of course, but this one was vacant. And the sweet old man who owned the building, Mr. Blumenhein, had saved a few of my things in a box for me."

"That's so sad," Holly said.

"Time moves on," Mrs. Comanici said. "I had a reason to stay here, even if it was foolish, and no real reason to move. So here I am. If your robbers were looking for state secrets, or the crown jewels, I'm afraid they struck out."

"I never heard the name August for a kid before," I said. "He's lucky he wasn't born in September. I bet the other kids would of teased him if he was named September."

"Yes, that was lucky," Mrs. Comanici said. "I hope he's been lucky like that his whole life."

In the middle of the night I woke up. An idea was buzzing around my head like a mosquito you can hear but you can't see good enough to catch. It had something to do with a dog not barking. Finally it come to me. It probably wasn't nothing, but I seen that Mrs. Comanici had give me another clue without even knowing it. I got out of bed, turned on the light and wrote it down on my yellow legal pad. Sometimes the best clues is the ones you don't pay attention to at first, so you can't throw any away until you know if they're extras.

Once I wrote it down, I felt a lot better. I went back to bed and slept like a puppy.

Chapter Eight
Some new clues, some suspected perps, and some red hair rings

Everybody's been in a rainstorm before, but in Colorado we got cool ones. It mostly don't rain much, so plants and lawns get dry if you don't water it. All the weeds and leaves and grass gets about as dry as tea in a box. When it rains, all that tea gets thrown into a big teapot and it smells as good as baking cookies. So that's one cool thing.

The next thing is that we got so many sunny days in the summer that the blue sky seems pretty ordinary. When the whole sky gets gray and cloudy everybody looks around and says hey, who changed the light bulbs? It's like at a movie after they showed the last preview of coming attractions and friendly reminders to turn off your cell phone. The screen changes and everybody gets quiet, since they know the main show is about to start. A cloudy summer day is like that in Denver. Sometimes then the sky dumps buckets on you and the lightning and thunder is like freight trains crashing together around you. The rain drops is big like grapes and cold as a Pepsi. It's pretty fun.

I was walking home from the grocery store when it started to rain like that. The drops seemed extra cold, and the air smelled good.

If I'd been running, I might not of noticed a tan van parked across the street from my building. I know most of the cars that usually park on my street, but this must of been visitors. Two guys was in it and they was looking right at my building, talking to each other and sometimes pointing at it. They didn't see me since they didn't have the windshield wipers going and the rain was coming down pretty good. They was about my age or a little older and didn't look fancy. They might be plumbers or carpenters who was supposed to work on something. Only that didn't make much sense because Mr. Sternberg usually lets me fix easy stuff, and I know the guys he calls to fix harder stuff.

Maybe they was workers looking at the wrong building and waiting for the rain to stop. It wasn't my business, so I just kept walking. As I walked past the van, one of the guys rolled down his window and took a picture of my building. Then they drove off.

There's lots of reasons you might take a picture and the building did look cool with its bricks all wet and red from the rain and all. And sometimes you get clues which ain't clues at all. Detectives call them phony clues "red hair rings," which is a name that don't mean nothing just like the clues don't mean nothing.

I was thinking of all the reasons a guy might take a picture but none of them made much sense to me. Obviously, this was a perfect time for a sidekick. I went inside and up the stairs to Holly's apartment.

When she answered the door, she looked at my head, which had wet hair and then down to my jeans and sneakers, which was also wet, but she didn't say nothing. She just threw a towel onto her couch and pointed for me to sit there.

"There was some guys in a van outside our building," I said. "So I was pretending they was the burglars," I said.

"Do you have any reason to think that?"

"No. Nothing you could use on a TV show. Or even in a law court. No law against looking at a building. But sometimes stuff you can't prove is true anyway, so I was just pretending about it. And then I thought, well, if it was them and they already burgled the place, why would they come back to look at it some more?"

"Maybe they want to hit those last two apartments."

"Yeah, that would work. Or maybe they was going to meet with their boss, a foreign guy who talks like a serial killer."

"Mr. Mitchell is not a serial killer."

"Maybe an alleged serial killer..."

"I don't think so."

"OK, so how about this? They come looking to swipe something and they thought they got it but then they figured out they didn't."

"Interesting," Holly said. "That would be a good idea except for one thing."

"Thanks."

"The one problem is this: you don't know the guys you saw in the van today were the burglars. So you don't know the burglars came back to the scene of the crime."

"They usually do, though."

"Fine. But you can't use things you make up as clues. That's not scientific. Did you have any other ideas?"

I looked at my legal yellow pad and read my notes. The idea of doing detective stuff with Holly had seemed more fun before we started doing it.

"Oh yeah, I did have one idea. Well, it's mostly just a clue I forgot to tell you."

"A real clue?"

"I don't know yet. But it wasn't one I pretended. Mrs. Comanici told me one more thing they swiped."

Holly leaned forward and looked surprised.

"Really?"

"Yeah. They swiped her picture album off her coffee table. We forgot to tell you that one."

"Oh," she said and leaned back in the chair. She looked disappointed that it wasn't as good a clue as she wanted.

"Why do you suppose they done that?" I asked.

"I don't know," she said. "It's probably not important. Nobody uses photo albums anymore. They keep their pictures on their computers. They probably just needed something heavy to hold a door open. Or to steady a couch."

Holly stood up and put down her teacup, which meant it was time for our meeting to be over.

"Thanks for telling me about it, though," she said, "You can't ever tell which clue will be important, right?"

"Right," I said. "See you later."

When I was walking down the hall I felt pretty dumb. I'd got all excited to have a meeting with my sidekick and all I had was one dumb clue that was real and one dumb clue that I pretended. If I didn't find better clues, Holly wouldn't even want to be my sidekick any more. I needed to come up with a plan for getting better clues.

Chapter Nine
Don't break into the zoo, plus another crime is committed

That night I decided to have a picnic. I put a can of spaghetti into my backpack, plus a fork and a can opener. The rain had stopped and the clouds all blew away, so I walked to City Park. Once it starts raining hard, people decide it's a rainy day so they don't go to the park even after it stops raining. I found a picnic table that wasn't too wet and sat down to eat my dinner.

The park has pine trees, which smell cool at night and it's always fun to look at the stars. If you watch them long enough, you can notice they all turn around the North Star, which is next to the Big Dipper. It's like being inside a big salad bowl that turns in slow motion, but you gotta watch for a long time to see it. Sometimes a plane flies past with its flashing lights, which makes you pretend you was on it.

I had a lot of good memories about City Park. From the picnic table I could see the lake where we released Bart the turtle. Over in another direction I could see the museum where they have big dinosaur bones. When I was little, my class went there on a school bus three times, so I pretty much memorized everything in it. I could live inside that museum easy.

A little ways from the museum, I could see the Denver Zoo, which I also knew by heart. I remember my mom liked the snow leopard. She said its eyes were a color called "celadon" which is between yellow and green, but really light. The color of celery, she said, and then she laughed. I don't know if she was right about the color but I always remembered the word and the way she sounded when she laughed. And I always liked the zoo. I talked to all the animals that was friendly and Mom and Dad never made a joke on it.

After Mom and Dad died, sometimes I'd sneak into the zoo at night after it was closed. If your sport is climbing trees and rain gutters so you can jump off of stuff, then climbing a chain link fence is like baby steps.

Some night guards are a lot faster runners than you'd think a grown up would be. But if you're quiet and don't scare the animals or make a mess and stay in the shadows, a guy could walk around all hypothetical for an hour without getting caught.

Lots of the animals sleep all day while the school bus kids stare at them, but they spend all night walking around and scratching and playing games with each other. The snow leopard looks like a white ghost walking through the shadows. When the moonlight hits his cage just right, he might open his eyes and look right at you like you was a meal. He sniffs the air, trying to decide what you'd taste like. Maybe the moonlight makes his eyes look like little flashlights aimed at you. And then you might whisper 'celadon' at him, like it was his name. But he's still thinking about your flavor. A minute later he moves back into the shadows and disappears like he got beamed back to his spaceship.

I didn't sneak in there too many times. Mostly I made a getaway without nobody noticing me, but I did get caught six times. If it was a young night guard, sometimes I'd just run my fastest to the chain link fence and climb out before he could catch me. That seemed like a fair race. But the main night guard was Mr. Riddle. He was so old it would of been mean to make him chase me and get a heart attack. If Mr. Riddle seen me, he'd yell, "Hey! What are doing there! Get over here!"

I figured it was my own fault I got caught and walked over to him to take my consequences. The first time he acted pretty mean and asked my name and address and who my parents was. I told him the truth, the whole truth and nothing but the truth, even about Mom and Dad being dead, but I didn't go into much details about who I was living with, since I wasn't living with no grown ups and I didn't want to get turned in to the services people who would help me by putting me in a better home where I didn't have so much freedoms. Pretty soon, he released me on my own recognizance but said next time he'd have to call the cops. The next time he caught me he said about the same thing only he didn't seem as mean. I didn't hold it against him. They probably made him say all that stuff. Nobody says words like recognizance unless somebody makes 'em.

By the time I finished my can of spaghetti picnic, it was dark enough to do some jumps. I climbed the biggest tree I could find up to the second row of branches and jumped off. It was a pine tree, which you could tell by the needles and the smell. The grass was extra soft from all the rain, so I climbed to a pretty high branch for the next jump. I done fifteen jumps from different heights and they was all pretty good.

That night I dreamed it was winter. One of them really cold days we get sometimes, like zero degrees, but the sun is shining. Little bits of ice dust blew off a roof. As they spun in the wind, the sun would hit them specks for just a second and they'd flash like comets about the size of a pinhead and then turn off just as quick. Sparkling ice dust is about the coolest thing in the world, like watching free fireworks with the sound turned all the way off, or maybe a swarm of little bitty lightning bugs, which we ain't got in Colorado. I seen it seven or eight times every winter, but only on real cold sunny days.

Once I talked to a guy who was older than me and lived in Colorado his whole life. He said he'd never seen that thing with snow in the sunlight. Maybe he was joking on me, but I don't think so. I think he just never paid attention.

Or else he needed glasses. You can't hold it against a guy if he needs glasses. But if he ain't ever noticed it, he probably don't dream it either. The more stuff you notice, the better dreams you're gonna have. That's just the way it is.

xxx

The next morning I got woke up by somebody knocking on my door, which ain't that ordinary. Mr. Silver thought somebody was coming to visit him, so he was chirping away like a little green opera star. I pulled my jeans on and opened the door. It was Holly. She was all excited.

"What time is it?" I asked, rubbing my eyes.

"About six," she said. "Put some clothes on and come downstairs. Mrs. Comanici got hit again!"

"Somebody hit Mrs. Comanici?" I started to wake up a lot faster. Holly was wearing sweat pants and a T-shirt and hadn't combed her own hair all the way. She still looked pretty good. Mr. Silver kept on whistling and chirping and hopping around his cage.

"No," she said, pulling her hand through her hair like it was a comb. Sometimes I thought she could read my mind. "They broke into her apartment again."

"Is she OK?"

"She's not even here. Remember she was going to a teacher's convention to see some of her old friends?

"She was?"

"She told us."

"Oh, yeah. Now I remember." That's what I said, and it probably should of been true, but my brain hadn't got up to full speed yet.

"The cops are downstairs. Someone was leaving for work and saw the door smashed in."

"Someone had to go to work before six?"

"I don't think that's the important clue here. They've called Mrs. Comanici at the conference. It's just across town, so she should be here any minute. I think we should be there when she arrives."

"Yeah, me too. I'll meet you down there in five minutes, OK?"

"Great," she said. "Poor Mrs. Comanici. Can you imagine being burglarized twice in one week?"

"Yeah," I said. "That would be twice as bad as getting burgled one time."

Holly left and I closed the door. While the microwave was heating me a cup of yesterday's coffee, I threw some cold water on my face and brushed my teeth. Mr. Silver tried to convince me he needed birdseed but I didn't pay no attention. He'd tell you he needed cable TV if you listened long enough.

Why would somebody break into the same unit two times in one week? Maybe it was different burglars and Mrs. Comanici just had bad luck. Thinking about her life, she wasn't the luckiest person so maybe that was it. I drank some of my coffee and took my cup with me downstairs.

Mrs. Comanici was already in the hallway when I got there. She was dressed up for the conference in a nice blouse and a black suit coat. She was talking to Holly. Mrs. Comanici was holding a briefcase thing in one hand, which had her laptop computer in it. Mrs. C. and Holly was both talking at the same time and both of them seemed pretty mad at the burglars.

The cops was already inside the apartment. A young skinny cop in a blue cop shirt come to the door. He wanted Mrs. Comanici to come in and see what was missing, but the way she was cussing in European scared him a little. Holly seen him and interrupted her.

"I think they want you to go inside now, is that right, officer?" Holly said.

"Yes, ma'am," he said. He looked happy somebody else explained it to Mrs. Comanici in case she wasn't done cussing.

"Jumper, why don't you and I stay here in the hall until they're done."

"OK," I said. I had my coffee cup so waiting wasn't a big deal. Mrs. C. grabbed Holly's elbow and give it a little squeeze and then she went in.

"I bet it was them guys in the van," I said.

"You've got absolutely no reason..." Holly started, then she stopped. She looked down the hall and kind of nodded. Then she started talking in a softer voice.

"You should probably tell the police about them. It could be nothing, but you're right. It wouldn't be smart to decide which clues are important before we have all the facts."

Well, that made me feel about a thousand percent better. But them police guys wasn't interested. When one older cop came back out to the hall I told him, "There was a tan van parked outside." He said, "today?" and I said no a few days ago. I told him it had Texas plates and he asked if I liked the Dallas Cowboys. Obviously I told him no, that they was a bunch of sissy cheaters and they won that last game on a holding penalty the Pope could of seen from his house in Germany. He probably agreed with me, since it was obvious, but he didn't write my clues down.

In a little while, the three police guys left the apartment and we went in. Mrs. Comanici was sitting on the couch. The place looked like a bunch of gorillas had a party in there. Stuff was on the floor. Chairs and tables was knocked over.

"Did they dust for prints?" I asked.

"They didn't dust for anything," Mrs. Comanici said. "They asked if anything was missing. Who could tell? I don't have anything valuable. That TV is too old to sell; I'd be embarrassed to leave it out on the street. I had my laptop with me at the conference. They already took my gold coins. It doesn't make any sense."

"No, it doesn't," said Holly. "We'll help you clean up."

Mrs. C smiled at that. I tilted her bookshelf back up. Her books was all over the floor, so I stated putting them back in.

"This probably ain't the right order, " I said.

"That's fine," Mrs. Comanici said. "No point putting them in order before they show up and knock it over again."

I let them talk and organize stuff while I cleaned up the obvious stuff. I picked some books off the floor and put them in the bookshelf. One was a crossword puzzle book. Three of them was about making wine. One was a picture book of horses, which looked cool. But I didn't pay too much attention to the books I cleaned up.

My brain couldn't stop thinking about the thing Mrs. Comanici said. She said 'it doesn't make any sense." But nothing makes sense til you figure it out. These burglars broke into Mrs. Comanici's apartment twice. That was about the best clue in the world if I could figure out what it meant.

With detective clues, you got to think up a bunch of suspected answers before you even start guessing which one might be correct. Maybe the perps accidentally left something in there, like incinerating evidence. Or maybe they was looking for something the first time which they didn't find and they come back to try again. Or maybe they looked at them coins they swiped and wondered if maybe she had a bunch more hid somewhere.

When I went to my own apartment I thought some more. Mr. Silver didn't care that I was trying to think. He was singing and trying to say words. It sounded like he was complaining that he wanted more interesting food than just seeds. "I ain't got any dinosaur food," I told him. "And even if I did, dinosaurs probably ate stuff like water buffalos. If I threw a water buffalo in there with you as food, I bet you wouldn't like it that much. Maybe you should just be happy with birdseeds."

Before you know it, it was night and I still didn't have good ideas.

Chapter Ten
Gang guys on Colfax Street and I zero in on suspected perps

Even I, who am a pretty good thinker, got to admit that sometimes you can think till your ears turn green and you won't figure something out. When I get stuck, I think about some different thing. It ain't like I give up on it, it's like my brain is a TV and I switch stations for a while.

Usually I go to the park and practice some jumps to change stations on my brain. But tonight I was in the mood to go walking instead.

I walked a couple blocks to Colfax Street, which is a street in Denver with lots of businesses on it. It stays busy until after the bars close, so there's always traffic and people walking around. The businesses have lights on their signs so it looks colorful. It ain't a fancy street, so you always got some gang guys, and ladies in short tight skirts, and a few tourists driving with both hands. They look like their big dream is to get somewhere else without their car breaking so they have to get out and walk. I turned left, which is away from the mountains, and started walking down Colfax on the sidewalk.

When a detective's working on a case, he keeps his brain on red alert all the time in case there's a clue he don't want to miss it. When your brain's on red alert, it notices just about everything, most of which ain't clues. Detective mode tires you out. But walking around is also a good way to change channels on your brain. Since maybe you ain't ever spent a night walking on a street in a town as big as Denver, I'll just tell you some of the stuff I seen so you can pretend you was there in detective mode too if you want. If that don't sound interesting, you can just skip ahead and you won't miss a car chase scene or nothing.

I seen several small guys walking with their elbows stuck out and their chests puffed up trying to look dangerous. I seen a young couple dressed like hippies even if their grandparents was probably little kids when the first hippies dressed like that. I seen a girl mad at her boyfriend. She kept yelling at him while the guy looked confused and tried to explain whatever dumb thing he done. You see that every night. I seen a skinny little black guy in his twenties wearing the bright silky basketball shirt of his favorite player. He walked real proud, like he hoped someone might mistake him for the big star, even though he was about as big as a twelve-year-old girl.

A 40-year-old lady who was probably on drugs crossed the road without looking. Her hair was messy, she had a few extra pounds on her, and her clothes was wrinkled. She wasn't paying attention to nothing. She threw her blue jacket down in the middle of the street when she crossed. Then after three steps it was like she figured out she wasn't in her apartment and went back to pick it up, even if the light had changed and a car could of creamed her. Instead, they just honked at her.

But mostly it was just lots of ordinary people wearing clothes you wouldn't notice, like jeans and T shirts in regular colors who wanted to get wherever they was going without much fuss.

The next interesting guy was in an electric wheel chair. He had a bright red shirt and had a US flag sticking up from the back of his wheel chair. His face looked like a picture I seen of a terrorist, all thin and pale with black hair and a beard, only this guy was licking a pink ice cream cone while he rolled down the sidewalk. Between his blue baseball cap and his US flag and the ice cream cone, obviously he was just unlucky to have a terrorist face and you had to cut him some slack. If I didn't just see the picture on the news, my first guess would be he looked like Jesus, which probably would not of been correct either. He was going the same direction as me, but a lot faster in his electric wheelchair. When he was a block ahead of me, a gym bag fell off his chair only he didn't notice it. He just crossed the street and kept going.

Six gang guys was crossing the street the other way, coming toward me. When they got to the sidewalk where the gym bag was, they picked it up. They could of been doctors, except they was all wearing Oakland Raiders baseball caps on backward, which is like the membership card of one gang I met before. They stood there laughing, holding the gym bag. They looked across the street at the back of the guy in the wheelchair, but they didn't go chasing after him.

I started jogging so I caught up to them before they decided on any good plan. One guy was holding the bag by its strap. I also took hold of the strap. The gang guys smelled like cigarette smoke.

"Hey, guys," I said. "Pretty lucky you found that guy's bag before he got too far away."

"This is my bag," the guy holding it said.

I laughed. "Well, right now it's kind of both of our bag ain't it? Only we need to get it back to the wheelchair guy in case it has medicine in it, or his school books."

"You can count, right?" the biggest guy said. "There's six of us. And one of you."

"Which is why it makes better sense for me to return it to him. You guys got more important stuff to do. Plus, you'd have to turn around and go out of your way. I'm already going the correct direction."

They kind of circled around me. I got the feeling they was thinking about making a example out of me for what happens when somebody messes with their gang. The odds for me didn't look good. But when you see for sure what the right thing to do is, the odds go out the window.

"Really, guys?" I said. "You want to make an incident out of a wheelchair guy's medicine and school books?"

I didn't let go of the strap and the other guy didn't either. They all looked at me pretty hard. Then the biggest guy talked again.

"Hey, I know you!" he said. "You're the fool who keeps blank paper in his wallet so it looks like you've got cash."

"It's just for insurance purposes," I said. "If somebody swipes my wallet, there ain't a rule says I gotta give them a big profit."

"Right," he said. "I remember. The duct tape guy."

OK, that might be confusing to you. When I was detecting on The Bones gang, I tied up some of them with duck tape, which they would of preferred I not do. Gangs remember things like that, even if it happened to a different gang.

"It's pretty handy stuff," I said. The big guy stared at me, thinking. Then he nodded.

"You know what, guys?" he said. "Mr. Duct Tape is right. We got more important things to do. Let him take the bag."

The guy who was holding the strap didn't let go right away. But after they looked at each other for a minute, you could tell the big guy was the scoutmaster of the gang and the other one let go.

"Thanks," I said. "You done the right thing, which is its own reward."

Them electric wheelchairs go faster than you'd think. It took me two blocks to catch it. It had a little wire basket on the back to hold stuff. When wheelchair guy stopped at a red light, I got up close behind him and put the bag into the basket, being careful he wouldn't notice I done it. You get bonus points in the Doctor Hudson game if you help someone out, but only if they don't know it. Sometime I'll explain the Doctor Hudson game to you, but for right now it don't matter. After I was sure the bag was stuck in there good, I went over next to the chair and jogged in place.

"Nice weather we're having, ain't it?" I said.

He just grunted in disgust, like nice weather was about the worst thing that could happen.

"Well, you have a nice day," I said. The light turned green and we both crossed the street. I just walked, so he beat me across easy. It felt good that I could help a guy who had such bad luck and was in a rotten mood. You should get double Doctor Hudson points for helping somebody in a bad mood. Maybe you do.

OK, all that stuff happened in the first five blocks of walking down Colfax. I think you get my point about detective mode. By the time I'd walked 19 blocks my brain was pretty tired from noticing stuff. I thought maybe I'd stop into Big Al's Diner and get a Coke before I went back home.

Big Al ain't its real name. I changed it for the book so I won't get in trouble for advertising something without permission. It's been in business as long as I remember and has a big electric sign and its own parking lot. On a busy street like Colfax, people like places with their own parking lot since it ain't that easy to park on the street. Big Al's is always busy, mostly cause of the parking lot but also because they sell patty melts which not many places do any more. I took a quick look around the parking lot before I went in in case somebody I knew was parked there and I could think of a joke to say to them ahead of time. Jokes always work best if you practice them.

I didn't see any friends' cars parked but I about fell over at what I did see. It was the tan van that had been parked in front of my building. I walked over to it real casual, but you could tell nobody was in it. There was a little scratch on the back door I seen before, so I was pretty sure. I took off my backpack and took out my legal yellow pad, plus a sharp pencil. First thing I done is write down the license plate number, which I should of done the first time. The front plate had the same number. You gotta check both, since sometimes crooks swipe plates and have different ones on the front so it's harder to catch them.

The plates was from Texas, but at least the van didn't have Dallas Cowboy stickers on it. The van was old, with some rust spots. There was some white paint on the back bumper, like from a spray of paint that didn't get cleaned up. I made a note of that and went inside.

Big Al's was extra busy. A pretty waitress in tight jeans and a black T-shirt walked past. She seemed busy. She waved her hand and said just sit anywhere. I said thanks and then she was gone. I looked around the room before I decided which guys might be the perps.

There was three guys at one table with dark hair. They was leaning toward each other and talking quiet. They all wore white T-shirts and white jeans and one had a white baseball cap.

My brain was working lightspeed on clues. The main color painters use is white, so lots of the time they wear white clothes. Then you can't see if some spills on them. There was paint splatters on the van bumper and even a good painter can screw up sometimes. Painters and other construction guys travel around the country looking for work, which means guys from Texas ain't off the hook. Everybody said there was three guys who burgled the apartments, and there was three of them. The burglars had accents. Guys from Texas sound different from regular Colorado people.

There was an empty stool at the bar next to the table they was sitting at. I walked over and sat on it. I put my legal yellow pad down on the bar and paid all my attention to it, even if it was a blank paper. I didn't look at the three alleged suspects at all.

"What'll you have?" asked the bartender.

"Just a Coke, thanks," I said. "I gotta study for a term paper."

I said that part loud enough the alleged suspects could hear me. Students is about as invisible as homeless guys.

When I got my Coke, I started writing stuff like pluses and minuses on the legal yellow pad and other fancy signs I just made up. Nothing makes a guy look like a student as much as making up fancy stuff nobody understands. Mostly what I was doing was listening.

But they talked quiet and the room was noisy so I didn't get many clues. They was arguing about something, so sometimes they talked louder and I could hear a few words. One guy sounded mad when he said, "She knows where he is!"

That seemed interesting, so I wrote it down under my fancy math design that looked like a spaceship. The guy had some kind of accent but it wasn't like Mr. Mitchell's. Just the idea that they talked funny was collaborating evidence.

Then one of them must of said a joke because they all laughed pretty loud and one said "Cool Bang!" Another one said that same thing back, which ain't a saying I ever heard before, so I wrote it down next to some plus signs.

That was all the clues I got and none of them was good enough to tell a cop about. I used to know a cop named Officer Mike who I could talk to like he was a regular person, only he retired. The new guy was young and wanted people to fill out forms and follow procedures. I didn't have any clues that was worth filling out a form over.

The three alleged suspects stood up to leave. They was all pretty skinny and didn't look all that scary, but you never want to mess with three guys. I just kept studying my math problems, especially the one that looked like a duck.

After they left I paid the guy behind the bar, put my backpack on again and went outside. You could smell cigarette smoke, and car smoke, plus the smell of meat cooking from inside. There was lights in the parking lot but there was shadows too. I found a shadow next to the building and leaned back against the brick wall like maybe I was gonna smoke or make a cell phone call. I seen the van's headlights come on. The van engine was noisy like it had a little hole in its muffler. They pulled out of the parking lot and turned east on Colfax.

My apartment was in the other direction, but I didn't have no appointments so I started jogging east. The van got stopped at the first stoplight, but I just kept jogging until I was half a block ahead of it. If they turned off, that was cool, then I'd know what their first turn was. But they kept going straight and passed me. There was so many cars they couldn't get up much speed and sometimes they had to stop. I just kept going. Sometimes I was ahead and sometimes they was ahead.

You can't beat a van in a race unless there's traffic and stoplights. But sometimes there is, which is why you shouldn't give up just cause it sounds like a dumb idea. I bet cavemen caught deers by not giving up until the deer was so tired he decided it wasn't worth it any more. I probably followed that alleged van for two miles before they turned on their turn signal and went down a side street.

Just to be safe, I kept going for one more block before I turned right myself. They might notice if a jogger took the exact same turns as them. I ran a little faster for three blocks, then turned on a street to intercept them.

They was going faster too, so they was two blocks ahead of me when I seen them again. They was driving toward a part of town that had a bunch of old motels. I stopped jogging and just walked. The suspected perps was probably staying in one of them old motels since they was from Texas. I didn't have to watch them drive. I just had to keep walking, then check all the motel parking lots. If their van was parked at some motel, that was probably where they was staying.

The big opera star voice in my head sang that I was probably chasing wild gooses, which a guy mostly never catches. It was just luck I seen the van outside my building in the first place and mostly luck I seen it tonight at Big Al's. And maybe these guys was innocent. Still, the only reason I got lucky is cause I was out looking for clues in the first place. If you ain't looking for nothing, that's what you'll find.

By the time I got to the first motel, it looked asleep. All the main lights was off, nobody was outside and the cars in the parking lot looked asleep too. There was empty parking spots, so you had to think there was lots of empty rooms, even if the no vacancy sign was on. But there wasn't a van.

I walked down the street til I come to another motel. It was also old, with peeling paint and downspouts so creaky a ten-year-old girl couldn't climb one without it breaking. Its name was in red neon lights, but that was the only interesting thing about it. There wasn't a van parked there.

I found the van at the eighth motel I investigated, which was called The Blue Moon. It had a blue neon sign with half a moon on it. There was lights on in three different units. I walked up the metal stairs to the second floor. Some of the stairs squeaked. A balcony walkway led around the building to all the doors. The balcony moved when you walked on it. The rooms that had lights on was 213, 222, and 233. Since the alleged suspects got there just before me, I figured they was in one of them rooms, or maybe in all three.

I went back downstairs and a block away to a streetlight. I took out my legal yellow pad and wrote Blue Moon and what street it was on and what rooms I thought they might be in.

Painters get up early. It takes so long to clean up their stuff, they get up early and work extra long days. That way, they don't spend so much time cleaning tools. If I wanted to surveil them tomorrow, I needed to get there early too. It didn't make much sense to walk all the way home, then walk all the way back here in the morning and then follow the van too. That's a lot of extra jogging for a guy who ain't training for some race.

I opened the dumpster lid and pulled out two big trash bags that was full of trash. I did it as quiet as I could and I don't think nobody heard me. Holding the sacks in one hand, I climbed up the downspout at the darkest corner in back until I was up on the roof.

It was a pretty good roof, mostly flat without much junk up there. I put the two trash bags down as a mattress and laid down on them. A trash sack full of old paper towels is about as comfortable as a fancy mattress. The stars was bright as Christmas tree lights. The air was still hot from the daytime, but there was a little bit of wind to make it feel about the right temperature.

I had a comfortable bed, with more stars to look at than I'd ever get around to before I fell asleep. Some crickets was chirping a slow song. Mr. Silver would be fine by himself for one night. He could last a week if he wasn't so careless kicking his food out of the cage, so I wasn't worried. Anyway, I had a plan. You can't complain too much about a night like that.

It was lucky them alleged perps was noisy in the morning or I would of slept through my own plan. The sun wasn't even up yet when I heard them joking on each other. They was in the parking lot walking towards their van. I could of jumped down to the little balcony and then walked down the steps, but that might wake somebody so I done it the hard way. As quiet as I could I grabbed up my trash bag mattress and climbed down the downspout on the back of the motel. I put the sacks back in the dumpster and looked around the corner of the building. They started up the van. Mostly what I wanted to do is see which way they drove. Since they ate at Big Al's Diner, which is pretty far from the The Blue Moon, I figured their work job was probably that direction too. But a detective can't just decide he knows something because it makes sense. He's gotta check stuff.

I was surprised when they went the opposite direction from Big Al's. I jogged after them for a while but they didn't pay much attention to stop signs and speed limits. That early in the morning there wasn't traffic or cops so they got away from me easy. After a while I turned around and started walking back home.

I didn't have good reasons to think they was burglars, I gotta admit that one first thing. Second, I didn't know their names or where they was working. If you look at it that way, you could say I ain't made much progress. But at least they was one idea for suspects. And if they was, I knew their license plate number, and that they was from Texas and they ate at Big Al's and stayed at the Blue Moon and probably worked at a job in the other direction. That was all good clues if they done it.

Plus, I still had Mr. Mitchell as a suspect since his apartment didn't get broke into.

I wished Officer Mike still worked in my neighborhood so I could just give him my clues. He was kind of old and serious but he was a good guy. Before he retired, sometimes he'd talk to me about my detective ideas. Mostly he said, "Young man, you stay away from them guys, they're dangerous." But it still felt good he'd listen to me. Sometimes the best way to help somebody think about an idea is just to listen to them and Mike was a good listener.

Then I had an idea. I knew one place Officer Mike used to go to. A friend of his owned The Train Track Inn before he died. It was in an old neighborhood with some crime issues. Motorcycle guys liked to play pool there. After his friend died, I don't know if Officer Mike kept going there or not. I ain't a big drinker, since it costs too much and usually gets a guy in trouble. But this was for business, if you looked at my detecting for free as a business. Guys do stuff for business all the time that ain't smart or legal or right. It don't matter; if it's for business, they ain't got much choices. They gotta do it.

It was Friday morning and Friday night is a popular time to go to bars. I decided I'd go home and do all my chores and then tonight put on clean clothes and put some cash in my shirt pocket and go to The Train Track bar. If Officer Mike was there, I'd buy him a beer and see if he'd listen to my latest detective ideas. I didn't see no hidden flaws with that plan.

Chapter Eleven
Officer Mike at the Train Track Bar

When I got home, I took a zip bag of liver out of my freezer and left it on the counter to thaw. There was three pieces of liver in every zip bag in my freezer. I always cook all of them, but sometimes I only eat one for dinner and save the others for breakfast the next day. There ain't many things as good as cold liver that's already cooked, plus it's about as easy as opening a can of spaghetti. You just add ketchup.

The other reason I froze three pieces of liver together is because I cut a big hole in the middle one and put another plastic zip bag in there with some paper money. I found some drug money by accident, which I won't say too much about in case you ain't read my other book. I tried to give it to the cops but they was pretty busy so I've been keeping it safe until they put out an APB on it. Lots of people hide money in their freezer, which crooks know, but most crooks won't bother to thaw out all your bags of liver looking for it. Them suspects that swiped my apple crate threw all my stuff from the freezer on the floor but they didn't find it. There was three one hundred dollar bills in each of my liver bags. If you add up all my zip bags of liver, that's a lot of money, but it ain't mine. I'm just storing it. On the other hand, I figure I'm like a bank, which takes some interest payments out of the money it stores for people whenever the bank guys need some cash. If I got a special reason to need some cash, I put on my banker hat and take an interest payment. Ain't no reason as special as business needs.

I made sure Mr. Silver had fresh water and a whole jar lid full of food. "If I'm going out, it's only fair you feel pretty comfortable," I told him. He didn't seem to care much either way. Sometimes he knows you're going out so he pouts, but you gotta ignore him. "Babysitting you ain't my only full time job," I said. "You ought to get a hobby." He just flapped his wings one time and turned away.

The Train Track Bar was kind of far from my apartment so I took a bus partway. I had took a shower and combed my hair and put on a clean blue work shirt with a one hundred dollar bill in its pocket. I buried the other two hundreds in my coffee can under all the coffee.

You could see the sign for the bar a long ways off. It was high off the ground, a big round plastic circle that was all white and lit up. There wasn't any words on it, just some lines that looked like train tracks.

It had a big parking lot. There was mostly old cars parked in it, plus about eight motorcycles. That seemed like a good sign since motorcycle guys know their bars and they're usually pretty friendly.

I walked in the door. The inside was darker than outside, so I seen stuff in order from brightest to darkest while my eyes got used to the light. A bunch of little round tables had red glass jars with lit candles in them. The place smelled like beer and candle smoke and pepperoni pizza. The walls had old red wallpaper, which had a fancy fluffy design. The walls was lit up by beer signs. The ceiling had speakers, which was playing Sweet Home Alabama loud enough you wanted to dance to it but not so loud you couldn't talk. Just inside the front door to the right was a little stage with guitar amplifiers and drums set up. I hoped I got to talk to Officer Mike before the band started since there wasn't much use trying to talk over electric guitars.

On the other side of the stage was a little room that had all kinds of mirrors on the walls. The sign said it was the dance floor, but it was more of a dance room. The main room, which had the stage and all the little tables, had a really long bar along one wall. Past that you could see a room with more light that had two pool tables, two foosball tables, and a pinball machine. The main room also had some more pinball machines. One tall guy just inside the front door was moving to the music and playing a machine, so it was clacking and ringing and the ball was banging into stuff.

Most of the tables was empty since it was still early. A couple guys with leather jackets and long hair was playing pool. One table had four pretty women drinking beers and laughing. I think maybe the light from the red candles made them look prettier, but that could be optical delusions. Six people was sitting at the bar. From the back, one of them looked like Officer Mike. There was an empty barstool next to him. I walked up behind him and leaned over to his ear.

"I'm gonna have to see some identifications, sir," I said to him in my most official voice.

That startled him, which was probably mean of me to do. He turned around pretty quick. His face went through a bunch of changes. First he was just surprised someone asked him for ID since he was obviously old

93

enough to drink beer. Second, it was pissed when he seen I wasn't somebody official. Third it looked surprised when he saw I was somebody he knew even if he never seen me in a bar, so his brain didn't remember who I was for a second. About a half second later his eyes got wide as he figured out who I was.

"Well, Mr. Jumper John Cable!" he said. He stood up and reached out his hand to shake. "I thought this was a higher class bar!"

"Yeah, I thought it had rules about who could get in too. I guess we both need to upgrade our bars."

"Sit down, sit down," he said motioning to the stool. "Let my buy you a beer. How have you been?"

I sat down.

"I been good. But I'm buying the beers." I pulled my hundred-dollar bill out of my shirt pocket and laid it on the bar. The motorcycle guy on the stool on the other side of Office Mike looked at it then looked back at his own beer. The bartender slid the bill into his hand.

"I'd like the same kind of beer as my friend's having," I said. "Plus one more for him and also one for his buddy next to him." The motorcycle guy heard that and nodded thanks to me. His face was pretty rough, like maybe he had lots of pimples when he was a kid and it never quite healed up. Even if he nodded thanks, I seen right away I should have stopped at a grocery store to get change for that hundred dollar bill before I come here only I didn't think of it. People see extra cash and it makes their brains get busy. Smart guys try to invest it away from you, pool players want to bet it anyway from you, and lazy guys just want to steal it from you. It's just how people are; you can't hold it against them. But it was dumb of me to bring enough money to buy fifty beers into a room full of strangers.

"What brings you all the way down here?" Officer Mike said.

"Well, I was just in the area and I seen this bar, which reminded me I was thirsty for a beer."

Officer Mike looked at me for a minute like he was watching my face for clues. Then he smiled a little bit and said, "Right."

The bartender brought each of us our beers, plus my change. I give him a good tip and then I folded the rest of the bills in half and put a paperclip on it to hold it together. I always paperclip money together like that. I put the bills into my shirt pocket and buttoned it so it wouldn't fall out if I leaned over or got knocked down.

"How about you?" I said. "What's it like to be retired?"

"It's about like your life," he said. "I do whatever I want. You still see Holly?"

I felt my face getting hot at that question. "Well, she lives in my same building so I see her sometimes."

"Oh?" he said.

"Sure. Plus she's been helping me with some detective thinking. Only I ain't as good a thinker when she's around."

"I see," he said. "So you've got some more detective ideas?"

"Well, I guess you could say that."

"And sometimes detectives like to talk about their ideas," he said.

"I seen it on TV all the time."

"So you put on a clean shirt and rode the bus all the way down here."

"Well, that was before I got here. Once I got here, I was just in the area. So I come in."

He nodded and didn't say nothing for a minute.

"There's a booth over by those pinball machines," he said. "Why don't we go over there so we don't bother anyone here at the bar."

"Cool," I said and started to get up but he touched my elbow in a way that told me to wait a minute. Officer Mike looked into the distance like he done sometimes when he was thinking. Then he turned to the motorcycle guy.

"You know, things aren't always the way they seem," he said. The guy didn't say nothing.

"Take me, for example. I'm a retired cop. You might not guess that. Concealed carry permit, the whole shot. And my friend Jumper here. He's got that big goofy smile and he acts pretty friendly..."

"Wait a minute," I said, but he looked over at me real casual and raised one eyebrow like Spock done sometimes and I closed my mouth. Then he went on talking.

"You remember that gang called The Bones?"

95

The guy's eyes got a little bigger. He looked at me, then back at Officer Mike.

"Jumper here took them out single handed. Broke a guy's leg and another guy's hand. Took out their three main guys. Their big leader from Chicago— six foot three, 240 pounds. By the time Jumper was done with him the guy just held out his hands for the cuffs and asked me to arrest him. Steve Atwater heard about it and gave him a signed jersey. Who'd guess something like that?"

Mike took a drink from his beer and swallowed it slow, like it tasted extra good. He was staring at the little cashew machine behind the bartender. It was like he was talking to the cashews.

"Yeah, sometimes things seem like a pretty good idea when you first think of them. And then they turn out to be about the worst idea you ever had."

I knew they was both thinking about the cash in my shirt pocket. It's a good idea to warn somebody their idea might have hidden flaws like what Officer Mike done with the motorcycle guy. But a good warning don't always stop a guy's plan even if has flaws. So it's smart to button up your pocket too.

"Come on, Jumper," Officer Mike said and he stood up. Then he put a hand on the guy's shoulder and smiled at him like they was old buddies. "You have a good night, all right?" He said. "A good smart night." The guy nodded and we went over to the booth. Once we got settled, Officer Mike leaned back in the booth.

"So, Columbo," he said. "What's the case you're working on this time?"

Officer Mike was pretty smart. He knew I wasn't an official detective like Mr. Columbo on TV so he was joking on me. When people joke on you and they ain't mean about it, they're telling that you're kind of a friend. You're gonna tell a friend stuff you wouldn't tell a cop. If you was questioning a suspected perp, you might try that. But I figured Officer Mike and me was sort of friends so he wasn't using a cop trick on me. I liked it that he was joking on me.

"Some guys swiped my apple crate," I said.

"What?" he said.

"Well, that's just how it started."

He looked away toward the bar, like he was hoping to see that cashew machine again. Then he started talking kind of soft, but still looking over at the bar.

"I remember The Bones claimed they lost a lot of drug money the night you caught them."

"You'd have to say we caught them," I said. "I couldn't of done it without you."

"Thanks," he said. "That money never turned up. But then, gang guys are pretty unreliable. They probably made that part up. Your apple crate wasn't full of cash, was it?"

"No sir, it didn't even have one dollar in it. I used it like a chair on my balcony. Somebody give it to me when I was a kid, so I liked it better than some apple crate that was a stranger. Every night when I sat on it, I felt kind of relaxed. Kind of like I was at home." I couldn't think of a smart way to say it, so I stopped.

Then I remembered what else he asked, so I started talking again. "But yeah, after The Bones killed that guy and swiped my turtle, you'd have to say they was pretty unreliable. I'd give them an A plus in unreliable."

"But you had your turtle after they went to jail. I bet there's an interesting story in there somewhere."

I could see why Officer Mike was a good cop. There was some parts of that story that probably never made it into the official police report. The alleged missing drug money was one of them sleeping dogs you try not to step on the tail of.

"The apple crate was just my part of the crime. Those burglars busted into almost every apartment in my building."

"Really? I hadn't heard about that. Was anybody hurt?" He leaned toward me, watching my face.

"Nah, but they swiped a lot of stuff. I think they used my apple crate to carry it in."

"I see."

"Like Holly's apartment and Mrs. Comanici's, where they swiped some gold coins. Almost everybody in my building got burgled. All they took from me was my apple crate, which ain't worth as much as a pair of sneakers except to me. Being expensive is just a guy's opinion."

I took my legal yellow pad out of my backpack.

"I been writing down clues," I said.

"That's smart. Why don't you tell me what you've got?"

"OK," I said and I read through all my clues. He didn't say they was dumb or make any jokes on them. He just listened pretty hard, like he was using his whole brain on it. A couple of times he asked questions about something I said, which is a smart way to prove you're listening.

"Interesting," he said. "So they never broke into Mr. Mitchell's place at all?"

"Yeah. And he always talks soft and polite, the way serial killers on TV do. But that ain't really a clue."

"Probably not. They broke into Mrs. Comanici's apartment twice?"

"Yeah. But the second time they just busted it up like they was looking for something. They didn't take nothing."

"And you think these three painters from Texas might be suspects?"

"I ain't got evidence. You'd have to say they was more like possible alleged suspects."

"When it gets right down to it, it's really just a hunch?"

Him saying that surprised me since I had in my brain it was better than a hunch. A hunch seems like a guess. I thought about that for a minute. The reason I got interested in them was mostly just coincidences. The more I thought about it the dumber it seemed.

"Yeah, I guess so. I ain't got any good clues for them."

"That's OK," he said. "You've had pretty good hunches before. Anyway, sometimes our brain figures things out before it gets around to explaining them to us."

The band was tuning up their guitars. One thing I know about Officer Mike is that he loves to dance, even if he's pretty old.

"OK, thanks for listening," I said. "I think I'll go home now."

"I could give you a ride."

"Nah, thanks. I like the exercise. And all the girls are gonna want to dance with you."

He laughed, but just then a pretty woman young enough to be his daughter's friend walked up to the booth and asked him if he was going to be dancing tonight.

Officer Mike looked around the room before he answered, like he was looking for someone.

"I seen that biker guy leave a while ago," I said. I stood up and turned to the girl. "Yeah, he's dancing tonight. Just don't let him wear out your shoes from stepping on them."

The room had got pretty crowded so it took me a minute to get through everyone to the front door. The night air felt cool as I stepped outside. The parking lot had lights so it wasn't that dark. A car turned in off the street and its headlights hit me in the face for a second. That's how come I didn't see what hit me in time to get out of the way. I just seen them headlights shine off a black motorcycle jacket. It was the biker guy from the bar, who moved from behind a parked car and without saying a word punched me in the stomach about as hard as he could. I didn't have time to block his punch or step back or nothing. At the last second I figured out what he was doing and tightened up my stomach muscles, but he still got me real good. The punch knocked me a step or two backward. I couldn't breathe or talk. I fell down on my knees on the pavement. He grabbed my shirt pocket and jerked so hard the button broke all the way off and part of the pocket ripped off too. Then he pulled out the cash that was in there, which was folded one time and held together with a paper clip. He stuck it in his jeans pocket and walked away real quick. I heard a motorcycle start up and then saw him racing away on it. It was a noisy, smoky bike, but it was real fast. He'd be a mile away before I could even catch my breath and start walking so he made a clean getaway. That was the only way to look at it. That ain't how I was hoping to end the evening, but you can't ever tell what might happen.

There was some weeds at the edge of the parking lot that looked about as comfortable as somebody's lawn so I got myself standing up and went over there. I could still smell the motorcycle exhaust. I was already starting to feel better, but I sat down on the weeds to rest up for another minute. While I was resting, I tried to think if there was a lesson hid in my night's adventure I ought to learn. It's pretty hard to think of lessons when you're stomach hurts and you can't breathe good, but lots of times lessons come about the same time as stomach aches.

Getting punched in the stomach was my own fault, I gotta admit that. A hundred bucks is a lot of money in a bar like The Train Track and I was asking for trouble by using it there. If a guy thinks you're rich, he figures he's got as much right to your money as you do.

It was a shame about my shirt pocket getting ripped, since this was about my best shirt. I could safety pin the pocket and wear it for most purposes, but if I needed a good shirt for detective business I'd have to go back to the thrift store and buy one.

On the good side, that biker guy didn't get as much cash as he was hoping. Besides my insurance wallet I had another policy in my shirt pocket. I pulled up the pant leg on my jeans and felt inside my sock. Yeah, the change from that hundred was still safe in there. Before I come to the bar I put a one-dollar bill around a little stack of blank wrapped papers, folded it once and held it together with a paper clip. I cut the blank pages out of an old book somebody threw away, which is about the best use for an old book. The pages is the right thickness. I put that phony wad inside my shirt pocket right next to my real hundred-dollar bill just in case. When I seen that biker noticing my cash, I paper clipped it and pretended to put it in my shirt pocket but really I kept it in my hand. First thing I done when we went to the booth was cross my legs and real casual slide it inside my sock. That's just being careful, which a lot of times don't do you any good. But every now and then it does, so if you got plenty of time and you think of some way to be careful, it don't hurt to try it. I only lost a buck, which is cheap insurance.

The problem was if I ever seen that biker guy again. About nothing pisses somebody off as bad as fooling them after they think they swiped all your money. But he didn't have a good right to my money either just because he wanted it, so I had a case for wanting to keep it too. Legal issues is complicated.

I took enough cash out of my sock to pay for the bus ride home and put it in my front jeans pocket and put the rest back in my sock. Then I stood up and started walking toward the bus stop. Nobody else was waiting for the bus, so I sat on the bench. It was across the street from an old brick apartment building with pots of blue flowers by the front door. A sign in the window said 'vacancy'. Lots of buildings had vacancies, since the economy wasn't all that hot. I looked down the street and seen the bus coming, which was good timing.

I stood up and looked around but my eyes kept coming back to that vacancy sign like it was a clue. Only that didn't make no sense.

Some trash paper was blowing around my feet. I ain't a big fan of litter so I picked it up to throw into the trashcan that was about three feet away from the bus stop bench, but then I stopped.

Sometimes your brain wants to tell you something but you get distracted doing something like throwing away trash and your brain gets pissed and won't say nothing. That's what happened to me. I kind of froze like a statue of a guy holding trash paper in his hand. Some idea had jumped up behind me and said "hey you, over here!" but when I turned around it had hid again so I couldn't see it. I maybe looked dumb standing there with my backpack on holding some red trash paper in my hand but bus drivers seen about everything in the world and the bus stopped right in front of me. I could always throw that trash away at home, so I just kept standing there thinking when the bus door opened.

The bus driver figured I changed my mind, so he started to close the doors. Just then I figured out what the clue was that my brain already knew which it had not got around to telling me. I quick got on the bus.

Them painters had been parked outside my building taking pictures of it. But why? I paint the units when they go vacant and there wasn't a vacancy sign on it anyway. So why was some painters from Texas taking pictures of my building? There wasn't a job for them and there wasn't a place to live. That was the clue that didn't make no sense.

I sat in a bus seat and opened my backpack. I stuffed the red litter paper into it to deal with later and took out my legal yellow pad. I wrote down the clue about how come them painters was interested in a building that didn't have any empty apartments to paint or rent. I ain't sure how good a clue it is, but you gotta write all of them down. I read my note on the Blue Moon motel, and all the ideas Officer Mike had said.

I didn't make no note about the biker guy punching me. Getting sucker punched for making a dumb mistake ain't a clue. That's just life.

When you want to think about one idea, pretty often your brain decides to think about a whole other thing. That night while I was laying in bed thinking about my clues, I had a pretty good idea for world peace. Instead of churches starting wars against each other, they should all start a league, like the NFL football league. They could have contests against each other in praying and feeding those less fortunate than ourselves. They could have rules and referees and a Super Bowl and whichever church prayed the best or fed the most kids could get a big trophy. I was pretty sleepy so it made sense to me, but there must be hidden flaws or else they'd already be doing it.

Chapter Twelve
A whole other crime happens, there's a fight, and somebody goes to the hospital.

The next day I decided to work on solving the clues and getting my apple crate back, but sometimes plans don't come in the order you wrote them down in. First, Mr. Silver spilled all his water and got his wings wet, which made him mad at me. He was flapping and jumping like a chicken in a cartoon. So I had to clean up his cage before my brain was up to full speed. "I'm gonna ship you off to the bird pound," I told him. "I swear I am. You got two things to take care of, your water and your food, and you mess them both up every day. It ain't a wonder your dinosaur buddies went extinct." He just turned away from me and pouted.

I microwaved a cup of coffee from yesterday and took my pad out of the backpack to study clues. I sat on the floor of my balcony and thought my hardest while I drunk my coffee. No ideas come to me right away. I seen that red litter paper jammed in the backpack. Well, I couldn't think about clues while I had unfinished business like litter. I got up, crumpled it into a ball, and threw it away, which felt like doing my part for the environment. I went back out to my balcony. It ain't all that comfortable out there without an apple crate to sit on, but it's where I drink my coffee if it ain't snowing. I sat down and started over.

Them clues felt like a school assignment and it's easy to think about everything else in the world if you got a school assignment. I thought about how cold it would be to sit out there if there was a bunch of snow. Then I thought about the thawed out liver in my refrigerator, which would make a pretty good breakfast if I cooked it. Then I started wondering about that red litter paper I just threw away. Maybe that was a clue the universe tried to tell me and I didn't pay attention. It ain't ever smart to ignore the universe.

I went back inside and took the paper out of the trash. It was just an ad somebody had stapled up somewhere and then the staples come loose. Just to be extra careful, I read some of the words on it and my mouth fell open from surprise. Maybe it wasn't a clue, but it was even better. It was an ad for a circus that was coming to town this next weekend. And not just any circus. It was the same circus I still had three tickets to go to in my cigar box.

After that, I was too excited to do much detective work. I had to figure out what bus went where the circus was going to be, and what shirt I should wear. Then I had to think about who I should take with me. Holly was the first person I thought of. But then I also thought of Linda, a little girl I done some art therapy with when she was sick. Kids like the circus, so that would be pretty fun. Then there was my buddy Greg who was a teenager who cracked me up. He wouldn't think the idea of a circus was cool, since he mostly didn't admit anything was cool. But he says funny stuff, so that would be fun.

I had three tickets, so I could bring two people, which only made it harder. Then I thought maybe my tickets had expired. The guy who give them to me named Gus said they wouldn't ever expire, but stuff expires all the time even if it ain't supposed to. Mr. Silver chirped.

"No, buddy, you ain't going to the circus," I said. "You can put your foot down on that idea."

Then I thought about the drug money in my freezer that I was taking care of for the police until they noticed they didn't have it. Even if my tickets wasn't good, I could use a tiny little bit of that money to take somebody to the circus. It would be like interest on an investment. If you put money in a checking account, the bank charges you interest for using an ATM card and for getting a box of checks. Even if you put a lot of money in a bank, them interest charges can use it all up.

Maybe I'd take all my friends to the circus and pay for it with interest on that drug money. But that felt like a little wrong in some way. Banks can't just charge you extra interest on your money they're storing for you because they want to go to the circus. Then I had an different idea.

Going to the circus would be pretty fun with my friends. That wasn't even a brainer. But maybe it would be even more fun to do what my Dad and I done when I was a kid. Maybe I'd go a couple days early, while they was setting up. Working for the circus was about the most fun I ever had. Even if my Dad wasn't there, maybe they'd let me do it again. Before I made any plan that was sitting in stone, I had to use my whole brain on that idea.

After I fried some liver and microwaved a potato, and ate them with ketchup, I went downstairs to tell Holly about my new idea, which was how come my hunch about them three guys in the van was suspicious. I already made my mind up not to talk about following the perps or sleeping on trash sacks on a motel roof without permission, or getting punched by that biker guy. You always got the right to remain silent, but it's about the hardest right in the book.

But Holly wasn't home. So I went down to the first floor and knocked on Mrs. Comanici's door. When she answered, I seen that Holly was already inside, sitting on the couch.

"Come on in, Jumper," Mrs. Comanici said. I felt a little weird, but then Holly seen me and smiled and waved so it felt OK. I stepped inside.

"Holly's helping me fill my new photo album," Mrs. Comanici said.

"Cool," I said.

"Mrs. Comanici has some wonderful old pictures," Holly said. "You'd like these pictures of old trains. And pictures from Europe with horses, and the zoo."

"I always liked zoos," I said.

"Do you want to help us?" Mrs. Comanici said. "I keep digital copies on a thumb drive. I took them down to the print store and they made wonderful copies. We're putting them all in order and mounting them in the new album." Mrs. Comanici sat next to Holly and pointed for me to sit in the chair across the coffee table.

On the one hand, if I stayed to help I'd probably get a free cookie out of the deal. And I like hanging out with Holly and also with Mrs. Comanici. Plus I wanted to tell them my new clue.

On the second hand, sorting pictures and putting them into an album sounded like the homework they give you as punishment when you forgot your first homework. And if there was two people besides Officer Mike who could get the truth, the whole truth and nothing but the truth out of me when I was trying to use my right to remain silent, both them two people was sitting on that couch.

"Well, if you really need me to help..." I said. Maybe I didn't sound as excited by the idea as I should have.

They both laughed. Then Mrs. Comanici said, "Of course we'd love your help. But maybe it would be more fun for Holly and me if we do this part by ourselves and then you can look through the book and see if we did OK. After we're done, you can give us suggestions, the way a supervisor would."

"Supervising is the most important job," Holly said.

"If that's how it would be the most fun for you, I'd come back after you're done and supervise," I said.

"Spoken like a born supervisor," Holly said with a smile.

I turned to leave.

"By the way," Mrs. Comanici said. "Was there something you wanted?"

At first I thought well, a cookie would be pretty good. Then I understood she was asking why I knocked on her door. I was going to tell them about why my hunch might be a clue, plus about the circus. But telling those things might get them all excited and they'd be saying lots of stuff and asking questions and before you know it I'd be sorting pictures.

"Nothing important," I said. "Just following up on clues and hunches. It can wait."

"All right then," Mrs. Comanici said. They both waved and went back to looking at pictures and saying how cute stuff was. I don't think they even seen me go out the door.

That night I went to the park to practice my jumping. The park's got nice trees there you can climb easy and then jump down onto the soft grass. There's always a few bugs and birds singing. Plus, you can pretend you're Tarzan of the Jungle and make up stories about fighting pirates. I always wait until there's nobody to see me because people think jumping out of trees is weird, even if they ain't ever jumped out of even one tree. It's just as hard to change an idea from someone who don't know better as someone who does.

I done twenty jumps which is more than usual, but the ground was soft and the air smelled like summer and I just kept climbing back up there and jumping again. Maybe it wouldn't of made any difference to what happened next, and I ain't making excuses. I'm just saying I climbed a tree and jumped out of it a bunch of times before I jogged back home. So maybe I was a little more tired than usual.

Then I run up the three flights of steps to my apartment since it's good practice for my speed running. I poured me a cup of water from the sink. My neighbor was playing an old TV western show pretty loud. Sometimes I listen by that wall, but tonight I wasn't in the mood. Mr. Silver tried to sing along, but I ignored him. He ain't ever got the hang of singing cowboy songs. I took my cup of water outside to my balcony to drink it.

My balcony looks out on the back yard of the apartment building. Past the yard there's a little wood fence and then the alley, which is where our Dumpster is. It's usually pretty quiet.

Only tonight there was people out there moving around in the dark and bumping into stuff. They didn't say nothing, like they was trying to be quiet, but they grunted like they was fighting without no words. One of them was a woman. I could tell from her voice only she didn't say nothing but "mmm!" She made pretty loud humming sounds, only they wasn't happy ones, they was mad ones. It was like she was trying to yell but couldn't open her mouth. I about decided to go down there and see if she was OK when she got her mouth open and said "help." It wasn't loud, but I heard it for sure and then she went back to making mad humming sounds.

Maybe it was just kids fooling around, but when somebody says help you don't wait to go help. I put down my cup of water and got up on the balcony railing. Right below there's a garage with a flat roof and a old mattress on top of it. I jumped it lots of times before even in the dark. But I always check to make sure nobody threw a bottle on it ahead of time. Now it was too dark to see and I didn't want to waste no time with stairs.

I jumped down to the garage roof. Even if my legs was already tired, I landed pretty good. Then I went over to the edge of the garage by the alley and jumped down to the ground.

That landing wasn't as good. One foot hit some gravel and twisted a little. It hurt to walk on it, so I had to limp a little to get over by the people by the dumpster. I climbed the wood fence to see what was going on.

What I seen didn't make no sense. Next to the dumpster was the tan van I'd been surveilling. The three painter guys was outside the van on its right side. The sliding side door was wide open. Two of the painter guys was holding a woman trying to push her into the van. Only she was wrestling back and they was having a lot of trouble. One guy had his hand over her mouth so she couldn't scream. She slammed her foot down on the guy's foot, which surprised him a lot but he didn't let go. Then she bit his hand so hard I thought she took off his fingers. He let go his hand off her mouth and started cussing like a pirate. The woman started yelling too, but not words I ever heard before. If she would of been thirty pounds bigger she might of made a fair fight out of it.

I was running toward them but my limp slowed me down. The lady seen me just then. "Jumper!" she said.

It was Mrs. Comanici. They pushed her into the van and slammed the door. Before the closest one could get himself set, I jumped right at his knees and he went down on the ground about as surprised as a guy could be. It was like tackling a teddy bear. I heard Mrs. Comanici pounding on the van window and yelling, "There's no door handles in here!" I didn't have a chance to open the door for her. I was still on the ground, mostly on top of the guy I tackled.

There was three of them and only one of me so I knew I didn't have much chances. The only idea I had was to fight them one at a time if I could. Maybe they'd forget about Mrs. Comanici if they was busy and she could escape and call the cops.

The first guy was still so surprised from getting tackled I figured I could slow him down before he got back in the mood to fight. He was on his back and his feet was almost under the van already, so I just rolled over to his shoulders and pushed real hard. His whole body slid underneath the van like he was a mechanic looking for expensive problems to fix.

By that time the other two figured it was their turn. One guy kicked me in the side about as hard as he could. It hurt like heck, I won't lie to you. But it didn't hurt so bad I wanted to stop fighting and just lay there so they could kick me some more.

When a guy kicks you when you're on the ground, what you want to do is grab his foot and lift it up as hard as you can. So his next kick, that's what I done. I grabbed his foot before it got to my stomach and pulled on it. This guy was a hard kicker for sure but balancing wasn't his best sport. When I lifted his foot up, he went crashing backward on the alley dirt. I ain't sure if his head hit the same time as his backbone, but it didn't sound good.

I'd stood up about the same time I lifted his foot up and now the other guy grabbed me from behind. He put me in a bear hug, holding my elbows to my sides. He was lifting my whole body off the ground. My first thought was that this skinny painter was a lot stronger than he looked. My second idea was that he was going to hold me there until his buddies got up and come over to start punching my face and stomach. Like I say, three against one ain't ever an easy fight.

But just cause something ain't easy don't mean you should give up. I could see Mrs. Comanici trying to open the van door which was locked somehow she couldn't figure out. If I didn't give her some time, she was gonna get kidnapped.

The guy kept holding me up in the air and I couldn't break his grip. Then I done three moves right after each other.

First, I jerked my head backward as hard as I could. My head whacked his nose pretty hard and he let me down a little from surprise. While he wasn't holding quite as hard, I jabbed backward with my left elbow and then my right elbow. I could feel his grip loosening just a little so I bent over forward. He was still hugging me but now his brain was also thinking about his nose and the new pains in his stomach from my elbow punches. My feet touched the ground just a little and I grabbed his left ankle as hard as I could. Then I stood straight up again, pulling his ankle forward between my legs.

His bear hug stopped as he went falling backward and I was free.

I ran over to the van and opened the door. Mrs. Comanici looked scared and mad at the same time. She didn't look at my face but looked over my shoulder.

"Jumper!" she yelled. "Look out behind..."

I felt a really bad pain across the top of my back and head. The guy I slid under the van had crawled out and whacked me hard with a board or something. It seemed like there wasn't nothing in the world except that pain. Then the pain kind of faded, and so did the light and all the sounds. Mrs. Comanici got blurry and I fell down on the ground.

Chapter Thirteen
Police got their own rules about who to believe, I make a daring getaway, and
we got to make a rescue plan

When I woke up, I was alone in the alley. The van was gone and so were the painter guys. It was still dark but the air felt colder so I think I must of been laying there a while. A gray cat jumped out of the Dumpster and walked over to me. He sniffed my foot for a second and then walked away.

Then I fell asleep again.

When I woke up it was still night but starting to get light. I heard a kid's voice saying, "He's right over there. I thought he was drunk until I saw the blood on his shirt."

Then a cop I ain't never seen was leaning over me shining his flashlight in my face. "Can you hear me?" he asked. Even if I was mostly asleep I thought that was about the dumbest question you could ask a guy. If you answered "no" they'd figure out right away you was lying. But I didn't feel good enough to make a joke on him, plus I didn't really care, so I just closed my eyes again.

The next time I opened my eyes I seen right away I was in a hospital bed with a nurse holding my wrist to see how my pulse was doing. It felt nice to just lay there in a clean room with somebody holding my wrist. Except that I hurt in a lot of places. My back, the back of my head, my stomach and my cheek all hurt. But the pain seemed kind of far away, like it was somebody else's body that got beat up and I could only feel it in the distance, like their body was telling my body how it felt over a telephone with a bad connection.

Then I remembered what happened and I tried to sit up. That didn't work. I'd forgot how to sit up and it felt about as hard as trying to fly. I laid back down.

"They got Mrs. Comanici!" I said to the nurse. I tried to yell it, but my voice come out like a whisper. "I tried to stop them but the one who was under the van snuck up on me!"

"He's awake now, Doctor," the nurse said over her shoulder but I didn't see no doctor. "You just lie back and relax," she said to me. "You've got some nasty injuries and the pain killers will make you feel confused."

"It was the painters from Texas," I said. "The one who eats scrambled eggs for dinner, he's the leader. He was under the van but he got out. Big Al's Diner. Scrambled eggs..."

"Right," the nurse said, like she wasn't even paying attention. "You didn't have any identification. What's your name?"

"Jumper," I said. The room had that hospital smell from using cleaners that kill germs.

"Think hard," she said. "We need to put your name down on your chart. Your full name."

"Jumper," I said again. "Jumper Cable. The principal always called me John."

"OK, then. We'll call you John. How about John Doe? Where do you usually sleep? Do you have a favorite underpass? A park maybe?"

"I usually sleep at home. But I like the underpasses by Speer Street."

"Fine. How would we recognize your home?"

"Not by my apple crate. Them painters stole that."

"That should make it easy. We'll look at all the cardboard nests under Speer that don't have apple crates."

"It had peaches on it."

"Your home has peaches on it?"

This nurse was really nice and she was trying her hardest but I ain't sure she was really smart.

"No. My apple crate. But it ain't there since the painters stole it. So if you find it, you'll find the painters too. Plus Mrs. Comanici. She's the one you should be looking for. Just don't call her a gypsy. She'll put the evil eye on you."

"Right. Why don't you get some rest? The police will be sending someone over to take your statement. I'll wake you when they get here."

"Mr. Silver probably pooped on his newspaper."

"Mr. Silver?"

"He used to be a pirate. He's green. But they got Mrs. Comanici."

"Yes, I wrote that down. And I'll be careful not to call her a gypsy. You just rest."

I was pretty sure she didn't understand. But I was sleepy and the bed felt good. Maybe the next nurse would be a little smarter. I closed my eyes again and went to sleep.

The cop who finally come to get a statement from me seemed too young to be a cop. Maybe he was old enough he had to shave and he could of had a wife and kids but he seemed like a second grader to me. Everybody's got to start on square one; you can't hold that against them. His hair was cut short, his face was skinny and his uniform looked as new as if he bought it this morning. He said his name was Officer Simpson and he took out a little pad to write on.

"I hope your first name ain't Homer," I said. Sometimes you can break the ice with a stranger by joking on him.

Officer Simpson didn't even look up. He probably didn't get the joke.

"No," he said. "Why were you in the alley last night?"

"I heard noises and then I heard someone call help. So I went to help."

"I see. Where were you when you heard this?"

"I was in my apartment." I give him the address and he wrote it down.

"Interesting," he said. "Isn't that the building that was burglarized?"

"Yeah," I said. "They swiped my apple crate."

"Really?" he said, but he didn't write nothing down. "They took an apple crate? Why would they do that?"

"I ain't sure," I said. "Maybe to carry stuff in."

"And where were you at the time of the burglary?"

"I was at the grocery store. I bought three cans of Dinty Moore stew and two cans of minestrone soup and four apples."

"Can anyone corroborate that?"

"I don't keep my receipts."

"Right. Did anyone see you there?"

"I didn't have on my secret invisibility cloak, so they probably seen me if they looked."

"Can anyone prove your whereabouts at the time of the break in?"

"Well, I still got all the food except one apple and two cans of Dinty Moore. But ain't we supposed to be talking about the guys in the van kidnapping Mrs. Comanici?"

"The nurse told us what you reported. We checked it out. Her neighbor said she often took little trips, it was probably nothing to worry about."

"Did he talk real soft and polite?"

"The report didn't mention that. No one heard anything in the alley, no one saw anything."

"But I seen it! I tried to stop them only there was too many of them."

Officer Simpson closed his little note pad and sighed.

"Yes, the nurse told me your story. There was a gypsy and an evil eye and a green pirate and you have a house made of peaches under an underpass. Look, the memory is a funny thing. You probably just had too much to drink and got mugged in the alley. We'll keep trying to contact Mrs. Comanici and her family. If she really is missing, we'll contact you again. Until we confirm your story, you're just not a very credible witness."

And then he left.

It felt like somebody slapped my face. It ain't fair if you tell the truth, the whole truth and nothing but the truth that the cops think you're probably lying anyway. His questions made it sound like he was wondering if I might of been one of the burglars instead of the guy that got beat up by them.

My next idea was that nobody was looking for Mrs. Comanici since they didn't believe she was even missing. So I needed to get out of the hospital and find her.

The next thing I thought was that nobody even knew I was in the hospital since they wrote down my name as John Doe, which is a cool name, but it ain't the correct one. My friends might start wondering about me in a couple of days, but there ain't nobody I see every single day. Nobody'd say, hey, I ain't seen Jumper today so I wonder if he's in the hospital.

Hospitals is like fancy hotels, where they give you orange juice and applesauce and you ain't got any jobs or assignments to do. Plus, they got great TV's with cable channels. If you feel OK, they're a good vacation place.

But I couldn't stay there extra days even if it might be fun. I sat up. I felt dizzy, so I rested a minute and then I started feeling ordinary again. My head and back hurt like heck when I got out of the bed. My clothes was all in a little closet. I changed out of the goofy hospital gown and got dressed. When nobody was looking I went out into the hall.

In my head, I pretended I was visiting some sick guy so I'd walk like a visitor and not like a patient. I must of done a good job since the nurses didn't even look at me. To be extra safe, I took the elevator down to the main floor instead of the steps, which everybody knows I would of chose. It ain't like somebody was following me, but that's sort of how I felt. When I stepped outside and took a breath of outside air, I felt like I just busted out of prison.

My whole body hurt too much to walk very fast, but I kept going as steady as a turtle until I got home. I had to stop and rest after I walked up the first flight of steps of my apartment building, but once I felt better I kept going until I got to Holly's apartment. I probably looked like a lost hobo. My hair didn't comb itself in the hospital and my clothes was still dirty from getting beat up in them. I ain't never knocked on a girl's door if I wasn't in clean clothes with combed hair. But if I went upstairs and took a shower I'd probably lay down for a minute to rest. If I laid down I wouldn't wake up for two days. So I knocked on her door.

When Holly opened the door her eyes got big and she didn't say nothing, but you could tell some of the stuff she was thinking. First, she was surprised to see me. Second, she was noticing the way I looked and thought of about six different reasons for it. Some of those ideas meant she could make a joke on me for doing something dumb, and some meant she should be pissed at me for doing something extra dumb. Then maybe she thought something bad happened so she should say something to make me feel better.

"Come in, Jumper," is what she said, and it made me feel better. "What happened?"

"I got beat up a little bit," I said. "So they took me to the hospital."

"That's terrible! Are you all right? What happened?"

If somebody asks you a whole bunch of questions you want to decide what's the big one and answer that. Otherwise you spend a lot of time talking about little stuff and maybe never get around to the main thing.

"Them painters from Texas kidnapped Mrs. Comanici in their van. I tried to stop them but they outsmarted me."

"Did you tell the police?"

"I tried to, but I ain't a credible witness so it don't count. Plus, they put my name down as John Doe and maybe Mr. Doe ain't credible either. They don't even think she's missing yet."

"When did this happen?"

"Last night. Wait. What day is it?"

Her eyes got bigger and she said, "Monday."

"Then it was two days ago, on Friday night. My neighbor plays old Gunsmoke TV shows real loud on Friday nights, which is the first reason I went out on my balcony. Only it don't seem like two days have went by."

"Sit down on the couch. Tell me what happened."

So I told her about hearing the fuss in the alley and about jumping down and trying to help. "I was already kind of tired from training," I said. "Plus I hurt my ankle a little jumping off the garage. I ain't making excuses since there was three of them, which ain't ever a fair fight. I'm just saying there was some reasons they got Mrs. Comanici and I got a hospital trip."

"And then the police wouldn't listen to you?"

"You can't hold that against him," I said. "Maybe if I was wearing a clean shirt..."

She wasn't listening any more. She picked up her cell phone and tapped some numbers onto it. She had as mean a face on as I ever seen a woman have and her voice sounded like she was talking to some kid who broke ALL the rules and was about to wish she'd just send him to the Principal's office to take his consequences.

"Hello. This is Holly Johnson," she said into the cell phone. "I need to report a kidnapping." She waited a second. "No, I won't hold. My aunt has been gone for three days and now I discover that Doctor John Cable saw her being taken against her will." She listened for a second. "Yes, of course he reported it. He was in the hospital being treated for the injuries he incurred trying to stop them. But you didn't bother notifying me. You didn't notify any of our family. You didn't notify our attorneys. Doctor Cable says you didn't seem to take him seriously either. Have you checked the morgue? Have you checked the hospitals?" She waited about a second. "No, 'I don't know' is not an acceptable answer. Let me talk to your supervisor." She pulled the phone away from her ear for a second. "Jumper, did you get a license number?"

I nodded, since I knew I couldn't say a whole sentence before she started talking again. "Write it down," she said and then went back to her phone. I found some paper and wrote down the license number.

"That's right, detective," Holly said. "Her name is Edith Comanici." She said the address, then waited a second. "On Wednesday night she was seen in the alley behind her apartment building being abducted by three men. They drove a tan van." She took the paper from me and read the license plate number.

"About fifty years old, black hair. Wait, I can get you a picture." She picked up the big three-ring binder she and Mrs. Comanici had been using as a photo album and turned pages until she found a picture she liked. She took a picture of the page with her phone.

"I'm sending you a recent picture right now." She waited a second and then the detective must of said he got it. She listened and nodded. "Yes, of course I can come in to make a full report. And then you can explain why I shouldn't have our family attorneys get involved."

She put the phone back down on the coffee table and smiled. "There," she said. "I think they understand now."

"I didn't know you had family attorneys," I said.

"I don't. But sometimes 'attorney' is a magic word that gets people's attention."

"I'll remember that" I said. "Hocus Pocus ain't been working so good for me lately." I started to get up from the couch.

"Where do you think you're going, buster?" she said. She stood over me with her hands on her hips.

"I'm pretty tired," I said. "I need to go up to my apartment."

"Not tonight, you're not," she said. "You're sleeping right there on my couch tonight. I'll get you a blanket. But first, you're going to eat some chicken soup. And not out of a can. I make big batches and freeze them. It will just take a minute to heat it up. How long has it been since you ate hot soup?"

"It's a lot easier to just open a can and eat it. Then if you drink a big glass of water, it's about the same in your stomach. Only no dirty dishes, plus it's pretty thick."

She said one of the bad sentences Mrs. Comanici must of taught her, which I ain't gonna even translate for you.

"Take off your shoes," she said. "You need to get your strength back if we're going to rescue Mrs. Comanici."

Obviously, I took off my shoes. That hot chicken soup was pretty good, even if it was a lot waterier than the way I usually eat soup. By the time I got done, Holly had took my bowl and threw a blanket on me. I slept about as good as I ever slept before.

The next morning I woke up slow. The couch was comfortable and the blanket was warm. The whole apartment smelled clean, like lemons. I smiled and opened my eyes just a little to remember for sure where I was. Holly's apartment has wood floors, but a dark blue rug covers most of it. Her living room is brighter than mine, maybe since she has two windows and I only have one and mine is in the kitchen part of the room. The coffee table with Mrs. Comanici's photo album on it was still right in front of the couch. The album was open to the picture of Mrs. Comanici that Holly took a picture of last night. I closed my eyes again. I about fell asleep again but something was bugging me only I didn't know what it was. I opened my eyes and sat up. Something seemed different about the coffee table. I stared at it.

"How do you like your coffee?" Holly's voice surprised me and I about jumped off the couch. Her apartment is bigger than mine. She's got a separate room for her kitchen and a whole other room for her bedroom. I ain't used to waking up when people just walk in from a different room. I rubbed my eyes.

"Your coffee," she said again. "How do you like it?"

"Well, it's a little better if it's hot, but I ain't picky," I said.

She laughed and handed me a cup. "You're in luck this morning," she said. "The coffee is hot. Did you sleep OK?" She sat down at the other end of the couch.

"I slept like a polar bear," I said.

"Good," she said. "I think."

"Did you do something different with your coffee table?" I said.

"I might have dusted it. Why do you ask?"

"It ain't a new one? Or in a different spot?"

117

"No. Well, I put Mrs. Comanici's photo album on it."

"Yeah, I seen that. Maybe it just reminds me of something."

"Well, it'll come to you. You've got a good memory. Are you feeling better today?"

"Yeah. I got a lot of sore spots, but I could probably play in the Super Bowl if the Broncos call me up."

"Good. But I think you've got a long time to heal before we have to worry about that. Doesn't look like they're going anywhere this year. Not even preseason yet and half the offensive line is injured."

"Well, we gotta keep our hopes up."

She reached over to the coffee table and closed the photo album. It made kind of a sound, like somebody snapping their finger. It was like a TV hypnotist snapping his fingers and waking me up.

"That's it!" I said.

"Excuse me?"

I stared at that photo album. For a minute, I thought there was a big clue there. But that wasn't exactly what snapped me awake. It was a detective idea.

"What?" Holly said. She looked confused.

"Nothing really," I said and felt dumb that I said 'that's it' like I discovered the moon or something. "It's just that I ain't thought much about her photo album as a clue."

"You've been pretty busy."

"Yeah, and it probably ain't a good clue anyway. But it makes me wonder if there's other clues I ain't thought about on account of they seemed too little."

"Like what?" she said.

"I don't know. Like the order they done the burglaries. I come up with one idea for that and then figured I didn't need to think about it no more. Or that they talked to some of the tenants but not to Mrs. Comanici. Or that they done it on a Tuesday."

"I see what you mean."

"Mr. Monk and Mr. Columbo sees clues that are too little for everybody else. That's why they got their own shows."

"You're right," she said. "We should keep track of all the details, even the silly little ones. You can't ever tell what might be important. But you've already written them all down."

I could tell she wasn't too interested in the idea, so I changed the subject.

"It's a good thing she had backup pictures on her computer," I said.

"I think we got all the photos mounted. Do you want to look through it?"

"Sure," I said. "Maybe there's a clue in there."

"OK. I'll take a quick shower while you do. Then I'll fix you some bacon and eggs. OK?"

"I ain't gonna argue with you."

Looking at old pictures ain't my favorite thing, only I boxed myself into that corner by saying there might be a clue. She left the room and I started looking at the pictures. There was old pictures of young guys on horses and some big buildings with signs in a different language. Then there was pictures you could tell was Colfax, only with old cars. There was three pictures of a train. There was a picture of Big Al's Diner, only the sign had a different name.

There was a bunch of pictures of a young man that I guessed was Mrs. Comanici's husband. In one picture he was on a horse and in another one he was climbing up a rock wall. That was about my favorite, since he was looking back down at the camera with a big smile on his face. He had a big fancy ring on one finger, which I would of put in my pocket before I went climbing. Seeing he liked to climb stuff meant he was like me in one way, so I felt friendly to him.

Then there was pictures of Mrs. Comanici when she was young. I had not pictured her being pretty.

There was some pictures of a little kid with a teddy bear riding a horse. In the first pictures, he was sitting in front of Mrs. Comanici's husband. Then there was some with him riding all by himself. He looked like a toy up on top of that big horse, but he was grinning like a cocker spaniel puppy.

In the last picture the man, young Mr. Comanici, was someplace I knew by heart. He was at the Denver Zoo, standing in front of Bear Mountain. He was pointing up, maybe toward a bird or something. There was a

119

bear behind him which I never seen before in that cage. Maybe that's why they call it Bear Mountain, if they used to keep bears in it. Now, even if it looks like a mountain with a cave in it and there's trees way up on top, they keep little animals that look like goofy raccoons or something. They mostly sleep and hide and they ain't that interesting to look at.

It was weird to see Mrs. Comanici's husband when he was about as old as me, doing stuff I like to do. He was a dead guy now, like a guy in a history book but one time he was just as living as me or you. Maybe he liked the smell of coffee and had favorite foods. Maybe he could whistle or juggle tennis balls or cross his eyes. Except for Mom and Dad, who I knew when they was alive, I always thought of dead people being different from me. But maybe they was just the same except for being dead.

Before I closed the book, I took one more look at Mr. Comanici. "Take it easy, buddy. See you later," I said to his picture. He looked a little like some guy I seen on TV or maybe at a grocery store but I couldn't think who. But I wasn't going to go goose-chasing trying to remember. It's OK to pay attention to stuff but a guy can get tangled up in his own brain if he notices all the little stuff and misses the big stuff. I learned that lesson about a million times. Especially when you're trying to think of what Star Trek guy a picture reminds you of, when he's probably a servant on a alien planet that got killed in the first minute of an episode.

Holly finished her shower and started cooking bacon, which smells great but ain't usually in my budget.

"There's some guys in the alley," she said. She had a window over her kitchen sink and was looking out. I went and looked too. Two guys in suits was out there taking pictures and measuring stuff.

"I bet they're police detectives," I said. One guy was writing stuff down on a legal yellow pad like mine. "Looking for clues about Mrs. Comanici."

"I think you're right. Do you want to go down and watch them?"

Well, obviously I did. But I ain't a professional detective. I seen a thousand times on TV some guy thinks he's helping and he just screws up the investigation.

"Nah," I said. "I'll let them find the easy clues first. After they leave maybe I'll go find the clues they miss."

Holly laughed. "Yeah, I bet you do."

The bacon and eggs was as good as a restaurant. I ate pretty fast. Holly smiled since she knew I wanted to go check the alley. For a minute I thought about going up to check on Mr. Silver, but birds ain't like people. They can live for a while even if they ain't got as much birdseed as they want. They get their toughness from being little dinosaurs. Plus, I wasn't ready to argue with him yet. When me and Holly was done eating, we both went down to the alley.

"I think the police collected all the evidence," Holly said. She looked around at the alley, which looked about the same as always. The Dumpster was empty, since the trash guys emptied it that morning. There was some cans and food wrappers and cigarette butts on the ground. There wasn't no scraps of the perp's shirt stuck on a fence like you see in the movies. If there was DNA evidence, the cops probably already got it, which is good since I ain't exactly sure what it is.

"Yeah, the cops do a good job," I said. "But everybody can use a backup guy checking on them just in case." The dirt was a little messed up where them guys and me fought, but not so much you could get clues.

"I guess that's it," Holly said. She was done looking for clues.

"Let's just walk all the way down to the street," I said. "Maybe something fell off their van or something."

"Fine," she said but I knew she thought I was time wasting. We walked for a minute noticing stuff pretty hard, but it all looked the same as every other time I walked down it. Then I seen something.

"That paint bucket lid is new," I said.

"You're kidding."

"Well, I don't mean new like brand new and ain't ever been used. That one's been used, since it's got dried paint on it. I mean it ain't been in the alley before."

"How do you know that?"

"I walked down here pretty often."

We stood over the lid and stared at it.

"We don't know it's from the burglars."

"Yeah, but it could be a clue. Maybe there's fingerprints. Or maybe we could find the store that sold that color of paint and ask who bought it."

"It's white paint."

"Maybe if they was painting a ceiling it is," I said, trying not to make her feel dumb for not knowing about paint. "There's probably fifty colors that all look like white but with special names, like 'antique white" or 'eggshell' or 'winter snow'. Maybe a paint store would tell us exactly which one this is and what job is using that color."

I took a clean piece of paper towel out of my back pocket, which I always carry in case I need a handkerchief. I picked up the lid using the paper towel so I wouldn't mess up any fingerprints.

"That's about all the clues I see," I said.

She looked at me kind of worried. "It might not be a clue," she said. "It might not have anything to do with the crime. I don't want you to be disappointed..."

"Yeah, detectives always gotta worry about that. You collect all the clues like Easter eggs, but they mostly won't hatch into chicks. Some of 'em are just breakfast so you don't want to name them. The eggs you name is about guaranteed to not hatch into chicks. And then you'll feel pretty dumb for eating scrambled Captain Kirk."

"I'll remember that," she said.

We both went to our own apartments. I put the paint can lid in a white trash bag so if it had any forensics on it they wouldn't get dirty from my own forensics, and leaned it against the wall so I wouldn't step on it. Mr. Silver was about as mad as I ever seen him from being ignored so long. "Here you go," I said and I put a handful of birdseed into his jar lid. "But I ain't cleaning up your mess right now."

Then I laid down on my couch and went right to sleep again, even if I ain't been up that long today. I slept all that day, got up long enough to eat a hot dog, then went back to sleep again. The next morning when I woke up, I wasn't near as sore and I was out of the mood for sleeping.

Chapter Fourteen
Paint bucket lids and circuses

It was weird to think about going to the circus before I solved the mystery of Mrs. Comanici. On the other hand, the cops was working on that mystery too and they had lots of advantages, like computers and APBs. On the third hand, the circus was only going to be in town one weekend, so it wasn't like I could wait for a better time. Today was Wednesday and the circus started on Friday night. I decided to kill two birds with the same mousetrap. After I cleaned up and put on clean clothes, I went down to Holly's apartment.

"You look a lot better," she said.

"Thanks," I said. "You look good too. Any news about Mrs. Comanici? I think I slept right through another whole day."

"No, no news. But the police are being very careful to keep me informed."

"Cool. Look, I know you're about going to work. But could I use your phone to call Greg?"

"That kid from the hospital?"

"Yeah. I think I need to take him on a field trip."

"That kid that hates everything and everybody?"

"Well, yeah, that's how he talks. But he and me get along pretty good since his art therapy lessons. Plus his parents like me and he got a driving license."

"I should think they'd like you. You kept him from killing himself or anyone else. What's the field trip?"

There wasn't no point trying to fool Holly.

"I'm going to take him to the circus tomorrow."

"I read about that. But I don't think it opens until Friday night. Tomorrow's only Thursday."

"Anybody can go to the circus when it's open."

"You're not going to get yourselves in trouble are you?"

"Nah. Only he won't go if he knows the exact place. So we got to be a little mysterious about that part."

Holly shrugged, dialed the cell phone and handed it to me. Greg's father answered the phone.

"Hi, sir. This is Jumper."

He waited a while to say something until he remembered who I was. You can't hold that against someone.

"Oh, Jumper!" he said when the right part of his brain turned on. "How nice to hear from you! Are you doing OK?"

"Yes, sir. I was thinking about taking Greg on a field trip tomorrow. Well, he'd have to do the driving since I ain't got a car. So he'd be taking me on a field trip."

"Greg has school tomorrow. Can it be a different day?"

"No, it has to be tomorrow, starting real early in the morning. Has he got some sick days or bonus points?"

Greg's dad laughed. "He's been doing a lot better at school since you knocked some sense into him. But he's already used all his sick days and angry days and bored days and he sure doesn't have any bonus points. What kind of field trip would this be?"

"I'll tell you if you want me to, since you're his dad and all. But it's got to be a secret from him or else he won't come. He'll say it ain't cool enough. If I ain't telling him, it seems more fair not to tell you either. I told Holly, so if there was an emergency she could find us."

He thought about that for a minute. Finally he talked again. "Nobody owes Greg any field trips. He's taken them whenever he wanted. But we owe you at least one. Just don't let him talk you into doing something stupid." Then he yelled, "Greg!" In another second he yelled, "It's Jumper the art therapy guy from the hospital." In a little bit I heard Greg on the phone.

"Doctor Bologna Brain!" Greg said. "The coo-coo farm lets you make phone calls now?"

"Nice to hear your voice too, Sunshine," I said. "I need some help."

"And you figured since we're such good friends you'd ask me?"

"Yeah, I guess so." I knew he was making a joke on me about being good friends. So my answer surprised him.

"If you need a kidney, my answer is no."

"Nah, I ate fried kidney once and it got moved way down my list of favorites. I need an early morning ride someplace tomorrow, and then I need you to be my sidekick for a while and then give me a ride home."

"Are you trying to break out of the loony bin?"

"Nah, this ain't that obvious."

"Well, I'd like to help but I've got school tomorrow and my parents have gotten sort of silly about me going there every single fluffing day."

"Your dad already give permission."

"So, you told him but not me?"

"Nope, that wouldn't of been fair. I just told him you wouldn't think it was cool and that talked him into it."

"You do make it sound fun."

"I done it once and it was more fun that it sounded. That's all I'm going to say. You won't have to read any books, or sit at a desk, or take pop quizzes. But you need to pick me up about sunrise. OK?"

There was a pause and then you could picture him shrugging his shoulders.

"What the heck. Sure."

"Thanks. Wear old clothes. Bye."

"You're a pretty good salesman," Holly said as she took her phone back.

"Thanks," I said. "It's pretty easy to sell people free stuff and days off."

"Do you think the circus has anything to do with Mrs. Comanici?"

"Nah. It was in a whole different state when everything happened. But tomorrow's the only day I can take Greg there and I been planning it for a long time."

"Planning everything except mentioning it to Greg?"

"Yeah. My Dad and I went to it once and it ain't been back in Denver ever since. But I'm going to work on my clues today extra hard and give any evidence to the cops and then take a vacation day tomorrow. It's the only day I can."

"That sounds fair. I'd love to help you, but I have to work. Is there anything you need?"

"Well, since I ain't got a phone..."

"Who do you need me to call?"

"Maybe Officer Mike. He give me his cell phone number. If I figure out some admissible evidence, I'll write it on a paper and slide it under your door."

"You know he's retired, right?"

"Yeah. Him and me had a beer a few days ago and he said I could call him. Sometimes cops listen to other cops before they listen to unreliable witnesses. Anyway, some of my detecting plans might keep me too busy to call him myself."

"Don't worry about it, I'm happy to call him. I better get ready for work."

"OK, I'll see you later."

I felt a lot better after so much sleep, and now I had a plan too. I felt pretty ordinary again, not like a guy who got beat up so bad they threw him in the hospital. But Mr. Silver stayed mad at me for a long time. Whenever I walked past his cage, he just turned to face away from me, like he was giving me the silent treatment. Which with him wasn't ever that silent. Since I might not get a chance to feed him, I made sure he had extra birdseed and put a slice of apple in there too, which he likes and it don't fit through the cage for him to kick out. He didn't even look at it. "Yeah, you're gonna stick your beak into that apple about one second after I go out the door, ain't you?" I said. "I see right through your dinosaur tricks."

Chapter Fifteen
Sometimes you gotta break into the zoo. And paint bucket lids is good clues.

Every paint can lid has a code on it that says what colors they mixed together. If you want the exact color two years later, you just tell the paint store that code and they make you a new batch.

If you ain't painted as many apartments as me you might not know that and I won't make a joke on you. Some cops might not know it either, except forensic cops. The lid I found in the alley had a code on it, plus the company name, which was Benjamin Moore. Luckily, that was my very favorite kind of paint and I know the biggest store that sells it in Denver. Plus there was another clue to that lid.

You can take a paint bucket lid off by prying on it, or you can punch a hole in the top to put a sprayer tube into. My lid had the hole punched out, which meant it got used by guys using sprayers not brushes or rollers, so it was probably a pretty big job.

I hope I don't get in trouble for saying Benjamin Moore is my favorite paint. I didn't ask nobody's permission to say the real name in a book. If Mr. Moore gets mad and sends me a letter I'll change the name to a pretend company. But he makes a pretty good paint, so I bet he's a nice guy who won't get bent into a new shape.

Just so I didn't make a mistake, I opened up the trash bag and wrote the code number on my legal yellow pad. I didn't touch the lid at all in case there was admissible fingerprints, and I didn't let it get close to any forensics. After I put it back in the bag, I started walking toward Mr. Moore's paint store.

The guy at the paint store was named Ernie. He always looked pretty comfortable, with a clean shirt and tan pants. He was probably 43 years old and had neat hair and a little pot belly like just about everybody gets. He smiled at every customer and remembered names about as good as anybody I ever met. I only bought paint from him six times but he smiled when he seen me.

"Mr. Jumper!" he said. "Are you painting another apartment?"

"Not today," I said. "I'm looking for some guys who committed a crime and they might of bought paint from you."

"I see," he said. His mouth was still smiling but the rest of his face wasn't buying it. "You don't think our store..."

"No, man, not even a little bit. It's just circumstantial they might of bought paint here."

"Good," he said. He waited to think of how to ask me something. "So, are you acting in some official capacity?"

"Like undercover? Nah. My apartment got burgled and so did my neighbors and then they did some other bad stuff." I pointed to my eye, which was still black. "The police took all the clues they could find and then I found a paint bucket lid they missed. It might not even be a clue, except these guys is painters."

"So what do you want from me?"

"Here's the code." I pointed to the numbers on my pad. "First I was wondering if you could tell me what Mr. Moore calls this color of paint?"

He looked at my legal yellow pad.

"That's easy," he said without even looking it up on his computer. "That's Arctic Snow. The hint of blue is too subtle to notice, but it gives it a nice clean feel."

"Yeah, I could tell it was a cool color. I might use it on a ceiling sometime."

"Good choice. It's a wonderful alternative to Ceiling White."

"Would it go good with Antique White walls?" I asked.

"Interesting idea. There might be too much contrast between warm and cool colors. But it's a creative thought. It might just work."

"Thanks," I said. There ain't so many guys who'll talk to you about paint colors these days. That don't say nothing good about our education system.

"So, is there some project using Arctic Snow right now? They're using sprayers, so it ain't a guy painting his kitchen."

He frowned, wondering why I'd ask that. Then he figured it out.

"Ah!" he said and his eyes got big. "That's pretty smart. Let me look it up."

He typed into his computer. Then he nodded and read off his computer screen.

"There's three. The biggest is Autumn Gardens, south of Cherry Creek. It's a complex for seniors. Upscale apartments. Eight units per building, looks like twenty buildings in the first phase. They're doing all the ceilings in Arctic White. Occupancy scheduled for next month."

"Who's the paint contractor?" I asked.

"Gold Rush LLC. Used to be my favorite customer. But ever since Bill Gold died, Jim Rush hasn't been able to keep his crew together. They must have a dozen painting subcontractors on this job alone, any one of them might have ten men. With Rush's financial problems, he can't be too choosy who he hires. All the paint goes through the corporate account, so I don't have names. Sorry." He sighed like he was disappointed. "But it was a good idea."

"Don't be sorry, you been really helpful. I'm going to give Officer Mike these clues and tell him they was from you. If he thinks of questions he might call you. He ain't scary like some cops."

I took his business card and walked outside.

Maybe it's just since I had some bad luck coming out of buildings recently, like that biker guy hitting me in the stomach, but I look around parking lots pretty careful these days. Plus, when I'm in detecting mode I notice extra stuff that ain't clues. And maybe my brain was still making up stuff. For just a second I seen a old tan van behind a row of cars. I wasn't sure, so I took a couple of steps to one side to get a better view and it wasn't there.

OK, it don't make sense that the perps might be following me. They seen me up close when they was beating me up and they knew where I lived. My brain was making up stuff just to goof with me.

The obvious answer, if it was the perps, is that they was just going to Mr. Moore's paint store to get more Arctic Snow paint. If I would of thought of that right then I would of hid and followed them when they left. Or called the cops. But I didn't think of it til later, and I ain't got a cell phone anyway. Right when it happened, I decided my brain was goofing on me and started walking toward the bus stop.

It was lunchtime by now. I had a plan to do something tonight in the middle of the night, which was the dumb idea I mentioned before. Plus tomorrow I had to get up early to go on the field trip with Greg. The smart thing would be to go home, eat a can of soup and then take a long nap.

Since I pretty much always like to do the smart thing, that's exactly what I done. But before I took my nap, I wrote a note for Officer Mike on a page of legal yellow pad. It said: I think the perps is painters working at the Autumn Gardens project. Since there's a bunch of empty units, I bet they got Mrs. C hid in there. Why I think it is they dropped a paint lid in the alley, which is the color arctic white paint made by Mr. Moore. The guy at the paint store is nice. There's two other projects he talked about, but Autumn Gardens is in the right direction from the Blue Moon motel, which is where the perps was staying. I'm taking a vacation day tomorrow, which is why Holly is going to call and read this to you. Sincerely, Jumper.

I really felt like taking a nap after writing that much words, but I took the paper downstairs and slid it under Holly's door. The cops was probably already way ahead of me, since they got computers and uniforms and DNA. But sometimes a private detective gets lucky, especially during a commercial, so maybe they didn't know all my info yet. If it was right, we'd all be glad I give it to them. If it was a goose chase then it was just one more clue that wasn't the important one. I'd learned my lesson about trying to capture perps myself without the cops. Nope, I was staying far away from them perps and letting the correct people handle the situation. I cleaned out Mr. Silver's cage and put a new apple slice in there. He'd already forgot about giving me the silent treatment. "Yeah, you got the memory of a dinosaur too," I told him.

The next step in my plan was taking a nap, so I drunk a big glass of milk and laid down on my couch to sleep.

My alarm clock woke me at two in the middle of the night. If my adding was right, I'd been taking a nap for thirteen hours, which is more sleep than some people get in a whole night. I ate some scrambled eggs and drank some coffee. Then I put on a black sweatshirt and a dark blue Denver Broncos wool cap, grabbed my backpack and went back to the bus stop on Colfax Street by my house. I had to wait a while for a bus, since they don't go very often at night. I rode to Colorado Blvd without nothing too interesting happening and then got off. It only took about eight minutes to walk to the Denver Zoo. I stood outside the fence in a extra dark place under a tree and did my thinking.

I got to admit, I was nervous. I was about to break into the zoo like I done when I was a kid, and there ain't no rules that say that's OK. Plus, now they might have laser guns aimed to zap burglars or other things I ain't even thought of. And like I said before, I already knew this was a dumb idea that probably wouldn't work. If you start with a dumb idea that you already know ain't considered "best practices" in the rulebook, and which probably has hidden flaws, the smart thing is to skip that whole idea and come up with a new one.

But sometimes an idea grabs your brain like a octopus and there ain't much to do about it. You get ready to take your consequences for being dumb and do whatever the octopus tells you to do.

When I was a kid, I figured out a good way to sneak into the zoo, which I ain't gonna tell you exactly since I don't want to be an accomplice of your own dumb idea. But you know I like to climb stuff and you know I like to jump off stuff so you can probably think of ways I might of got in.

A concrete path goes around the middle part of the zoo in a big loop with some other paths going off of it. On the middle of the loop, there's lots of animal homes, with lions and deers and cheetahs and hippos and rhinoceroses. On the outside of the sidewalk there's other animal houses and more trees so you can't see the outside fence or parking lot. They done it that way so you'd think you was walking through the wilds of Africa and just happened to run into a bunch of animals. There's also buildings hid between the outside fence and some animal areas. Some of the buildings is mostly underground or disguised to look like nature. There's other paths and tunnels back there for the zoo guys to use which you won't ever see if you just come in the front gate, even in the daytime.

Everything looks different at night. If a guy climbed over the fence to get into the zoo at night, he might be in the tool area, or he might be in a polar bear place which is a lot easier to get into than out of. Polar bears is about as big as Godzilla. Since stuff is more fun if you're a little bit scared, them polar bears was a nice touch.

I had a flashlight in my backpack, but it was light enough from stars and the moon and zoo lights I didn't need it. The air smelled like mowed lawn and dried hay and a lot of animal poop. I walked in the darkest shadows in case a guard was making his rounds. Most of the animals was asleep, but I seen a few moving around. The lions heard me and they was staying in the shadows of their areas but watching me in my own shadows like a cat watches a bug on the carpet, waiting for him to make one false move.

When I walked past one spot, the animals started squawking like gooses but I didn't see them and I don't know what they was. The whole place was spooky with shadows and smells and quiet animal sounds. The moon kept going behind clouds and then coming out again.

Then I seen somebody walking right toward me on the sidewalk. There was some bushes next to me so I went in them to hide.

It was two people, a man and a woman walking along like it was Sunday afternoon, holding hands and talking. Sometimes they laughed. They wasn't young like me, but they wasn't old either. Since they just kept walking and laughing I figured they didn't see me and I stayed still.

"We haven't been to the zoo like this for a long time have we, Larry?" the woman said.

"Not like this we haven't," the man said. "I'm just glad you're well again, Janice."

"It's like magic," she said.

By now they was right next to me and I could see them real good. He looked at her face like it was the best painting at the art museum.

"Yes," he said. "It's just like magic."

They kept walking. After a minute I got out of the bushes and kept walking the other way from them. I ain't never seen regular people at the zoo in the middle of the night before. Maybe they got special hours for some people. Maybe if you're really rich they let you in whenever you want. Larry and Janice looked as happy as rich people so I bet that was it.

I decided right then if a night guard caught me I'd just tell him I was really rich.

But I didn't see nobody else and pretty soon I got where I was going.

I already said Bear Mountain was a cool part of the zoo. It looks like ancient cliff dwellings or an Egyptian cave with really old stuff you might find by a Pyramid. The cave part is in the side of a hill that goes about straight up and then has trees and stuff on top. It looks like they moved a part of the Rocky Mountains to the zoo but if you read the sign, they tell you it was built by people in 1918. A metal fence about waist high keeps people out and then a deep moat of water keeps the animals and people from getting close enough to bite each other. On the left side, the hill comes down almost to the fence and left of that is a bigger place where they keep the grizzly bears. It's got a bigger moat and a place where bears can play with pumpkins like they was footballs, which is pretty funny until they smash the pumpkin by biting it.

They don't keep bears in the Bear Mountain cave any more. The sign showed some goofy looking animal with a striped tail which didn't look all that scary. Anyway, I wasn't going where the animals lived. I looked around to see if the coast was clear, then climbed over the fence between Bear Mountain's moat and the grizzly bear moat. There was bushes growing there so you might of thought you couldn't get through but I was careful and didn't have no issues.

The hill was steep but it wasn't as hard as climbing a downspout. If I lost my balance I didn't have much good choices. I might fall into the grizzly bear's home and he'd probably think my head was a new kind of pumpkin to play with. If I fell into the Bear Mountain cave side, I'd land in that moat and the sides was too smooth to climb. I'd have to swim around in that moat until the zoo guys come around to save me. They'd call the cops on me and it wouldn't be the best day I ever had. Or, if I got lucky, maybe I'd catch myself at the cliff dwelling part, but there wasn't any way I'd escape from there. I started wondering if that goofy animal with the striped tail was poisonous.

I decided I better use my whole brain on climbing and not falling off either side. There was a few little bushes and rocks sticking out for hand-holds and footholds so I didn't have no incidents. From the ground, you could just see a few bushes up there and the tops of some trees so your brain thought you was in the mountains. Climbing up, you could pretend you was climbing a mountain and maybe you'd see more mountains on the other side. Once you got to the top, it was cool, but not the same as you thought it was going to be.

The top was mostly cement, so you could tell it wasn't a real mountain. Flat brown flagstones was stuck into the cement, which made it like a patio. The stones was mostly about the size of a man's hand and all different shapes, with some bigger ones. They was probably the extra pieces left over from some big patio job. There was also holes in the cement as big as a couch filled with dirt and that's where the trees was growing.

I sat down for a minute. I hadn't thought up the next part of my plan yet and this seemed like a good time to do that. This is what my dumb idea was: Mrs. Comanici's husband liked to climb stuff, just like me. And guys was trying to beat him up at work to get his cool ring. And he was in a picture in front of Bear Mountain sort of pointing up. About the best place to hide a secret ring would be a place you wasn't supposed to go that was guarded by bears.

Only now that I was up there, there wasn't no hiding spots. It was like a rock patio with a couple of big pine trees and that was it. So now you know that even guys like me who figure out a lot of hard stuff ain't right every time. Sometimes you get a good idea, like inventing Jell-O, but other times you invent Brussels sprouts. One dumb idea ain't a big deal and you shouldn't feel bad about it.

There was a good view of Denver lights from up there. In the daytime you could probably see the whole zoo. For about three seconds I thought about camping out up there so I could see that, but I put my foot down on that idea. I had a appointment in a couple of hours with Greg, so I needed to get back home.

I stood up to leave. There was one big pine tree that had good branches and one extra good branch about halfway up. A guy could probably sit on that big branch easy and see the city lights even better. It would only take about two minutes and then I could say I really checked for hiding spots every place I could think of.

It's slower to climb in the dark but I didn't want to use my flashlight and get seen by a night guard. Anyway, it was a easy climb. Before I thought of any new interesting ideas I was halfway up that tree and sitting on the limb. It was just as cool as I thought it would be. From up there you could see the sky starting to get light for morning, which meant you could see the mountains like a big black outline on the other side of Denver. I could of sat there for all day but it was time for me to go. I heard a car pull into the parking lot. The early crew must be showing up already, I thought. You could tell it was workers and not a boss because the car was pretty noisy. Plus bosses ain't usually the guys that show up first to clean animal cages.

I put my hand on the main trunk and reached my foot down to the next branch but then I stopped. The trunk of the tree felt goofy, which I had not noticed before. I felt it more careful. The bark pattern was weird.

The branches hid me pretty good so I shined my flashlight on it. It looked like bugs ate out some lines in the bark, which the tree was trying to heal over. Then I seen it wasn't bugs. Somebody carved their initials up there. I brushed some dirt off and seen it said DC and EC. But instead of a heart shape under it, it had a weird shape like two parts of a star sticking out of a box.

134

Well, them initials could of been Mrs. Comanici and her husband's since they was the correct letters. If I had a cell phone I would of took a picture of it. Mrs. Comanici would think it was cool her husband carved their initials, even if she might of liked a heart under them instead of some voodoo shape. But maybe in Moldova that's what heart shapes look like. I balanced pretty careful and took my legal yellow pad out of my backpack and drew the letters and the voodoo shape as careful as I could.

The sky was getting lighter when I was finished so I climbed back down the tree. Before I started down the side of Bear Mountain I looked around to make sure I didn't drop something.

I didn't see nothing I dropped, but I seen something else. One of them rocks stuck into the cement was the exact same shape as the voodoo sign carved on the tree. Maybe that shape happened all the time and I just ain't noticed it before. Maybe people write that shape and put it on potato sack labels and church walls all the time. If you ain't looking for something you don't see it.

But maybe it only happened this one time and it was a clue. I got a big screwdriver out of my backpack. Screwdrivers is like duck tape. You might need one any time. I kneeled down by that stone and cleaned the dirt and crap around its edges. Then I pushed the screwdriver down and pried on it.

That stone looked like it was cemented down forever, but it wasn't. In about twelve seconds I lifted it up. The cement under it wasn't flat or even. There was patches of dirt in the cement holes where the workers was stingy with the cement. One hole was about as big as a tennis ball. I poked the screwdriver into it and dug out the dirt.

That's where I found the ring.

It wasn't pretty like I thought it would be, but it was covered with dry mud and it was still too dark to see good. Maybe it would look better if it was all cleaned up. Even if it was ugly, I gotta say I felt about as excited as if I found a million bucks. Every time you have a dumb idea which everybody would laugh at but it works anyway, you feel as good as if you just invented electricity or apple pie. I stuck it in my jeans pocket and started climbing back down. Mrs. Comanici would like that ring even if it was ugly, I thought. By now maybe the cops would have rescued her from the Autumn Garden apartments.

I was thinking that and trying not to fall into the grizzly bear home so I wasn't paying good attention to other stuff. I was just climbing over the last little fence by the moat when I seen two guys with flashlights walking toward me. I didn't know if they seen me, so I stood real still for a second. I don't think they seen me yet, but they was getting closer and they would in a second. If they was using flashlights they was either guards or really dumb. Then I heard them talking and they said some words Mrs. Comanici had taught me from Moldova. Maybe it was just some night guards who knew Moldova words. But the odds seemed pretty unlikely for that. If it was the perps, they must of figured out Mr. Comanici hid the ring by Bear Mountain just like I did and was going to steal it. Some crooks will work pretty hard to steal stuff that ain't worth that much, since crooks ain't that bright. But there was two of them and only one of me and I sure didn't want to fight two guys again if I didn't have to. Before they seen me I started running away. I tried to be quiet, but they shouted something, so I figured they seen me. They started running after me and yelled stop but I didn't even slow down.

I'm a pretty fast runner, and I know the zoo by heart, so I kept ahead of them easy. But I didn't want them following me to my secret place where it's easier to get out of the zoo. They could figure out their own way out and maybe they'd try to go through the place where night guards drink coffee, or maybe they'd wind up on the gorilla's lawn, which would surprise the heck out of everybody. But they could follow me just by listening to my sneakers on the cement, which was making it too easy on them. So, when I run past the monkey house I yelled "Hey, wake up, I got bananas!"

Them monkeys started making a lot of noise. I could see the light from a flashlight hit the trees I went past so I knew them guys was still chasing me.

But I'm a faster runner than most grown-ups. You might guess that it would be easier to get out of a zoo than into it if you're a human. But some places fool you. You climb over one fence and go around some bushes and you're right next to a building where they keep tractors and stuff or maybe money since it's so hard to get out of. I learned that lesson only one time and I ain't never tried to use that place again. I call it the kid trap. The fence to the outside is the tallest and has barbed wire on top. If there ain't a guard you can get out, but it ain't easy. But this time I headed right toward the kid trap. I climbed up the first chain link fence about halfway and stuck my Denver Broncos wool cap into the fence. Then I climbed back down and ran over to the easy place escape from, which I ain't telling you where it is. I stood real still in a shadow and listened. In a minute, I heard them guys start climbing the chain link fence into the kid trap. They seen my Broncos cap and figured that's where I went so my plan worked perfect.

I climbed out of the zoo. Once I got to the parking lot I looked around for the tan van but I didn't see it. There was a few cars there that got left from yesterday. One was a nice new car, which had windows that was all steamed up. Maybe the third perp was waiting in it so they could make a getaway. One guy was a fair fight, and I owed these guys something. I ran up to the driver's side and shined my flashlight in the window.

The flashlight surprised the driver and he jumped and shouted. Then the window rolled down.

It wasn't the getaway driver. It was Larry, the guy I seen walking around in the zoo a little while ago. His wife Janice was right next to him. Larry looked pretty surprised, but Janice was giggling.

"I'm sorry, officer," Larry said. "We just stopped for a minute to... to..."

That give me another idea.

"It's OK," I said. "I ain't a officer. But there's some suspected criminals chasing us and we ought to leave pretty quick. Could you give me a ride to my apartment? It's only about ten minutes away in a car and I got a appointment to take a teenager to the circus."

"The circus doesn't open until tomorrow," Larry said, looking confused.

"I know. We're going to help their twenty-four hour guy with setting up and cleaning up elephant poop. It's the best part of the circus."

You could see different ideas going through their brains. I was a guy who just come running away from the zoo in the middle of the night who they didn't know from atoms. I could of been a dangerous killer or a crazy guy. Maybe they was thinking that, but they didn't say nothing. Then they might of thought that if I had a problem of getting to my apartment it wasn't their problem and they should just roll up their window and drive away. They didn't say that idea either.

Larry looked at his wife. Janice was still giggling a little. "The really dangerous ones make up a story that sounds completely believable," she said. "I think he must be telling the truth." So then Larry started giggling a little bit too and unlocked the doors.

I got in the back seat and told them my address. I didn't see nobody following us when we left the parking lot. Larry and Janice acted like a couple of teenagers on a date, smiling at each other and touching each other's arm when they said something. I think they forgot I was even in the backseat until we got to my apartment.

"Is this it?" Larry said.

"Yeah," I said. "Thanks a lot. I think we made a clean getaway." They just smiled. I looked out the back window before I got out but didn't see a car following us so I got out and they drove away.

Greg was already parked in front of the building. I went over to his car and he rolled down his window.

"Doctor Bologna Brain," he said. "You been out making house calls?" Greg is a skinny teenager with messy black hair. He likes to wear black T-shirts and sometimes has rings in his nose or cheek. He might look scary to a grown up since he likes to dress like a black vampire and talk mean like he hates everybody. But he's about as scary as a kitty once you get used to him. Only it wouldn't be nice to tell him his Halloween costume wasn't working on you, so I just ignore it.

"Nah, Sunshine, I was just the third wheel on a date. Could you wait here one minute while I go to my apartment?"

He shrugged. "Hey, the meter's running and it's your dime."

"Thanks."

I ran up the stairs to my apartment. I didn't want to take the ring with me to the circus. I was pretty sure them burglars didn't follow me, but there was always a chance. If they was still following me, they'd probably try to beat me up all over again and swipe any stuff in my pockets. But they also knew where I lived and if they burgled me again they'd take anything that wasn't hid pretty good.

The ring didn't look like it was worth much so I was probably worrying just for the fun of it. Mr. Silver started whistling and chirping at me. "Not this time, buddy," I said. "You got plenty of food." Then I had one idea.

I opened up my trash and dug down through it till I found a plastic sack that was tied shut. I had got some fresh broccoli at the store a couple of weeks ago. I tried cooking little bits of it different ways, in the microwave and boiled and fried with an egg. It's supposed to be good for you but I didn't find any way to cook it that tasted good. Then I forgot I had it and it started to rot in the fridge. That sack of rotting broccoli smelled like an outhouse on a hot summer day, so I tied up the sack and threw it into the trash. I would of took it out to the Dumpster but then I got beat up and went to the hospital so it stayed in there a while longer. I held my breath, undid the twist tie, dropped the ring in with the broccoli and quick tied it up again. I dropped the sack back into the trash, put some other stuff on top of it and let out my breath.

If you're making cheese and you let it sit for a while it starts smelling a lot stronger. They say the cheese is "maturing." When I breathed in again, I could tell that broccoli had matured about as much as it could. Nobody was going to open that sack long enough to find the ring. And, like you probably guessed, my apartment don't come with a maid who comes in and throws out the trash sacks on Tuesday mornings. Or any other morning either. It was a safe hiding place. If burglars swiped the ring out of that trash sack, they deserved to keep it.

I washed my hands, locked the apartment and went down to Greg's car.

"So, what's our big adventure?" he said when I got in.

"My main adventure is getting into a car with you driving," I said. "Go down to Colfax and turn left."

"You're pretty mysterious for this early in the morning."

"The sun's almost up already," I said. "Some guys already been at work for an hour."

"Not going to tell me, eh?"

"We're going to help some guys do their jobs."

"Let me guess. They're international spies and they called in a favor from your last job with James Bond."

"That's pretty close. Only they ain't spies. And they don't know we're coming."

"Perfect," Greg said. "I think your phrase is 'I don't see no hidden flaws with that plan.'"

"Great," I told him. "I don't either."

Chapter Sixteen
Returning to the scene of the adventure

The circus was getting set up on the exact same spot it did when my Dad and I come there. We parked in the same parking lot next to trucks just like back then. The sun hadn't come up yet, but it was light enough to see pretty good. There was a little bit of fog, which ain't that ordinary in Denver, so it looked like a dream. For a minute I felt like I was a little kid again and my Dad was still alive and we was about to go shovel elephant poop.

It was a happy idea. Maybe my parents being dead and all the rest of the stuff that happened after that was a dream and when I opened my eyes I could go eat a bowl of Cheerios before Mom told me to get moving, mister, or I'd be late for school.

"Are you OK, Bologna Brain?"

I just nodded my head. It felt like if I said something my voice would come out weird. I got out of the car and so did Greg. We walked past the trucks. Some of them said the name of the circus.

"OK," I whispered when we got close. "This is going to seem goofy to you. But then every adventure starts out by doing something that seems goofy."

"We're going to a circus that isn't open? Yeah, that sounds like the goofiest kind of adventure I ever heard of."

"We ain't just going to the circus," I said. "We're joining the circus for one day."

"And we're going to jump off the high wire?"

"That would be pretty fun, but no, that ain't it. All them acts is for the gillies."

"The who?"

"The gillies. The Townies. The outside folks who pay to get in. It also means the carts they haul stuff in, but sometimes now it means anyone who ain't in the circus. Watching acts made for gillies ain't the most fun part of the circus."

"I don't think I want to know the answer, but here goes. What's the most fun part?"

"I wanted to surprise you..."

"Consider me surprised. What's the secret fun part of a closed circus?"

There wasn't no way to hide it from him since we was getting pretty close.

"Elephant poop," I said.

"What?"

"Shoveling elephant poop."

"You've got to be kidding!"

"Well, it ain't a fancy job. But we ain't got circus tricks. It's how everybody starts."

"I'm not shoveling elephant poop! I might as well be studying algebra!" He stopped walking.

There wasn't no good argument between algebra and elephant poop. I tried to think of a smart way to change his mind but no ideas come to me. My throat started feeling like I swallowed a walnut without chewing it first. I hadn't thought of him just saying no. I didn't have no Plan B.

"When I was a kid, my Dad took me..." I said. Even I could tell my voice sounded weird and my face felt hot. "It was about the last adventure..." I couldn't say nothing else. I just looked at my shoes for a minute. Greg didn't say nothing. When he talked again, his voice was the softest I ever heard him talk.

"OK, Boss," he said. "Lead me to my shovel."

We stood next to the last truck, where it was still all the way dark. I seen a guy off to the right with a wheelbarrow and shovel. It was a lot like when I come with Dad. He was shorter than Gus, the guy my dad and I helped, but with the fog and the dark it was easy to pretend it was the same guy. But I knew it wasn't.

"This was a dumb idea," I said. I couldn't time travel back to being a kid and maybe that's what I was trying to do. "Let's just go home."

Greg kind of laughed, which ain't all that ordinary for him, since he likes to be mad all the time, making fun of stuff and complaining. It surprised me to hear him laugh.

"I don't think so," Greg said.

"What? Now you want to shovel elephant poop?"

"Well, you made it sound so fun," he said.

"It ain't fun!" I yelled at him. "It smells bad and it's hard work and we'll probably just piss off the guy for doing his job the wrong way."

"Yeah, all that's probably true. But there's some reason you thought this was important."

"Nah, I ain't got reasons. It was just another dumb idea."

"Maybe. But it's too crazy of an idea to just walk away from. There's the shovels." He pointed to a cart with tools. "Come on."

He started walking down the path. He picked out two shovels and started walking toward the guy by the wheelbarrow. I just watched him walking away for a minute. In a million years I didn't think Greg would be the one wanting to do some smelly work and me being the guy wanting to go home. It felt kind of like a dream where stuff gets all mixed up and flowers come to life and start dancing and lawyers smile and let you cut in line in front of them. Greg was almost to the wheelbarrow guy. He was pretty sure to piss the guy off the first time he said something, since he usually did. Even if he mostly acted tough he was just a kid and it would be my fault if he got beat up by a circus guy.

I ran and caught up with him and took one of the shovels.

"Don't say a word," I whispered to him. "He might not be that friendly."

Greg nodded.

The guy by the wheelbarrow was pretty small, not even as big as Greg. He wore a black sweatshirt with a hood so you couldn't see his face. With it being dark and foggy he could of been a evil villager in a kid's fairy tale just slowly scooping piles of poop into his shovel then dumping it into the wheelbarrow. The wheelbarrow was in the middle of the path and the guy in the hood was mostly working on the right side. There was some piles on the left side, so I scooped one into my shovel and dumped it into the wheelbarrow. The guy in the hood looked at me for just a second and I seen he was just a kid, with big eyes and smooth skin. I didn't say nothing and he looked away quick, like he was shy. Greg done the same thing as me, shoveling some poop into the wheelbarrow.

It wasn't just elephant poop. There was a good variety. Some piles was pretty big and stuck together good and others was little and wetter. A bunch of different kinds of animals must of been on that path, which made it kind of interesting, trying to guess what they was.

With three of us working, that wheelbarrow filled up pretty fast. None of us said nothing or looked at each other. Then Greg made a mistake which anybody could make. He was kind of tossing shovelfuls into the barrow a few inches before the shovel was right above it. You could tell he was making a game of it, which is always smart. But one time he didn't aim right and he missed. Poop splashed all over the path in a bigger mess than before he scooped it up. The kid in the hood got pissed.

"Haven't you ever used a shovel before?" he yelled. It surprised me and Greg since it was the first words anybody said and it was so loud we didn't expect it. But what mostly surprised us was how high the voice was. "Who are you guys anyway? Who said you could be here?"

"I'm Jumper," I said as polite as I could make my voice sound. "And this is Greg. I used to work for a guy named Gus at this circus."

"You worked for Gus?" he said. "And he didn't train you on operating a shoot shovel?"

"Greg's brand new," I said. "I figured he'd get on the job training. We'll clean up after ourselves. You don't have to worry about that. What's your name?" Sometimes if you get people answering easy questions they forget they're pissed.

The kid pushed the hood off his head. Only it wasn't a boy, it was a girl, maybe a little bit younger than Greg with long blonde hair tied up in the back.

"They call me Pickle," she said.

OK, so that ain't a very ordinary name, but Greg shouldn't of laughed anyway. That girl named Pickle dropped her shovel and jumped right at him. He took a step backward but she was too quick and he was too surprised to do much. She grabbed his shirt and sort of lifted him a little bit while she pushed him backward.

"You think that's a funny name?" she yelled. Her face was close enough to his I was afraid she might bite off his nose. "You know what I think's funny?" she put her right foot behind his ankles then pushed his chest hard and let go of his shirt. He tripped over her foot and fell hard on his back.

"That's funny," she said.

Greg was too surprised to even yell and insult back at her, which means he was as surprised as I ever seen him.

"Why don't you get up and let's do it again," she yelled. "I could use another good laugh!"

We all heard footsteps at the same time and looked up. It was a guy riding a horse. The horse was sort of casually walking toward us across the field. The sky was pink and blue and the fog was moving around like ghosts as big as houses. The horse was a tan color and his mane was almost white. The man was big and didn't look excited. He looked like a guy who don't scare that easy. He was wearing a white baseball cap and a blue work shirt. The horse didn't have no saddle but the man stayed on top of him easy. They stopped when they got close to us.

"He laughed at me," Pickle said to the man. She pointed at Greg, who was still flat on his back.

"Yeah," the man said. His voice was low and real calm. "People laugh at the circus a lot. What did I tell you about your temper?"

"You ain't my real dad," she said.

"I'm the closest thing you have to a real dad and you know that. Now what's going on?"

"They're gillies!" Pickle said. "They just snuck in here and started shoveling without permission. And then they laughed at me."

The man sat up straighter on his horse and took off his cap to look at us better. "Is that right?" he said.

When he done that it was like I was looking at an old picture I seen a bunch of times. I knew who he was. I was sure of it.

It was Mrs. Comanici's husband Dobre. I seen a picture of him on a horse leaning forward just like that. Only that didn't make sense, since Mr. Comanici was dead and if he wasn't dead he'd be as old as Mrs. Comanici. This guy was just a little older than me.

It only took a second for me to figure it out: this guy was a ghost. When Mr. Comanici died, he didn't know where he was so he joined the circus. Somehow my brain had figured it out and told me to go to the circus too. I ain't never known a ghost before so I was a little nervous. Do you say, hi Mr. Ghost, or call him by his human name, or do you pretend you don't even notice he ain't that ordinary?

144

I'd been awake for a long time so maybe I wasn't doing my best thinking. When he talked again, I figured out I was wrong. He was a whole different person than I thought.

"Gillies volunteering to clean up," he said. "That's only happened once before." He looked at me pretty careful. "A couple of guys decided to just drop in for a morning of shoveling crap. A man and his kid who turned out to be a chimp whisperer. I don't think these two are gillies at all."

"Gus?" I said. Once I figured out who he was it was pretty obvious. "You got a little older than you was."

He laughed.

"Yeah, I guess I have. So have you, Mr. Jumper. Looks like you've been lifting weights."

"Nah. Unless you count elephant poop."

"Who's your friend?"

"This is Greg," I said. "He's a pretty good artist if you like pictures of dead stuff."

Greg stood up but kept a little space between him and the girl.

Gus looked over at her. "Now, Pickle," he said. "Mr. Jumper here is a friend of the family. Do you know what that means?"

She looked down at her shoes.

"Yes, sir," she said softly.

Gus climbed down from his horse and shook my hand. Then he shook Greg's hand. "Pleased to meet you, Greg. I'm Gus," he said. "If you're a friend of Jumper, you're my friend too. I don't think you'll have any more trouble today."

"Now, Pickle," Gus said to her. "We're all going to be helping you this morning. So I'll need a shovel and we'll need a second barrow. You and Greg take this load to the bin and bring back what we need. I'm guessing Greg hasn't ever gotten to use wheelbarrows like ours. So you're going to teach him. Gently."

"Aw, crap, I don't want to waste my morning with some candy face gilly..."

Gus held up his hand and she stopped.

"Gently," he said. "I don't remember asking for your opinion. Friends of the family."

Greg didn't look all that happy about the whole deal either, except he kept looking at Pickle. Even if she was kind of dirty with mud on her face and poop on her boots and she'd thrown him down on the ground, I think he was wondering what she'd look like if you hosed her off and gave her clean clothes.

"Nobody asked what I wanted to do," Greg said.

"Yeah," I said. "That's how life is. Them wheelbarrows is kind of fun though once you get the hang of em."

The two teenagers walked off with Pickle pushing the full wheelbarrow and Greg trotting along behind her. Both of them was insulting the other every step of the way.

Gus turned back to me. "It's good to see you again. Your Dad was a good man."

"Yeah, he was. Only he's dead now."

"I figured that. I could tell he was sick when you were here the first time. I'm sorry. I bet you still miss him."

I nodded and changed the subject.

"I thought Greg might like the circus."

"Maybe. It's changed a lot."

"Well, you still got a lot of poop to shovel up if you let the animals walk around to stretch their legs."

He smiled. "That's true. But we don't throw it away anymore. We sell it."

"You sell poop?"

"Of course not. You call it poop when you're buying. It's compost when you're selling. Gardeners pay a fortune for little bags of exotic compost."

Now he started talking in a big voice, like he was doing a TV commercial. "Why bore your plants with common barnyard compost when you can treat them to a product made by the creatures of the darkest jungles. Circus Gold, the soil of the Garden of Eden." He smiled and winked at me like he was telling me a inside joke. "Plus, the smell of tigers and bears scares squirrels and rabbits away from your garden."

146

"Man, you make it sound like something I want to put on my bowl of cereal."

"These days you have to monetize everything," he said.

Greg and Pickle come back with two wheelbarrows and a shovel for Gus. You could hear them arguing from two blocks away. I never seen anybody who cussed as much as Greg did, but Pickle maybe had him beat. They sounded as mad at each other as you could sound. Gus smiled at me.

"I think your friend is enjoying the circus already," he said.

"Yeah," I said. "As long as they don't start throwing compost at each other."

The four of us filled one wheelbarrow and then Greg wheeled it away with Pickle steadying it.

"Don't lift it so high!" she yelled. "Let the tool do the work. You know, the tool with the wheel."

"You're tilting it to the side!" he yelled back.

"No I'm not. Geez, can't you aim it in a straight line?"

"I could if you weren't pushing it sideways!"

They kept on like that till they was too far away to hear. Gus and I moved the other wheelbarrow to the next piles and started to fill it. We didn't say much. I always like it when someone don't need to be talking every minute. He looked at my hands.

"I should find you guys some gloves," he said. "Greg's gonna get blisters for sure."

"I brought some," I said. "Only I forgot them in Greg's car. I bet I can get 'em before they get back with that empty barrow."

"I bet you can," said Gus. "You were always pretty fast."

I dropped my shovel and ran to the parking lot. Greg's car was unlocked so there wasn't no adventure in getting the gloves.

The whole sky was pink and blue by now which was cool. Sometimes I have dreams where the sky is pink like that so I took one minute to look at it. When I was looking around at the sky, I seen something else. In the corner of the parking lot was a tan van.

OK, there's lots of old tan vans, but I couldn't pretend I didn't notice this one. I ran over to it. Before I got to it, I seen it had Colorado license plates, so I figured I was wild goose chasing, but I went up to it anyway. There was paint splatters on the bumper in the shape of a duck, just like the van of the guys I was looking for. The doors was locked but you could see nobody was inside. They must of swiped someone's license plates. I said the plate number about six times so I'd remember them, then remembered I still had on my backpack with my legal yellow pad. I took it out and wrote down the number. Then I run back to Gus.

Greg and Pickle was just getting back and they was still arguing as much as guys on cable TV news shows do.

"Here's some gloves," I said to Greg and tossed him a pair. Pickle almost made a joke about gillies with soft hands from never doing any work. I could see it in her face, but Gus looked and her and she didn't say nothing.

"Do you got three painters from Texas working at the circus?" I said to Gus, trying to sound about as cool and casual as James Bond.

"Don't think so," he said. "Why do you ask?"

"I thought I recognized a van in the parking lot."

"We do our own painting," he said.

We kept on working like before with Gus being mostly quiet and Pickle and Greg arguing. While I was working, I had some detective thinking to do.

That van didn't show up at the circus by accident on the same morning as I was there. Them painters must of followed me home from the zoo after all, then followed me and Greg to the circus. But that didn't make no sense. I was going to tell Gus about it only I didn't know what to say. There's a van in your parking lot that belongs to some painters? Every way I thought to say it, it sounded like I was goose chasing or being a idiot. I decided to wait until better words come into my brain, which they usually do if you wait long enough.

It was light enough to see by now and I didn't see nobody spying on us. Maybe that ring was worth more than Mrs. Comanici thought. Maybe they figured it was in my pocket. Was that what they was after? Bad guys don't like fair fights, so they'd probably wait til I wasn't with other people to jump me. They figured they had surprise on their side, but it ain't as good a surprise attack if a guy knows it's coming. And I had one surprise for them too. My pockets was empty and that ring was locked up in the Safe Deposit Bank of Rotten Broccoli.

When we was done shoveling, Gus told us we should put away our shovels and wheelbarrows and then go feed the animals. We followed Pickle across the field. She pushed one wheelbarrow and Greg pushed the other one. "Are you drunk?" she said to Greg. "Even a gilly ought to be able to drive a wheelbarrow straight."

"Maybe if you stopped getting in my way," he said back.

I stayed a little bit behind them since there wasn't nothing I could say to them that would make them get along. Plus, I wanted to keep my eye out for them painters. Even if I wanted to tell Gus about them, it wasn't his problem and he had other stuff to worry about. He walked along next to me, holding his horse's leash. We talked about regular stuff, like we was friends who seen each other every day and didn't need big stuff to talk about. Things was getting pretty busy with people putting up the big tent and lots of little tents. Older guys moved carts around that was set up with games. Like one game, if you hit something by throwing a baseball, you got a prize. And a tent with a fortuneteller lady. Mostly people was wearing jeans and T-shirts but some people had on bright circus clothes. Some clowns was in their clown outfits whispering to each other. A lady in a sparkly blue dress walked around carrying a snake as big around as my leg, practicing singing some song. But nobody was joking. They set up a thousand times before and they knew what to do so they just done it. People kept coming up to us and asking Gus questions, which he always knew answers to.

"So, are you the boss now?" I asked Gus after a skinny little guy asked him a question about the high wire and Gus told him to do it just like last time.

Gus laughed. "Nah, you can't ever get promoted over the owner's nephew. I'm just a little easier to talk to than him."

A really pretty lady come over to us. Her skin was pale and her hair was long and black. She was dressed in regular clothes of jeans and a pink shirt only a little bit tighter than most people wear. She looked at the rest of us but smiled big at Gus.

"They need some help with the anchor pole," she said to him. She looked at the shovels and wheelbarrows. Then she kissed his cheek. "Did you insult Charlie again?"

"No, ma'am," he said. "I volunteered for this duty. Do you remember our old friend the chimp whisperer?" He pointed to me.

She looked at me all confused. I was just as confused. She looked a little familiar but I'd remember if I met someone as pretty as her. Then her face lit up and her eyes got big.

"Jumper? Is that you?"

"Yeah," I said. "You must be the fortune teller lady if you know my name." I reached out to shake her hand but she gave a little squeal and jumped at me instead, like a tiger attacking a deer. She grabbed her arms around my neck and her legs around my waist and I about fell over from surprise, plus from her weight. Circus ladies ain't like other ladies I guess.

Gus laughed. "You remember Thumbelina, don't you?" he said. "She's trying to overcome her natural shyness."

She just kept hugging me the way a cat hugs some animal it's about to eat.

"Thumb?" I said. "Wow, you grew up."

Finally she let go.

"So did you," she said. "Maybe Gus has some competition at last."

"Good thing you already said yes," Gus said. "Jumper would be strong competition."

"You guys are...?" I asked. Sometimes you think you understand something, but it's better if people just tell you in case you're wrong.

"Engaged," she said. "But I could always change my mind." She smiled at me but everybody knew she was joking. You could tell by the way she looked at Gus that he was the only guy in the world she could see, even if he was a few years older than her.

"OK, I need to go help supervise the big tent," said Gus. "Pickle, you and your crew get the animals fed and watered, OK? And then bring our friends over. I want to introduce them to some folks."

Pickle wasn't happy about getting a job but she nodded. Gus got back on his horse by putting his hands on its back and then jumping while he was pulling with his hands up on the horse's back. He done it about as easy as a kid jumping up to sit on the kitchen counter, which was neat. Then he reached down. Thumb grabbed his hand and climbed up behind him. They trotted away and we went back to work.

The field was even busier now with circus people walking around, carrying poles and ropes. Some had weird tools that you could spend all day wondering what job they done. One skinny guy in a tuxedo walked by on stilts, which made him seem about ten feet tall. He had a Abraham Lincoln hat on, which he took off for a second when he walked past, like he was waving hello. There was too much stuff to notice and I felt my brain getting filled up. It was all cool stuff I wanted to notice. Two kids maybe ten years old walked by juggling bright green tennis balls. Some clowns walked by going the same direction as Gus went on his horse. One looked at me sideways, then looked away quick. You wouldn't think a clown would be shy, but maybe that's why some of them decide to be clowns. A shy guy can hide inside a good costume, like a suit and tie, or a minister's robes. I ain't all that shy, but I wondered if maybe clown would be a good job for me.

We finished up with the compost business and putting tools away, then Pickle led us to the cages with animals. I wondered if Chimp the monkey still worked for the circus but I didn't want to come right out and ask. Some animals don't live very long, so he could be dead by now.

"What animals do you have?" I asked instead. "I got a parakeet."

"Elephants and tigers are the big ones," Pickle said. "They eat a ton. We have to do it in the right order or they get upset."

"I like to eat in the right order too," I said. "Them clowns was interesting,"

"Clowns are jerks," she said. "Almost as bad as gillies."

"Well, they got cool outfits. I like the goofy noses and the big clown shoes..." Then I stopped. In my brain I was just noticing something I seen a while ago. Only I had to wait for my brain to tell me what it was.

"Whatever," said Pickle.

"Them clowns didn't have the funny shoes," I said. "They was just wearing sneakers."

"So what? They weren't on stage," Pickle said. "They were probably just practicing a routine. I'm sure you'll get to see the funny shoes."

151

"That ain't it," I said. "There was something about their sneakers. What if somebody snuck in? Could they find all the clown uniforms and swipe one?"

"Sure," Pickle said. "We don't keep them in some secret vault. But the other clowns could tell."

"So just because a guy is wearing a clown suit don't mean he's a real clown. Just like anybody can wear a tie but that don't make them a lawyer."

"Look, Bologna Brain," said Greg. "In the great detective story of your life you got to let go now and then. Not everything is a clue."

I stopped walking so I could use my whole brain on thinking. Pickle and Greg stopped too. They made some jokes on me but I didn't pay attention. I stood staring at my own sneakers to listen to whatever my brain was trying to tell me. Then it come to me.

"Paint splatters!" I said. "Their sneakers had paint splatters!"

"Maybe that's the latest craze in clown shoes," Greg said.

"No," I said. "It's just really long odds."

"What?"

"It means some bad guys followed us here, and they're trick or treating on us as clowns. And I think I figured out why. Do you have your cell phone?"

"Sure," Greg said.

"OK, you need to call Holly. You got her number, right?"

"My dad made me program it into my phone."

"OK, so you need to call her right now. Tell her the guys who kidnapped Mrs. Comanici are right here at the circus and they ain't done doing bad stuff. Have her call Officer Mike."

"And you think the police will drop everything they're doing and send a SWAT team just because you saw paint on some clown shoes?"

"Good," I said. "You understand. Now tell me back what you're going to tell Holly. Quick, I gotta go try to stop them."

So Greg said back everything I told him. He's got a good brain for remembering stuff if he ever wants to.

"Listen Pickle," I said. "I been wrong lots of times. If I'm wrong, you guys can joke on me all you want later. I think maybe Gus is in trouble. Which way is the tent he's at?"

"Gus can take care of himself," she said. "The animals need to be fed and I'll be in trouble if I skip chores just because some dumb gilly..."

Greg grabbed her elbow tight. She stopped talking from surprise and looked like she was about ready to bite his hand off with her bare teeth.

"You go feed them," he said. "I'd just slow you down anyway. But I've seen that look in Jumper's eyes before and I'm going with him. Which way?"

Pickle looked at him hard. First she looked mad, then surprised and then one second later her face changed to a whole different look, like maybe Greg didn't seem so much like a dumb gilly to her any more. She nodded for a second, thinking, then raised her arms and pointed.

"He'll take his horse off to the left to avoid all the ropes and little tents. If you go straight that way and cut through the vendors, you'll get to the big top about the same time as him."

"Thanks," I said. "Greg, you call Holly first. That's the most important. Then I'll meet you over there." I started running toward the big tent. If I was wrong, I was about to feel about as dumb as I ever felt.

There was too much stuff to notice while I was running. Guys was pounding stakes into the ground for tent ropes. Some kids was chasing each other and giggling. Somebody was cooking bacon because you could smell it. Guys in pickup trucks was driving pretty fast with boxes of stuff piled in the truck bed and other guys standing on the back bumper and hanging on with one hand like they was trick riders on a rodeo bull. Kids jumped out of their way at the last second like it was a game.

The little tents and buildings where there was stuff for sale made a circle around the big tent, with a wide path for customers to walk down. It was tricky to run between the tents since ropes was tying them to the ground and people was so busy doing stuff they wasn't paying attention to a guy running. I didn't see no clowns and I didn't see no horses, but a dog run in front of me so close I had to jump over him, which almost made me miss a tent rope I had to jump. I got over that one and nearly hit a older woman who was about as big as a linebacker who was carrying a big laundry basket full of flags. She yelled at me. I said I was sorry and kept running.

The main pointy top part of the big tent was already up but guys was tying canvas pieces all around it to make the straight up walls. I went through one of the spots they didn't do yet and got inside.

The inside of the big circus tent is a lot bigger than you think. Lots of people was in there doing stuff, but it still looked about empty. There wasn't enough lights in it yet, so it was too shady to see good. Nobody paid attention to me. I didn't see Gus, but after a minute I seen Thumb talking to some other lady so I run over there. She seen me and smiled.

"See, Mom," she said to the lady. "Here he is now. You remember Jumper, don't you?"

"Of course I do," the lady said. She smiled at me too and reached to shake my head. "You were a quick study as a box drummer." The lady was Charm, the lady who was a good dancer who all the men watched. She looked about the same as before except a little older. I shook her hand.

"You're Thumb's mom?"

Charm smiled again. "You thought we were sisters?"

"Yeah," I said, which was a white lie since I hadn't thought about it at all. But if I thought about it I might of thought that since they looked kind of the same. Charm just smiled some more and looked right in my eyes and my face got hot. Charm didn't care. She was used to guys' faces getting hot when they talked to her.

"Where's Gus?" I said to Thumb.

Her face changed from smiling to worried in about one second.

"What's wrong?" she said.

"Maybe nothing," I said. "Some guys broke into my apartment building. They was looking for something which they might think Gus has."

"What is it?"

"It's a ring which is hid real good but that ain't the important part. Gus looks kind of like the guy who used to own it. If they seen me talking to him they might of put one and two together."

"Are they dangerous?"

"Well, they beat up me pretty good and they kidnapped this old lady..."

Charm stopped me and turned to Thumb.

"Where is he?" she said.

"He was just going to tie Brandy by his truck and then meet me. He should have been here by now."

"Where's the horse?" I asked.

But the two of them was already running through the big tent and they was pretty fast. A second later I was running after them. They went through a opening in the big tent and I followed them.

As soon as I got outside I seen them running toward a old blue pickup truck. Gus's horse was tied to the back bumper and there was a bucket of water in the bed of the truck and some hay. The horse was just standing there eating hay like he was on lunch break but Gus wasn't around.

Thumb petted the horse's forehead.

"Where's Gus?" she asked the horse. The horse just kind of nodded and kept eating his hay. "What did they do to Gus?"

Charm looked worried.

"I'm sure he's OK," she said, looking around. Her eyes said she didn't think that at all.

"Yeah," I said. "He's probably OK, but I ain't taking chances. My friend Greg is already calling the cops."

"We're not big fans of the cops," Charm said.

"Nobody is if they don't live in one spot all the time," I said. "Cops like people in houses. But my friend Officer Mike is pretty cool. Anyway, they're just my backup plan. We gotta a look for clues ourselves."

"What are we looking for?"

"Anything that seems goofy. Footprints would be good. You guys look for footprints and I'll check out the truck."

Thumb and Charm done what I said, which surprised the heck out of me. Women almost never do that. I walked toward the driver's door, but seen something in the hay the horse was snacking on. I could only see a couple of inches of it since hay was on it, but it looked like a black pipe. When the women wasn't watching, I pulled some of the hay off it to get a better look. It was a tire iron, a tool you use to loosen bolts on a tire when you get a flat. There was blood on the end of it which was still wet and red. Blood turns black when it dries, so this was brand new.

I was careful not to touch it in case it had forensics on it. I covered it back up with hay since it would upset the women. Maybe somebody just cut theirselves changing a tire, but maybe they whacked Gus with the tire iron and took him away someplace. But if I said that before I knew it I'd scare Charm and Thumb without doing no good.

"You guys find any footprints?" I said.

"There's footprints everywhere," Thumb said. They both seemed a little nervous, since we didn't find Gus yet, but they wasn't really scared or anything. I think seeing his horse being tied up made them feel more comfortable. Only they ain't seen that tire iron.

"How about wheel tracks," I said "Like from a wheelbarrow?"

"There's some deuce cart tracks," thumb said. "Is that important?"

"What's a deuce cart?"

"That's just what I call them. It's like a wheelbarrow but with two wheels instead of one. Easier to control."

I went over to her. She pointed to the ground. The tracks was pretty clear. They headed off toward some big cottonwood trees at the edge of the field.

"Could a deuce cart hold a man?" I asked. I tried to sound casual, but they both looked at me quick and you could tell they was wondering if I meant Gus. Then they looked at each other. I quick tried to change the conversation.

"What's over there?" I asked. I pointed to the trees in the direction the tracks led.

"Not much right now," Charm said. "That's where the train's parked. But the offloading is mostly done, there shouldn't be anyone over there." She started to sound more nervous.

"Wait a minute," I said. "There's a train?"

"Sure. That's how we move from town to town. We have sleeping cars and a pie car for meals and all the animals have cars. Most of the cars carry tents and trucks and all the scenery and equipment. We spend more of our time on the train than we do at a site. Do you think he's down there?" She pointed to the trees where the cart tracks led.

"You're telling me the circus has its own train?"

156

But they wasn't listening to me. Thumb ran back over to the horse and untied him from the bumper. She stepped up onto the bumper and then threw herself on top of the horse. She pushed her heels into his side. In about a second the horse was running like a racehorse toward them trees with Thumb on top, hunched over like Tonto on the Lone Ranger TV show.

"I'll get some help," Charm shouted and started running back to the big tent. For a second I was just standing there alone. Then I took off running after Thumb and the horse. I didn't want her to run into them painters all by herself.

But I gotta admit, if I'm telling the whole truth and nothing but the truth part of me was pretty excited. I might get to see a circus train.

I run through the open field of weeds toward the row of big cottonwood trees. Thumb was way ahead of me on the horse. After she got past the first trees I couldn't see her any more. It felt good to run, like my legs was loosening up after sitting too long. The sun had burned off the fog, the sky was blue and meadowlarks was singing in the weeds. Bindweed, which farmers hate, was blooming with white and pink flowers that smelled sweet, like the perfume part of a clothes store.

When I got to the trees I slowed down so I didn't just run into the wrong place at the wrong time and get myself whacked on the head again. These clowns was mean and I had to remember that even if they looked goofy.

Nobody was in the trees. I walked through them and seen they was just a little strip of trees by a dry irrigation ditch. Past them was another weed field. On the other side of that was more trees. I could see a train beyond them. Thumb and her horse had already got to them and she was stopping the horse and sliding off his back at the same time. I probably shouldn't of wasted time but I stopped and stared. I didn't have no choice. I just couldn't believe what I was seeing, like if a movie come to life in my kitchen or if I seen ghosts come floating out of my refrigerator.

Just past Thumb and her horse was a big fence made of one white rope held up by metal fence posts every fifteen or twenty feet. The rope was maybe five feet above the ground, so you could duck under it easy. The fence closed in a place about as big as a basketball court. In the middle of the fenced-in place was one big Cottonwood tree. Underneath the tree was a big gray elephant with huge floppy ears and a long wrinkled elephant trunk nose.

If you're noticing an elephant under a tree in a big weed field your brain ain't got room to notice much else, so that's all I seen for a minute. The elephant looked nervous, lifting his legs one after the other so he looked like he was dancing in place. He lifted his trunk-nose and made a big elephant noise like you see in the movies. He shook his head so his ears flapped around. His front legs was pounding on the dirt and making little clouds of dust and weeds. He was mad about something.

Thumb ducked under the white rope and ran to the back of the elephant. That didn't look safe at all, since he was moving around a lot and not paying attention to what he might step on. Then I seen what she was doing. Somebody was laying down on the dirt right by the elephant's back legs. From the color of his shirt I figured it was Gus. The elephant took a step backward and Gus was right between his legs. Thumb grabbed under Gus's armpits and dragged him backward. I would never in a million years think she was that strong, but she had her mind made up to save Gus. She got him most of the way out, but then one of the elephant legs hit her sideways and knocked her away. She yelled so loud I could hear it all the way across the field. She grabbed her leg and rolled back.

I started running across the field toward them. Thumb only took a second yelling about her leg, even though you could see how bad it hurt. She grabbed Gus again. She couldn't stand up because of her leg, so she sat behind him and pulled as hard as she could, pushing against the dirt with her good leg. She tried hard but Gus was a big guy and she could only move him a few inches at a time. Meanwhile, elephant feet as big as car tires was pounding up and down around them.

Obviously I ran straight toward them. Before I got to the white rope fence I seen why the elephant was in such a bad mood. In front of him, by his trunk, them three painters in clown suits was yelling and waving their arms. One had a board as big as my arm that he kept poking at the big guy's trunk. Another had a garbage can lid and was banging it like a drum. They was jumping in at the elephant and whacking him with the stick, then jumping back to keep him confused. Elephants is pretty casual and they don't like to lose their temper even when somebody's being mean to them. When you're the biggest guy in the jungle, you cut everybody else some slack. But sooner or later, even the nicest guy says that's it. I'm trampling these clowns and the straw huts they live in.

These clowns had a easy plan. They was getting the elephant nervous so he'd trample Gus without even knowing it and everybody would think it was an accident. In another ten seconds, both Gus and Thumb would be goners; the clowns would leave before anybody knew who they was. There wasn't no time for fancy plans.

I ducked under the rope, ran behind the elephant and leaned down under his tail. I grabbed the back of Gus's shirt, right by his neck, and grabbed Thumb's shirt in the same place and just dragged them backward. Thumb screamed when her hurt leg hit a rock, but I didn't stop. I could always apologize later if she didn't get killed. I got them out from under and kept pulling them. I got them as close to the big cottonwood tree as I could and let go.

"Jumper," Thumb sort of whispered. "They hurt Gus."

"Yeah," I said. "And they ain't done. You got any hints about elephants?"

"Daisy's usually a sweetheart. She loves music. I ride her all the time. What's wrong with those guys."

"They ain't sweethearts," I said. "The police is coming but I don't want these guys to run away if they hear sirens. They're kind of getting on my bad list."

I stood up. The clowns was herding Daisy back toward us and them legs looked huge. We didn't have time to wait for cops. I looked back at Thumb. "You got any more ideas?" I said.

Thumb looked at me kind of funny.

"Yeah," she said. "Maybe one," She put two fingers in her mouth and let out the longest, loudest whistle I ever heard.

Daisy must not of heard the whistle since she kept backing up. Them big back legs was getting close to me. Them clowns kept yelling and poking with the stick and banging on the garbage can lid. Maybe Daisy was too polite to charge at them mean guys. But I ain't that nice and I just got pissed at them. I should of found another cheek and turned it, but I didn't. Even if I ain't a elephant, I just wanted to smash somebody's straw hut.

"That rope is an electric fence!" Thumb yelled out. "Don't touch it!"

When you get really mad, you don't think of all the smart ways to do stuff. You just go straight ahead. Instead of running around Daisy, I ran right up to her tail, dropped down to my hands and knees and crawled right underneath her. Them legs was pounding all around me, but I didn't care. I crawled as fast as I could past her back legs, under her belly, between her front legs and then come out right under her big trunk nose and stood up.

The clown with the board was right in front of me, with the board raised up above his head like a pick ax. He was going to whack Daisy's nose but when he seen me his eyes got big and his changed direction to hit me on the top of my head.

Well, that was his plan. He was mad but I was a whole lot madder, which means everything seemed a lot slower to me. He put all his strength into knocking my head down my neck and into my stomach, but I stepped sideways and he missed me clean. He was trying so hard the board hit the dirt. Before he could pull it back, I stepped on it with one foot. He tried to pull it but couldn't. That was his mistake. He should of let go.

"I'm getting pretty tired of you hitting me with boards," I said. And then I punched him in the face so hard his fake clown nose busted and fell off. His head snapped back, his eyes closed and he fell backward onto the weeds. It probably shouldn't of made me feel good, but it did, just a little. But there was still two more of them.

The guy who was beating the trash can lid with a tent stake took a couple steps backward when his buddy fell down. The other guy stayed behind him. My first idea was to move these guys back from Daisy so nobody got stepped on, so I walked right up to them.

"It'd be a lot easier if you'd just surrender now," I said.

"That's what your mama told me last night," he said. His voice had an accent. Then he raised the garbage can lid like a shield and raised the tent stake like it was a sword.

"Ban-khul" I said. If you don't remember, that ain't a nice thing to say to somebody if they know words from Moldova. You only say it when you smash your thumb with a hammer. But it ain't as bad as him talking about my mom like he knew her. His face looked real surprised that I knew them words. Then he swung that tent stake at me.

OK, it sounds like a goofy weapon, but it was dangerous. If he hit my eye I'd be blind forever. If he got my neck I might bleed to death right there in the weeds. Anywhere he hit me would hurt like heck. I didn't have no weapon and I couldn't punch him or I'd just hit the trash can lid. About all I could do was dodge and take steps backward until I come up with a better plan. At least I tried to back away from Daisy so all of us was getting farther away from her.

I seen his buddy move around the side to circle around behind me. That was the oldest trick in the book. His buddy was going to get behind me on his hands and knees until I backed into him and fell down. Or else he'd grab me from behind, which is the second oldest trick in the book. Either way, I didn't have much time. The next attack, I stopped backing up and just dodged the stake. When he pulled his arm back to poke at me again I took a quick step closer to him and grabbed the trash can lid with both hands. He tried to stab me again, only I had two hands on his shield and he only had one. Plus, I'm pretty strong, and I was still mad, and he wasn't expecting me to grab his shield. I pushed it sideways which blocked his stab, then I pulled it toward myself. Just by instincts, he tried to do the opposite. So he was pulling it toward himself. Then I switched direction and shoved it toward him really hard. Since he was already pulling it too, that garbage can lid whacked him really good in his chest and head.

The stake flew out of his hands and he stumbled backward. His hand was still holding the trash can lid and maybe it was stuck in the handle since he didn't let go. The lid also had some old wire on a screw, maybe to hang it up with and that wire got hooked on my shirt. I tried to pull loose but it got me like a fishhook snags a carp.

We was stuck together, that clown and me while he was stumbling backward. Before I thought of a good plan for that problem, we both fell to the ground, stuck together by a garbage can lid. I know that sounds like a country western song, "stuck to a clown by a garbage can lid," or maybe an opera, but sometimes songs talk about real stuff.

The bad part is we twisted around and he fell on top of me. My right arm was caught on a garbage can lid, which was under him, and most of him was on top of my legs. The even worse part is that third clown. He had picked up his buddy's two by four and was walking over to us.

I tried to roll over, I tried to get my arm loose, but I was in one of them pickles there ain't a easy way out of.

"You've been most inconvenience to us," the guy said. Even if he used big words, he had a accent just like the other one did.

"Well, you ain't exactly been the Easter Bunny to me either," I said.

"You give us ring, we let old lady go." He was standing right over me with the two by four raised above his head. I kept trying to get loose from the guy on top of me, but I was stuck.

"Mrs. Comanici?" I said. "Over at Autumn Gardens? Man, I think the cops already let her go for you. So you can check that off your list of stuff to do."

He looked surprised, so I must of guessed right. But he wasn't a guy who used lots of words.

"Give me ring now!" He raised the board even higher.

"I ain't got it on me. But I know where it is. Why do you want it anyways?"

He thought about that for a minute, deciding if there was any reason to tell me. He must of decided there wasn't a good reason to keep it a secret any more. He shrugged and kind of shook the board.

"Proof of grandson," he said. "Our father died, we claim estate. Old country laws, you don't know. Oldest grandson gets the ring. Man with ring gets estate. Stupid old men and their foolish ways! Nothing to do with you. Now where is ring?"

"Well, you already figured out it was at the zoo, right?"

"We followed you."

So they hadn't figured out exactly where Dobre hid it. Maybe I could stall until the cops got there.

"I seen an old picture with Dobre at the zoo. So that's how I figured out where he hid it. It had to be someplace safe, right? Somewhere nobody'd go snooping around. I'll give you three guesses."

"No guesses! No games!"

"OK, OK. I'll tell you where he hid it. But you've got to promise you'll let me and my friends go."

He smiled but didn't lower the board.

"I promise," he said.

"He hid it in the bear exhibit," I said. "Up high where the bears couldn't reach it. I seen it. It was easy once I figured out where the clue was. But there's no way I'm climbing into a grizzly bear home unless the zookeepers got the bears taking naps someplace else."

OK, so all that was true in a lawyer sort of way. He did hide it in the bear house, only there ain't bears in it now. And it ain't a lie to say I ain't climbing into a grizzly bear cage. And I did see the ring. The whole truth and nothing but the truth is that I took it away from there but I figured these guys don't deserve no doubt benefits.

"Good," he said. "Ring can stay there. As long as he doesn't show up with it," he pointed to Gus, "the elders grant estate to us. Your use for me is over." He took a step toward me and pulled back the board again like a batter getting ready to swing, or an ax cutter about to whack into a log.

"Wait!" I yelled. "You promised!"

"Fingers crossed," he said.

There wasn't nothing I could do except hope the guy had as bad an aim with a board as the last Colorado Rockies pitcher had with a bat.

But before he could swing, there was a weird sound from back behind the elephant. It sounded like a kid screaming in a grocery store when his mom don't buy him candy. The clown heard it too and stopped for just a second to look. It wasn't no kid. The clown's eyes got bigger. I heard that sound before, only I didn't remember where. It went "Eek –eek- eek!" real high and loud. Something brown and furry come out from under the elephant. It was maybe five feet tall and moving too fast for my eyes to keep up with. It run right at that clown like a big furry spider screaming eek eek.

"Chimp!" I said. It was the monkey I made friends with when I was a kid. Only he'd growed bigger than any monkey I ever saw. His arms was long and hairy, kind of reddish brown. His voice was about the same as ever, only louder and he sounded mad. He was running twice as fast as my fastest speed, so there wasn't much time for thinking about it.

When the clown figured out that Chimp was aiming at him, he turned to face him so he could whack him with the board instead of me. But Chimp had his whole brain aimed at that clown like a dog aiming at his food dish and he didn't pay no attention. In about one second he was between me and the clown.

Maybe the clown's idea would have worked if he started it sooner. But nobody thinks as fast as a monkey. And nobody's as strong as a monkey that big. The clown swung the board but Chimp had already jumped on him so it only hit air. Chimp put them big furry arms around the guy's neck and wrapped them big furry legs around the guy's waist. With his face about an inch from the guy's face, he kept screaming eek-eek-eek! The clown could see his big yellow teeth and probably smelled the bananas he ate for lunch. I figured out that when Thumb whistled before she wasn't whistling to the elephant. She was calling her buddy Chimp.

So the clown kept trying to swing the board but there was too much monkey in his way. Since his hands was above his head to start with, when Chimp jumped on his chest he started stumbling backward. He was half falling and half walking backward, trying to catch his balance at the same time he was trying to get the monkey off his front. Chimp didn't bite him, but I bet the guy was worried his face was about to be a monkey snack.

I raised my head off the ground a little bit and seen they was about to stumble backward right into the electric fence. I don't know how them things work exactly, but if it makes a big enough spark to scare an elephant it would probably knock a man down along with any monkeys he was carrying.

"Jump, Chimp!" I yelled. "Chimp! Jump off!"

But Chimp was still busy yelling at the guy's face and didn't pay no attention. They was only about one step away and there wasn't nothing I could do.

Then I heard two whistles, real loud and short one after the other. As if he was on a leash somebody pulled, Chimp jumped off the guy. The man took one more step backward and turned to run away. Only his arm touched that white rope and it was like a lumberjack punched him. There was a snapping sound, the guy straightened up and fell flat on the ground.

So one guy was unconscious on top of me and one was unconscious by the electric fence. The third guy looked at each of them for a second then turned around. He ducked under the rope and started to run away. I worked at getting unstuck from the garbage can lid, but Chimp had his own ideas. He come over and give me a big hug, which would of been cool except I was pinned on the ground and a suspect was making a getaway.

"I like you too," I said. "But I ain't done yet!"

But Chimp didn't care. I was his long lost buddy and we just had fun playing the clowns with sticks game and he was ready for some birthday cake and song singing. He kept petting my face and sitting on my arm and going eek-eek-eek but in a friendly way.

"That last guy's getting away!" I yelled at him.

"No, he ain't," someone said. I turned my head as much as I could and seen Greg and Pickle jogging toward us. There was a bunch of circus guys following them across the field. It was Greg who I heard. Even though Pickle was jogging pretty fast beside him, Greg shifted into a whole other gear I never knew he had. He took off after that clown about as fast as a Denver Bronco punt returner. The clown wasn't no slouch of a runner. He was older, and bigger, and he had a head start. But nobody runs as fast as a teenage boy who wants to impress a girl. In about ten seconds Greg caught up to him and jumped at his waist. It was a perfect tackle and the clown wound up with his face in the dirt and weeds. He squirmed around trying to get loose, but Greg wasn't having none of that. He put his knees on the guy's elbows and grabbed his hair and pulled the guy's head up off the ground just enough to convince him if he moved around too much he'd probably get his head pulled off. Some men from the circus caught up to them in a minute. They grabbed the guy by his arms and Greg got up off him.

Finally I got the dang garbage can lid loose from my shirt. Chimp figured out I wanted to sit up so he got off me for a second and I managed to wiggle out from under the clown.

"What in the whamaframitz was that all about?" a man's voice said. I turned and seen Gus and Thumb walking toward me. They had their arms around each other's waists and was helping each other walk. Gus had his other hand on the side of his head, which was bleeding. Thumb held her one leg up in the air a little bit so she didn't put weight on it. They was limping along pretty slow. I stood up and dusted off my jeans.

"I think I figured it all out," I said. "When you was a kid, did you live in Texas for a while?"

Gus looked confused.

"Yeah, for a while. Do these guys hate Texas?"

"Nah," I said. "They is Texans. Well, at least for a while they been. There's somebody you got to meet. Both of you."

"That sounds mysterious," Thumb said.

"Yeah, everybody says I'm a mysterious guy. Just like James Bond." Somebody bumped me from behind, which surprised me. What surprised me even more was that it was the elephant's big trunk nose pushing on my back.

"What the heck is she doing?" I asked. She was bending her front legs and lowering her head down right next to me. "Is she OK?"

"Wow," said Thumb.

Gus laughed but you could tell he was still feeling weak and dizzy by the sound of his laugh. "She's inviting you to ride her."

"The elephant?" I said.

"She knows you got rid of the guys that were pestering her," Thumb said. "She's very smart. But she's still nervous and needs to go for a walk, work off of all that energy. She figures you're her new friend and maybe you can convince Gus to take down the electric fence. Let her go walking through this big empty field. She's a circus tramp through and through. She knows a soft touch and an easy mark when she sees one."

"I used to drive a Pinto car," I said. "But I ain't never drove an elephant."

"Nothing to it," Gus said. "Just climb up her face and sit on top. You can hold her ears to steady yourself if you need to. Let her walk for a few minutes across the field. When you want to come back, just tell her 'home'."

"I ain't got insurance for driving an elephant."

"That's OK. We do. But just to be safe, Pickle, why don't you and Greg take Brandy and follow them. Pickle can maneuver an elephant like it was a forklift. If you get in trouble, she'll catch up and help you out."

I wasn't so sure, but the elephant was still kneeling down and Pickle went off to get the horse.

"OK," I said. I started petting the elephant trunk between its eyes. If you're gonna climb on someone's face it seems fair to warn them first. "I'm gonna climb up your nose," I said. "And I'll try not to hurt you..." While I was explaining it to Daisy what was going on, Chimp jumped on my back, then climbed right over the top of my head and up Daisy's face. When he got on top of the big gray head he stood there looking back at me going eek-eek-eek like he was saying he won the race and now I owed him a banana or something.

Well, I hate to let a monkey make me look silly. It ain't that hard to climb an elephant who wants to be climbed and in about six seconds I was right up there with Chimp. I got behind him, since I was taller and could see over him easy. I remembered Thumb said that she liked music, so I started singing real soft. The only song that come into my brain was Oklahoma where the wind comes whistling down the airplane. That's about the best song to sing in your big opera star voice, but I wanted to calm her down, not attack a village, so I sang real soft. Chimp made weird little noises that could of been his idea of singing too, and which me feel pretty good about my own voice.

Meanwhile, a bunch of stuff was going on while I sat up there. About thirty circus guys was around the painters in clown suits. A pickup truck come across the field with two cops in the cab and two in the back. Their cop cars couldn't of got through the field so they was riding with circus guys. When they got out, I seen one was Officer Mike. He wasn't wearing a uniform, since he's retired, but he had on a Denver Bronco T shirt. The other cops put handcuffs on the perps, who was all able to walk but didn't look all that happy. Officer Mike seen me sitting up there. I waved but didn't yell since I was trying to keep Daisy calm.

"I'm not going to have to arrest you for grand theft pachyderm, am I?" he yelled at me.

I shook my head no.

"We found Mrs. Comanici. She's fine, she'll be back home soon. They're keeping her overnight in the hospital for observation. You did some pretty fine detective work, Jumper."

I give him a thumbs up sign, since I was trying to be quiet.

"OK, see you later," he said. He got in the front of the truck with another officer driving. They put the three perps in the back with two more cops. They drove through the field fast enough to kick up a bunch of dirt. Them was going to be some dusty clowns by the time they got to the station and if they had hay fever they'd be coughing and sneezing. I felt bad for them, a little bit, but part of me also smiled at the idea.

What was also going on was that Pickle come back riding Gus's horse Brandy that was mostly tan with a blonde mane. Greg and her was going to ride together on one horse in case she had to drive the elephant then he'd be the one to drive the horse. Greg didn't look like he wanted to get up there on that horse, but he also didn't want to look scared. A circus man in a black T-shirt with big muscles put his fingers together to make a step. Greg looked around at me like he was asking what to do.

"Put your left foot on his hands, step up, throw your right leg over the horse," Pickle said. "Or didn't your city school teach you which one is your left foot?"

Greg did what he was told and in a second he was sitting behind Pickle on top of that horse, with no saddle and no place to put your feet or hang onto. He looked pretty confused.

"You're going to have to put your arms around my waist if you don't want to fall off," she said. He did that, but careful, like she was a vase of flowers he didn't want to break.

"Geez," she said. "You're going to have to do better than that. I promise I won't tell your girlfriend."

"I don't have a girlfriend," he said.

"Why am I not surprised?" she said. It was supposed to be an insult, only she was smiling just a little. Greg's face looked red. So that was all going on.

When Pickle and Greg was ready, and Chimp and I was sitting on top of Daisy's back, just behind her head, Gus told the men to take down part of the electric fence.

"The boss won't like that," a guy said.

"The boss doesn't like anything," Gus said. "I bet he wouldn't have liked a story in the Denver Post about one of our elephants trampling people to death either. We've got some heroes here, both human and animal, and they deserve to take a little walk. If he wants to fire me, let him. Take down the fence."

The man shrugged. Once they turned off the switch they could touch the rope like it was nothing. I kept singing Oklahoma real soft. Gus and Thumb was petting Daisy's trunk. When the fence was down, Thumb said, "It's OK, girl. Time for a walk. Go on." The elephant stood up.

Them big gray shoulders rolled from side to side under me as she started walking. She had big wrinkles in her skin and they looked cool when they moved. She wasn't clumsy like a Godzilla doll, the way you think an elephant would be, but felt as alive as a puppy dog or hamster. She walked out of that roped-in pen as easy as a little kid. You think of big animals as a lot different from ourselves until you're sitting on top of one. Then they seem as ordinary as any other friend. I could hear her breathing in and out, and felt a little bump every time her feet hit the ground. Flies buzzed around her ears, and sometimes she sneezed. When she did, she shook her head a little bit and her ears flopped.

Chimp was having his own little party up there in front of me. Balance is one of a monkey's best things and he stood there like a king standing in a Cadillac convertible in a parade. If there would of been crowds of loyal subjects, he would of been waving to them. He'd rode elephants before, you could tell, and the swaying was just part of the fun to him.

I felt like I was riding a dinosaur, or maybe a submarine. I should of thought of a story to have in my brain, only I ain't ever pretended to ride an elephant. What popped into my brain wasn't a perfect match, but a story don't ever need to be perfect. When we was past all the people and just had a big empty field in front of us, I had one ready.

"OK, chimp, did you ever see them old Westerns on TV? Sometimes you see them late at night." Chimp just kind of grunted. I decided he was trying to say, "Why, yes sir, I know exactly what you're referring to. They're my very favorite form of entertainment."

I was glad we was on the same page.

"So this time you get to be the Lone Ranger and I'm Tonto. We're riding on Trigger, which is a horse. Some cattle rustlers tried to get us, but we're making a getaway. They ain't never gonna catch Trigger, since he's about the biggest horse in the whole world."

Chimp went eek-eek-eek and kind of jumped up and down like he already liked the game. Plus, he was probably glad he was the Lone Ranger, since he's got the most lines to say. Chimp being excited made me laugh. I went "High Ho Silver... AWAY!" pretty loud.

Maybe that started Daisy or maybe she was playing the game too. She started walking faster and I had to quick lean forward and grab her ears so I didn't fall off. In about three seconds she was running full speed.

Maybe you think of elephants as slow walkers since they look fat. But even without knowing you, I bet you could not outrun Daisy. She was fast and you could tell she loved to run. Her ears flopped up and down and her feet kicked up clouds of dirt. It was like being on top of a locomotive.

After I seen that I could hang on easy and so could Chimp, I started laughing. We was all making a getaway from cattle rustlers and mean clowns and electric fences. If I closed my eyes I could see a whole tribe of Apache Indians riding their brown and white ponies right beside us, whooping and holding their bows up in the air. Their faces was painted with war paint and they had bands around their heads with a feather stuck in it. I wasn't scared. I was Tonto, who is also an Indian, so they was my buddies.

A bunch of geese flew right over us, honking like a traffic jam. They looked like Klingon space ships which is usually pretty dangerous, but me and Chimp was riding the big gray Starship Enterprise and we obviously just scared them away before they hurt the peaceful people on this planet stuck way out in the middle of the galaxy that looked like a weed field.

It was about the most fun thing I ever done. I decided I didn't need to sing soft any more. Nobody was nervous, we was just having fun. I thought of the song I should of been singing the whole time. In my biggest, loudest opera star voice I started singing:

"Daisy, Daisy give me your answer do

I'm half crazy, all for the love of you

It won't be a stylish marriage

I can't afford a carriage.

But you'd look sweet, upon the seat

Of a bicycle built for two."

I sung it three times with Chimp doing his monkey harmony. I closed my eyes again and for a minute I was riding in a car in the middle of the night. My dad was driving. I knew we was going to the circus but he wouldn't tell me, and I didn't say nothing to spoil the surprise. We was both singing in our big opera star voices and he didn't cough once.

Daisy slowed back down to a walk. She'd got it out of her system and so had I. I scratched her between her ears. "Home, girl," I said. "It's time to go home."

Daisy walked back to where we started from. I'd got used to the way her shoulders rolled from side to side like a boat. Pickle and Greg followed us on the horse. I could hear they was still arguing, but they was too far back for me to tell what they was saying. Their voices didn't sound all that mad. It was like they was only playing a game of arguing.

I wasn't playing a game any more. I wasn't Tonto, or on a space ship. I was just a guy riding an elephant through a field with his monkey. By now I'd got used to it and it felt pretty ordinary, just like anybody's life. The difference in adventures is mostly the way you think about them, which is a good lesson. If they ain't careful, anybody's life could go ordinary on them. If you think your life is mostly ordinary, you should look around just to make sure. Maybe you and your monkey is riding an elephant across a field too and you just ain't noticed.

When we got back to where everybody was standing, Daisy bent her front legs and lowered her head down, Chimp started to climb down her face like he done it a thousand ties. He was feeling pretty proud of himself that he was going to win the race of getting to the ground first. But while he was still climbing down, I stood up on Daisy's shoulders and jumped straight to the ground. Then I turned back toward Chimp, who was still up by Daisy's eyes, put my hands out on each side of my head like big ears and went "Eek-eek-eek!" to him. He stopped and looked at me all surprised, with his big monkey eyes wide open. Nobody beats a monkey at climbing down an elephant nose. Then he lifted his face and shook his head from side to side and started laughing his monkey laugh. He knew I outsmarted him on that game, but we was buddies so it was OK.

Greg and Pickle caught up to us. Greg slid off the horse and then Pickle did.

"Hey, Greg," I said. "I need to call Holly on your cellphone."

"Sure," he said. His face still looked a little red and he didn't look over at Pickle. But they was both almost smiling, if a guy used his imagination. He poked at the phone screen with his finger and handed it to me.

"Hello?" Holly said, like it was a question.

"Hi, it's me, Jumper," I said.

"Where are you?"

"We're still at the circus. Everybody's fine. Did you hear they found Mrs. Comanici?"

"Yeah," she said. "She's at my hospital."

"Is she OK?"

"Yeah, they just want to check her out."

"Good," I said. "We caught the perps. But there's two more people coming to your hospital for precautions. Their names is Gus and Thumbelina. I think Mrs. Comanici would want to meet them."

"I don't understand," Holly said. "She's been through a lot."

"Yeah. But if she stayed at the hospital overnight for observation, and so did Gus and Thumb, we could all have breakfast tomorrow in the hospital cafeteria, like at nine. I think they'd all like it, even if they don't know it now. It would be like a family reunion."

"But if they don't know each other, how could it be...?"

171

"Maybe you could bring her picture album," I said. "It would be a lot easier to explain to everybody how they got in their fixes if they had pictures to look at."

Holly didn't say nothing for a long time. When she talked again, her voice was soft.

"The doctors don't listen to me much about who needs to stay overnight for observation," she said.

"You probably ain't ever had a case like this," I said. "Tell them it's for insurance purposes. Doctors are pretty careful when it comes to doing stuff for insurance purposes."

"I'll see what I can do."

"Thanks," I said. "Greg, I think we need to take Gus and Thumbelina to the hospital, since you got a car. You know the hospital where Holly works? That's where they need to go."

Gus waved his hand to say no. "We're fine," he said. "We don't need a hospital."

"Sorry," I said. "Insurance purposes. Somebody's insurance guy might pay you money for getting hurt, but only if you got a note from a doctor. Your brains could be leaking out that cut in your head right now, and Thumb's got to have somebody look at her leg. The circus insurance ain't gonna be happy if your brains leak out, are they?"

"Probably not," Gus said with a little laugh. "They'd promote me to manager."

"See?" I said. "That's what I mean. It ain't worth ruining your life over."

Chapter Seventeen
A big meeting in the hospital cafeteria

The hospital cafeteria is like the lunchroom at school, except without the food fights. It's got light blue and green colors with lots of tile and stainless steel that clean up easy. The cafeteria at Holly's hospital was way better than the others I've eaten at. The food is good and they give you big amounts. The only minus is that the hospital was started by a vegetarian religion. Holly says that's why you can't get sausages or bacon or hamburgers, which might be true, but I got my suspicions. I think they mostly done that so people wouldn't come and eat there if they wasn't sick or visiting somebody. Once I had dinner with Holly there and it was mostly baked carrots and mashed turnips with some green weeds on the side. I gotta admit, it tasted better than it sounds but not so much I'd sneak in to eat it if I wasn't pretty sick.

But they do a good job with breakfast eggs and potatoes and pancakes. If I was going to pretend to be sick and sneak in to eat, that's the meal I'd rate the highest. Last night I had told Gus and Thumb to meet me in the cafeteria at nine sharp for breakfast and don't eat breakfast first even if the nurse brings you green Jell-O. They knew I wanted them to meet somebody and they promised three times, so I figured they'd show up.

I walked into the cafeteria by myself at about thirteen minutes before nine. I would of got there sooner, but Mr. Silver had some issues with his newspaper and his apple slice and his birdseed so I had to clean up his cage and explain how even pirates and dinosaurs got to be more careful sometimes. By the time I was done, I had to run most of the way to the hospital to get there in time. In the cafeteria, people was sitting at round tables eating, but about half the tables was empty. I seen Holly and Mrs. Comanici sitting by a table and walked over to them.

"Hey, Jumper," Holly said. "You look all dressed up this morning."

"It's my favorite T shirt," I said. "So I don't wear it that often." It was black with a picture of the Starship Enterprise on it. Plus I had on my cleanest jeans and white socks that was almost new. I'd scraped my sneakers clean, spray painted them white, and left them on my balcony to dry. Some people think that's weird, but a can of spray paint is way cheaper than new sneakers and it makes them look about new. What seems weird to me is buying new sneakers for the price of a whole car tire when all you need is a can of spray paint that will paint shoes a bunch of times.

"You guys look nice too," I said.

"Holly brought me some clothes from home and helped me this morning," Mrs. Comanici said. "She said sometimes the best way to start feeling better is to dress up a little bit. And she was right. I already do feel a little better." Mrs. Comanici was wearing a bright blue blouse that looked like silk and her hair was combed straight back and tied in back. There was a bandage all the way around her head, just above her eyes, but she'd stuck some flowers in it so it looked like a hippie headband. Even with the bandage, she looked more dressed up than I ever seen her and way better than most hospital patients. I looked at Holly and she smiled.

Well, Holly always looks nice. She was wearing a light green uniform since she had to go to work right after we was done. All the nurses wear that. But when Holly smiles it's like she's wearing a diamond necklace right on her face. All the fancy clothes in department stores ain't as good as a pretty smile. I was careful to only look at her a little bit or my eyes would get stuck watching her all the time.

"I understand I owe you a big thank you," said Mrs. Comanici. "Holly told me how you figured out where they were keeping me."

"I got lucky on that one," I said. "Them suspects wasn't very careful with their clues. It don't take Columbo to figure out who's buying Arctic White paint."

They both smiled.

"Well, the police didn't figure it out," Mrs. Comanici said. "If not for you I don't know if anyone would have ever found me."

"Speaking of finding stuff," I said. "I was wondering if this looked familiar to you." I reached into my jean pocket and pulled out the ring. I'd dug it out of the bag of rotten broccoli in the trash and washed it three times. It smelled a lot better now, but I wasn't going to be in the mood to eat broccoli for a long time. I set it down on the table in front of her.

Mrs. Comanici's eyes got wide and her mouth come open. She stared at the ring for about a minute and didn't say nothing. Holly stared at it too, but with a confused look. She knew she'd seen it someplace, she just couldn't remember where. Then she remembered and her eyes got big too.

"Is that what I think it is?" Holly asked.

"Yes," Mrs. Comanici whispered. "How did you... where...?"

It makes you feel good when you surprise somebody that much. I felt better than I maybe deserved to feel, but I was also nervous in case the rest of the breakfast plan had hidden flaws.

"Your husband left us good clues, so you gotta give him most of the credit. He hid it at the zoo, on top of Bear Mountain. Then he had you take a picture of him standing in front of it pointing up. You didn't get it since you thought guys beat him up and stole it. He didn't get a chance to explain because of the mine accident. I bet he didn't mean it to be a secret on you."

"But when could he have done that? I was right there with him the whole time."

"I figure he done exactly what I done. You said he was a good climber, so I bet he snuck into the zoo at night by climbing over the fence. Or really early, before work maybe."

"You broke into the zoo?" Holly said. I didn't have time to take any consequences right then so I just went on talking.

"It was an easy climb up to the top of Bear Mountain, since it ain't a real mountain. He was a lot braver than me, though, since they kept real bears in it back then. It was under a flagstone."

"How did you know which flagstone? Mrs. Comanici said.

I pulled out my legal yellow pad and showed her my drawing. "He carved your initials in a tree up there, which has a good view. See? Like this. It was mostly luck I climbed the tree and seen it. Then he carved the shape of the stone. It's better than a heart shape since it was the hiding place of the ring, but I bet he meant the same thing. Sure enough, there was a stone in just that shape, and the ring was under it. I thought them crooks figured out it was at the zoo from the picture in your album, just like me. They tried to follow me, but they was too slow."

"That's amazing," Holly said. She picked up the ring and held it up to her face to take a good look. She wrinkled up her face. "What in the world...?"

"That smell is my fault," I said. "I hid it in my trash with some bad broccoli in case they broke in again. Some hydrogen peroxide and baking soda will get it smelling better only my supplies was low. Sorry about that."

"Don't apologize," Mrs. Comanici said.

"I still ain't sure how come they wanted it so bad."

Mrs. Comanici sighed. "Just as insurance," she said and she looked a little sad. "My Dobre and his father got in some sort of a fight, he never talked about it. In anger, his father said he might leave the winery to Dobre's worthless brother Vidal. But there was never a deed, never a will. When their father died, Vidal just moved in. Legally, even now, years later, the winery still belongs to their father's estate. Vidal died last year. I got a letter from one of my aunts. If no one puts in a claim, his sons will get title because they're the only heirs the court knows about. But if Dobre had a son, and he showed up with his grandfather's ring, the council would know he was the right heir. They'd have to give the winery to him. It's a silly old custom, from a time before laws were written down. Certainly before DNA testing. But in the wine country of Moldova, sometimes the old customs are the only laws that matter."

"I ain't sure I got all that," I said.

"It's simpler than it sounds," Mrs. Comanici said. "If I ever find my son August, this ring could mean a lot to him. Even years from now, it could matter. He could claim the winery, which is worth a small fortune today. They wanted to make sure that never happened." She looked down at the table.

"Now, of course, it's just a symbol," she said. "But it reminds me of Dobre and August and hope. I can never thank you enough for that."

"No problem," I said. "Anyway, I got a couple more friends showing up for breakfast since you're all accidentally staying at the same fancy hotel here. They're circus people and they helped me a lot, so maybe they'll help cheer you up too. Plus, this place has great scrambled eggs and hash browns and I'm about as hungry as a hippopotamus."

Mrs. Comanici smiled a little smile. She rolled the ring around in her hand and stared at it. She was happy to think about her husband and her kid, and the ring reminded her they was real even if she couldn't see them no more. But remembering also made her sad which is how remembering works.

"Listen," I said, looking up at the clock on the wall. It was about five til nine. "There's something else I gotta tell you."

"Sure, Jumper," Mrs. Comanici said. Holly was watching me pretty careful in case I stuck my foot in my mouth.

"It could be weird to meet my friends. You know how sometimes one guy looks a lot like another guy? So that can be weird. And how sometimes you got to go slow in getting to know somebody else? Like a dog who had a bad owner who takes time to figure out strangers in case they're bad too. You want to move slow with dogs like that."

Just then the cafeteria door opened and Gus and Thumb walked in. She had a cast on her foot and one arm was in a sling. He had a bandage around his head just like Mrs. Comanici only without the flower. They was wearing jeans and T shirts, not goofy hospital gowns, so the doctors must of decided they was OK to leave.

I waved my arm and they seen me. They smiled and started walking toward our table. I stood up.

Mrs. Comanici's face looked as surprised and confused as if she opened her refrigerator door only now it opened to a beach in Hawaii. She stared at Gus and Thumb and her face couldn't decide what to do. Holly looked about the same. Holly put her hand on Mrs. Comanici's elbow, like maybe something was dangerous and that would protect them.

I was the only person Gus and Thumb recognized, so they come right up to me and didn't look at the others. Gus shook my hand and Thumb give me a big hug.

"They're still talking about you at the circus," Gus said. "Nobody's seen Daisy move that fast in ten years."

"Well, it's the fastest I ever rode a elephant, " I said. "And also the second fastest and the third fastest. Gus and Thumbelina, I wanted you guys to meet my friends. This is my friend Holly."

"Nice to meet you," Gus said and shook her hand. While Thumb shook Holly's hand, I explained. "Holly's a nurse here at the hospital but she also lives in my apartment building. Them suspects we caught yesterday swiped some stuff from her."

"I hope the cops get it all back to you," Thumb said.

"I think they will," Holly said. "They just have to inventory it."

"And this is Mrs. Comanici," I said. Gus smiled at her and reached out his hand to shake it. Mrs. Comanici didn't do nothing for a second. Then it was like she woke up and reached out her hand too.

"You say your name is Gus?" she said.

"Yes, ma'am," he said. "It's not fancy, but it's easy to spell."

She smiled. Her face looked about twenty years younger for a few seconds.

"It's a wonderful name," she said. "Here, you sit next to me, OK? You remind me of someone."

"That's the best offer I've had all morning," he said

Holly jumped up. "Here, Thumbelina. You sit next to me. Jumper says you're with the circus. That must be so interesting."

Thumb sat down and I sat across from them.

"Probably not as interesting as a hospital," Thumb said. They both laughed like they was old buddies.

"Well, the hospital probably does have more clowns," Holly said.

They both laughed at that too. They was already talking like they just seen each other two days ago even if they ain't ever met before. When women start talking to each other like that, pretty soon I don't understand all the stuff they think is funny. So I started listening to Mrs. Comanici and Gus. She kept asking him questions about the circus and riding horses. She smiled at all his answers and looked at him real hard, like he was the most interesting person in the world and his horse must be pretty interesting too. Some people are extra good at doing that. They act like you're interesting until you decide you must be pretty dang interesting even if nobody else ever noticed. You wind up liking that person for being so smart to notice you. But Mrs. Comanici wasn't pretending. Gus's horse with the tan sides and the white mane was about as interesting a horse as I ever met.

After everybody had talked enough they seemed comfortable, I said, "Well, it ain't really a breakfast unless we eat some food."

So everybody got up and stood in line. Holly kept talking to Thumb and Mrs. Comanici kept talking to Gus while we got our food, which was good. I'm always happy if somebody else will do the talking and I can think about my scrambled eggs and potatoes. The ketchup was extra good, and the coffee tasted like they just made it today. Plus, nobody made me eat any weeds.

After everybody had eaten, and was just drinking coffee, Holly pulled out Mrs. Comanici's photo album and put it on the table between her and Thumb. "Jumper asked me to bring this, and I think I know why," Holly said. She leaned close to Thumb and talked soft. "These are pictures from Edith's younger days, back in Moldova and then here in Colorado. She had a hard life. Her husband died, her son was taken away from her. I'd like to hear what you think about a couple of these pictures."

"Sure," Thumb said. You could tell she was just being polite. They opened the book. Mrs. Comanici and Gus was talking about horses and didn't pay no attention to anything else. People who like horses is like that. You can't hold it against them.

"This is Edith's parents," Holly said. "She got her mother's eyes, didn't she?"

"Yes," said Thumb. "The country looks so beautiful."

"Edith can tell you all about it." Holly turned the page. "And this was her husband Dobre when he was about twenty. He loved to ride this horse."

I watched Thumb's face. Her eyes opened wide. She stared at the picture, then looked at Gus, then back at the picture. She started to say something but Holly give her one of them little looks has that only other girls understand.

"I see what you mean," Thumb whispered.

"They had a little boy," Holly said. She turned a couple of pages. "Here. His name was August. He loved animals."

"August?" Thumb kept whispering, even if Gus and Mrs. Comanici wouldn't of heard anything that wasn't about horses even if she yelled it.

"That's right," Holly said very calmly. "What are the odds?"

"So Edith is his...?"

"Jumper thinks so. But now they're strangers."

"Did you tell her?"

"No. What if we're wrong? What if they hated each other?"

"It doesn't look like they hate each other," Thumb said. Gus and Mrs. Comanici was laughing at each other's jokes and talking about horse feet and saddles. The rest of us watched them for a few minutes without saying nothing.

"She knows, doesn't she?" Thumb said pretty quiet.

"A mother always knows," Holly said.

"Honey," Thumb said a little louder. Gus stopped talking like he'd been unplugged and looked at her. "Holly's been telling me a little bit about Mrs. Comanici. I'd like to hear the whole story from her. And then I want you to look at her photo album. OK?"

"Sure," Gus said. "She's already told me about her favorite horse. That's gotta be the most important part."

Thumb got up and walked over to stand behind him. She put her hand on his shoulder. "Start at the beginning," Thumb said. "Especially the part about your son."

Mrs. Comanici looked up at her and blinked a few quick times like some people do before they cry. She shook her head 'no' and then looked down at the table. Holly moved over next to her and put her hand on top of Mrs. Comanici's hand.

"It will be all right," Thumb said. "I promise."

Mrs. Comanici nodded her head yes.

"Well, since I already heard this, how about if I get everybody some more coffee?" I said. Holly give me one of them looks that guys don't understand but since she didn't say nothing I went and got a pot of coffee and refilled cups. The lunch lady didn't want me to take the pot, but I explained it would be faster than bringing all them cups up one at a time so she finally said OK. By then Mrs. Comanici was at the part about going to jail and her kid getting took away.

I took the coffee pot back to the counter. When I come back, she was telling the part about her kid getting took to Texas and her staying in the same apartment building so he could find her if he ever come looking. She said she hired a private detective to find him, which she had not said before. Only he didn't have no luck.

"So people probably called your son August 'Gus' for short," Gus said. "Just like me." Gus thought that was funny and laughed a little. Mrs. Comanici smiled but nobody else laughed.

"Plus, since I lived in Texas for a while when I was a kid, maybe we even met each other."

"Stranger things have happened," Mrs. Comanici said.

"I would have remembered running into another kid named Gus," he said.

"Here's the deal, Gus," I said. Everybody seemed so careful they wasn't getting anywhere. It was like listening to guys in Congress explaining stuff in a way to make sure everybody stayed confused.

"Jumper," Holly said. "I don't think you should..."

"It's OK," I said. "Everybody else knows what's going on except Gus."

Gus looked confused. "Something's going on?" he said. It felt weird somebody else was confused instead of me.

"Yeah," I said. "You look like Mrs. Comanici's husband did when he was young. Which is what her kid might look like by now. So them kidnappers thought you was her kid. That's how come they tried to kill you with Daisy."

"But why would they care whose kid I was?"

"Because there's a farm where they make wine..."

"A winery?"

"Yeah, you could call it that. A winery back in Moldova, which is on the other side of the ocean, that her kid might have a chance to own. It's got a big house made of rocks that looks like a castle, and tunnels with caskets of old wine that might be worth money. Plus barns with horses and a river and big fields of grape plants. It sounds like more of a summer camp than a farm. Them guys was following me from the zoo and they seen you and they put two and two together."

"That's crazy!" Gus said.

"Everything's crazy the first time you think of it," I said. "Even gravity was crazy when Mr. Newton invented it but now we use it all the time."

Mrs. Comanici was looking down at the table with a little smile on her face. It was about as much smile as Mona Lisa had when Mr. Vinci painted her picture.

"Of course it's crazy," she said. "But since it caused you so many problems, maybe you'd like to see my pictures. Just so you understand."

"Sure," said Gus, but he didn't sound all that sure. He thought we was all goose chasing. Mrs. Comanici put the book down on the table between them. She flipped through the first pages real quick. "You don't need to see my grandparents," she said. "Here, this one is the winery."

"That looks pretty fancy," Gus said. Gus's face didn't look so happy any more. He looked a little mad and you could tell his brain was working extra hard. He didn't look at Mrs. Comanici and his jaw muscles was tight. Something was bugging him only he was trying to stay polite and not talk about it.

"At one time, yes. I'm sure it needs a lot of work now." Mrs. Comanici looked at Gus, but he didn't look back. "And this is Marinela, my horse. Isn't she lovely?"

"Is she a vanner? They're pretty rare these days."

"Not in Moldova," she said. "Work like a mule, gentle as a lamb. This next picture is Dobre's horse Noroc. It means Lucky."

"Beautiful animal," he said. She turned the page. "And this is Dobre on Noroc. He was about your age when they took the picture."

There was some fog behind them in the picture. Dobre had turned his head sideways a little and was staring at the camera. He looked about ready to make a wisecrack. Gus stared but he didn't say nothing.

"See what I mean?" Thumb said. "You could be brothers."

"Yeah," Gus said. "That's a weird coincidence. I can see why those guys got confused." He looked off into space. It was like he was talking to the clock on the wall when he talked. His voice was soft. "So, did you abandon him when you came to America?"

Mrs. Comanici stared at him for a minute.

Gus looked down at the table. "I mean the horse," he said. "Did you have to abandon your horse when you moved?"

When she answered it was real soft too. "Not by choice," she said. "We were ripped away from each other." She stopped for a second. "I never stopped loving him. I never stopped missing him."

Gus didn't say nothing, but he kind of nodded. They was talking about a horse, but I think they was talking about him too. I was trying to picture what it must feel like to him, to think his Mom deserted him and then have some woman show up and try to make everything right over a cup of coffee. There wasn't no easy way for this conversation to go. If she was his mom, he'd be mad she left him no matter what she said. But mostly he wouldn't believe it. He'd already set up his life to work the way it was and changing it was a big deal that probably wasn't worth it.

"The world is full of coincidences," he said. "Coincidences don't prove anything."

"Yeah," I said, even if it wasn't really my conversation. "But coincidence is just another way to say long odds. Something being unlikely don't prove it's wrong either."

"You have to indulge an old woman by looking at just a couple more," Mrs. Comanici said. She turned a few pages. "This is my little boy August, with his teddy bear. He carried that thing everywhere."

"I had a teddy bear just like that," Gus said.

"Really?" Mrs. Comanici said.

"Yeah, I called him..."

Mrs. Comanici interrupted him. "Cookie Monster?" she said.

I laughed. "That's pretty funny," I said. "It don't look nothing like Cookie Monster on TV!"

"Yeah," Gus whispered. "Cookie Monster."

Nobody said nothing for a while. They was just staring at each other like they got beamed into a new planet where the sky was green and everybody had a whole family they never knew about.

The cafeteria door opened and in walked Officer Mike. He was carrying my apple crate. I got up right away and went over to him.

"They told me you'd be here," he said. "I convinced the DA we had enough evidence without the box they used to carry stuff. Maybe you should write your name on it so we don't have to go through this every time you lose it."

I took the apple crate from him. "I ain't losing it any other times," I said. "But I'll put my name on it too. Thanks."

Right behind him was Pickle and Greg. They was still arguing, only in whispers since it was a hospital. Officer Mike looked back at them and they hushed.

"Your friend Sunshine Speedboat here is going to give Gus and Thumbelina a ride back to the circus," he said.

"Come over to our table and meet my friends," I said. I was hoping there wasn't enough chairs so I had a good excuse to sit on my apple crate. There was extra chairs, but I sat on it anyway.

Pickle looked at Gus and Thumb. "You guys look like crap," she said. Greg tried not to snicker and made a snorting sound by holding it in.

"You know what you need?" Gus said, looking at her pretty hard like a principal might look at you before he told you what your consequences was going to be.

"Whatever," she said.

"You need a change of scenery. And a change of jobs. I think you need to work at a winery for a while."

"What the..." and then she said a bunch of words that ain't polite. Gus just let them words roll off him. When she was done, he started talking again like she hadn't said nothing.

"Yeah, I think that's just what you need. Thumb and I are thinking of moving to Europe to run an old winery. We're the closest thing you have to parents so I think you should come too."

"You don't know the first thing about running a winery," Pickle said.

"True," Gus answered. He stared off into the distance for a minute and nobody talked. Then he nodded. "But my mom here does. She's coming with us."

"Your mom?" Pickle said. "You ain't got a mom. You got found by a Dumpster in Dallas. You said it a hundred times."

"There was more to the story," Gus said. "It's going to take some time to get used to it."

Greg didn't look very happy and Gus noticed. "How much longer before you graduate?" Gus asked.

That surprised Greg. "I guess that depends," he said. "I'm a little behind."

"Do you think your parents would let you study abroad during summer vacation? My mom here is a fully accredited teacher. You could learn algebra and history from her while we're all learning about the wine business."

"I don't know," Greg said.

"Well, you think about it. Pickle could use a good influence. Just for the summer."

That time I about snorted coffee out my nose. Nobody would of thought Greg was a good influence. But then you can't ever tell all the things that might be inside a person. Maybe there was a good influence inside him just waiting to show its face.

Gus turned to Mrs. Comanici. "You know the customs over there, but it sounds like we've got competition for the place. Talk about your long odds. Hard to believe that we'd wind up with it."

"I'll tell you what the odds are," she said. She took her cell phone out of her purse. It took her a minute to find the number she wanted to call. Then she hit the call button and put it on speakerphone. After five rings a man answered. He sounded sleepy. He talked with an accent that was a lot like them painters.

"Who is this?" he said. "Do you know what time it is?"

"Minister Postan, I'm sorry to awaken you. It's Edith Comanici, Dobre's widow. I'm calling from America."

"Edith? Can it be you? It's been so long..."

"We can catch up later," Mrs. Comanici said. "I wanted you to be the first to know, so you can prepare papers. The American police have Vidal's sons in custody. After so many years, I did not recognize them. There will be no winking judge, no gypsy-cousin justice for them this time. They have earned long term accommodations in an American prison and have no use for the winery. Plus, I have found August. We have the ring. We're coming home."

Chapter Eighteen
The end

Night is my favorite time to practice jumping, which I probably already told you. First, nobody sees you, which means they ain't got any opinion about what you're doing. If they don't see you, they don't have to feel bad since you got a sport they can't do as good. Even in the summer, it ain't too hot outside in Denver at night, so you don't get sweaty from climbing back up to jump again. Sometimes there's stars or the moon, which is interesting. There's lots of advantages of night training, plus it's fun. So that night, after everyone got themselves used to having new families and new plans and went home to their own apartments, I went down to City Park and climbed a big tree. I sat on a thick branch and waited for it to get all the way dark. After all the excitement, I just wanted to think for a minute, do some practice jumps, and then go home and sleep. What I thought was this:

You never know where your next adventure will come from. Once I was just taking a nap in a park and these gang guys thought they wanted my wallet more than I did. They was not correct about that, but if I hadn't took that nap I would of missed out on a lot of cool stuff. Then with my apple crate, if I hadn't bought me some legal yellow pads and started interviewing victims, Gus and Mrs. Comanici might never have found each other, and Greg would not of met Pickle, and I never would of made friends with a elephant. Taking naps and writing down clues is obviously smart ideas.

After that, I thought this:

Sometimes you just got to do stuff even if you ain't figured out step two. The universe helps you have adventures, but mostly after you're already started. It's hard to row a rowboat when it's standing still, but it ain't that hard to steer it once it's moving. I think the universe is lazy; it might help you out but it ain't gonna start rowing before you do.

The other thing is you got to notice when you're having an adventure. Lots of people have exciting adventures, like getting lost, or having it rain on a picnic, or having the dinner they're cooking catch on fire and they don't even notice how fun it is.

Sometime I might write down rules for myself. If I did, them would be the first two: do stuff and notice your own adventures. I would of started writing that list right then, but I didn't have no legal yellow pad with me up in the tree. So maybe my third rule would be to always have a legal yellow pad with me in case I get smart ideas. But since I ain't actually wrote down my list, I ain't taking any bonus points off for not having some paper with me.

It had got pretty dark by the time I thought all that so I stood up on the branch I was on and looked around. I didn't see nobody else in the park. I took a deep breath. The air smelled clean and green like grass and trees. Crickets was starting to sing to each other. It was a pretty good night.

And then I jumped.

END